THE SQUAD

Killer Spirit

KILLER SPIRIT

JENNIFER LYNN BARNES

Published by Laurel-Leaf
an imprint of Random House Children's Books
a division of Random House, Inc.
New York

This is a work of fiction. Names, characters, places, and incidents either are the product of the author's imagination or are used fictitiously. Any resemblance to actual persons, living or dead, events, or locales is entirely coincidental.

Visit us on the Web! www.randomhouse.com/teens
www.meetthesquad.com

Educators and librarians, for a variety of teaching tools, visit us at
www.randomhouse.com/teachers

Library of Congress Cataloging-in-Publication Data
Barnes, Jennifer (Jennifer Lynn)
The squad : killer spirit / Jennifer Lynn Barnes. — 1st Laurel-Leaf ed.
p. cm.
Summary: As if it were not bad enough that sophomore computer hacker Toby Klein has to be a cheerleader to be part of the elite group of government operatives called the Squad, now she is part of the Homecoming court and has agreed to attend the dance with the most popular boy in school.
ISBN 978-0-385-73455-4 (mass market pbk.) [1. Spies—Fiction.
2. Cheerleading—Fiction.   3. Dating (Social customs)—Fiction.   4. High schools—Fiction.   5. Schools—Fiction.   6. Computer hackers—Fiction.
7. Robots—Fiction.   8. Humorous stories.] I. Title.   II. Title: Killer spirit.
PZ7.B26225Sqk 2008
[Fic]—dc22
2007017733

February 2008
Printed in the United States of America
10 9 8 7 6 5 4 3 2 1
First Edition

For my biggest cheerleader, who's been there through every step of everything I've ever done, and who would have loved me just as much if I'd never done any of it at all. A girl couldn't ask for a better friend or a better mom, and I hope I grow up to have a daughter half as lucky as I've been to be yours.

CHAPTER 1
Code Word: Body Glitter

Once upon a time, I thought that the cheerleaders at my high school were no more capable of intelligent thought or true athleticism than the average dachshund. Suffice to say that unless the wiener dogs of the world have been holding out on me—big-time—I was very, very wrong.

"Amelia Juarez. Jacob Kann. Anthony Connors-Wright. Hector Hassan." Brooke set the files down one by one, careful to avoid any undue wear and tear on her French manicure. "That's four TCIs arriving in Bayport in the past two days. The question is why."

Personally, I could think of a few other questions, starting with "What's a TCI and why are cheerleading spies so fond of acronyms?" and running straight through to "Do you have any idea how incredibly uncomfortable this godforsaken polyester uniform is?"

To my credit, though, I somehow managed to remain remarkably quiet. Experience had taught me that if I waited long enough, someone would answer at least one of my unasked questions. Experience had also taught me that the fashionistas among us got, for lack of a better word, *cranky* when you criticized their fabric choices.

"What level threat are we talking about here?" Tara asked from my right. It wasn't exactly one of my questions, but close enough.

"Nothing higher than third or fourth tier," Brooke said. She arched an eyebrow at Zee in silent command, and our resident profiler obligingly picked up where Brooke had left off.

"According to our data, their connections to known terrorists and/or terrorist organizations are weak, but the links *are* there, and in each case, there have been enough person-to-person interactions with suspected terrorists to warrant full profiling and a place on the watch list." Zee tucked a strand of jet-black hair behind her ear, a gesture I associated more with her ability to dispense gossip than her skills as a profiler. "All four are ambitious, and they all feel that they have something to prove. Amelia Juarez and Jacob Kann are terrorist-connected through their parents— lots of money, lots of power, long, drawn-out history of high-level crimes in both families. Hector Hassan is a businessman—again, young, smooth, very ambitious. And Anthony's father is an independent operative working primarily for the U.S. and U.K. governments."

Tara rolled her eyes. "Teenage rebellion?" she inferred, as if the children of operatives often rebelled by going over to the dark side and becoming wannabe evil masterminds.

"Try midtwenties rebellion," Zee said, "but, yeah, more or less. Anthony's driven by his father's career choices as much as Amelia and Jacob are by theirs, but in a different direction."

So far, we had a crime prince, a crime princess, an

intelligence brat, and a young businessman, all with some kind of vague-ish connections to terrorist groups. The part of my brain that's tuned in to patterns and codes played back everything that had been said in the debriefing so far, and zeroed in on the combination of words most likely to fit the acronym.

"Terrorist-Connected Individuals," I guessed out loud. "TCIs."

At the head of the table, Brooke rolled her eyes. "Very good, Toby," she said, her voice syrupy sweet. "Do you want a cookie?"

As a matter of fact, I would have loved one, but somehow, I didn't think Brooke's offer was anywhere near the ballpark of sincere. She was our Squad captain. In operative terms, that meant she was technically my commanding officer. In cheerleading terms, it meant she was a bitch.

Either way, I wasn't getting a cookie.

"No offense, Brooke, but it doesn't seem that complicated to me." I was completely unwilling to back down from the challenge in Brooke's eyes or the condescension in her voice. "An influx of TCIs to Bayport can't be a good thing, even if they're only fourth tier. We need to know why they're here."

Before Brooke could roll her eyes again, I plowed on.

"It sounds like we're looking at some pretty basic surveillance maneuvers—minimal interaction, bugs in their hotel rooms . . ."

"Trackers on their rental cars," Tara volunteered.

Brooke didn't acknowledge the fact that I'd actually come up with a decent (albeit obvious) plan. Instead, she turned to Chloe, the original "gadget girl in Gucci." "Can you get the necessaries by this afternoon?"

Chloe nodded. "I'll have the bugs and tracking chips in the guidepost by the time the pep rally's over this afternoon."

Tracking chips and pep rallies—par for the course.

Without a word, Brooke picked the folders up off the table, and began handing them out. "Chloe, you and April take Amelia Juarez, Zee and I will tail Connors-Wright, Lucy and Bubbles, you've got Hassan."

There was only one folder left and two teams. In the split second before Brooke made her decision, I swore to myself that if she put the twins on active duty and left Tara and me at the school to clean up after the pep rally, someone was going to die. Painfully, and without so much as a single "Go Lions!"

"Jacob Kann is all yours, Tare." Brooke handed the last folder to Tara, and by the transitive property, she handed it to me.

"We'll tag the TCIs tonight and report back here afterward to debrief," Brooke said. "No matter what, with the bugs up and running, we should have some major intel by this time tomorrow afternoon." She smiled then, a tight, broad smile that took up most of her face, and with that relatively small change, el capitan went from Squad mode to squad mode, from agent to cheerleader. "Next order of business: What color body glitter should we wear today? Blue or gold? Thoughts?"

From TCIs to body glitter in less than three seconds. Confused? Join the club.

I'd been a member of the Squad for less than a month, and I still woke up most mornings thinking it was all just some crazy Twinkie-induced dream. Then I looked in the

4

mirror, noted my perfectly sculpted eyebrows and artificially tanned face, and the truth sank in.

This wasn't a dream. I, Toby "Antisocial" Klein, had really been recruited to the varsity cheerleading squad, only to discover that said squad was actually a cover for an elite team of government operatives. The most popular girls at my high school were actually secret agents affiliated with a top-secret branch of the government somehow related to the CIA.

Yeah. Try to wrap your mind around *that* one.

I'd joined the Squad as a computer hacker with a third-degree black belt, and they'd turned me into a cheerleader. After a series of more-than-intense makeovers, fashion interventions, and instructions on the finer points of the toe touch, I looked like a cheerleader, cheered like a cheerleader, sat at the popular table for lunch, and spent my afternoons training for and going on missions that would blow most people's minds. That last part, I loved. The rest of it was pretty much Toby torture.

I checked my watch. It was only seven-thirty in the morning, and between the Great Body Glitter Debate of 2008 and Brooke's refusal to give me any actual cookies, I was already up to two woe-is-me moments today. Considering there was a pep rally in my near future, I could only conclude that things were going to get much, much worse.

"Blue's got better contrast."

"But gold accents our tans!"

Apparently, the debate was getting pretty intense. How messed up was it that we could unanimously agree on how to handle potential terrorists, but nearly came to blows over body glitter? After a few more minutes, Brooke decided to put the "issue" to a vote, and as the others weighed in, I looked at each girl in turn. I had to actively remind myself that, sparkly cosmetics aside, these girls were a force to be reckoned with, and pretty much no one knew it but me.

Zee Kim, in addition to being a first-class gossipmonger/party queen, was a former child prodigy. She'd gotten her PhD in forensic psychology at the age of fifteen, and soon thereafter transferred to Bayport High for the sole purpose of joining the Squad. The fact that she got a second chance at living the high school high life was just an added bonus—one that Zee took full advantage of, one A-list affair at a time.

Brooke I-Am-Captain-Hear-Me-Roar Camden was the very definition of A-list. She decided who or what was in, and behind closed doors, she was the one who ran our decisions by the Big Guys Upstairs, our vague and anonymous contacts in Washington. Brooke was a legacy, raised by a mother who'd been part of the Squad pilot program back in the day. As a result, Brooke had been taught from the cradle to do two things: to cheer and to lead our team like the little diva/dictator she was. Of all the girls, Brooke was the only one who could match me in hand-to-hand, which meant that when it came to combat, she was (as much as I hated to admit it) darn near amazing.

To Brooke's left, the twins were adamantly voting for their body glitter of choice—gold. Brittany and Tiffany were absolutely identical and shared matching aptitudes for fashion and the manipulation of the so-called stronger sex. All things male melted into a pile of XY chromosomal goo in the twins' presence. When they weren't playing the seduction card, the twins designed our outfits for missions. They'd also appointed themselves the masters of my personal wardrobe, which was why I now owned more pairs of shoes than most of Young Hollywood combined.

Tara Leery—the most down-to-earth and therefore least Hollywoodesque of the girls—was a British exchange student whose parents were operatives overseas. She'd moved to Bayport to become part of the Squad, and as far as I'd been able to tell, she lived with an "aunt" who may or may not have been CIA. Tara spoke somewhere in the neighborhood of eight zillion languages, and could read and write more than that. She was my Squad partner, and from the beginning, she was the one I counted on to have my back.

Since I'd joined the Squad, my back had needed a lot of covering, due in part to the great deal of enmity that Brooke's second in command, Chloe Larson, seemed to have for computer geeks in general and me in specific. A former child inventor, Chloe was now one hundred percent high school power player, and despite the amount of brain cells she reserved for playing the popularity game, Chloe's grasp of microtechnology put mine to shame. Needless to say, she could also without question outsnob, outsnark, and outcheer me any day of the week.

That just left our peppy-to-a-fault weapons expert, Lucy Wheeler; our contortionist and resident space cadet (figuratively speaking), Bubbles (yes, *Bubbles*) Lane; and April Manning—the only other new recruit this season besides yours truly.

Looking at the girls, split 5–4 on the body glitter issue, I thought about everything that I knew they were capable of doing. They were smart. They were athletic. They were beautiful, and they were continually and severely underestimated.

They were, in other words, perfect spies.

"Toby? Earth to Toby?"

I registered Brooke's tone and sent her a look that some people might have described as surly. "What?"

"Blue or gold?"

Apparently, they were still waiting for my vote. Let's see, I thought, what color body glitter do I want to wear?

"Neither."

Brooke smiled. "Blue it is."

Damn.

CHAPTER 2

Code Word: Interesting

By the time we hit the locker room, there was exactly half an hour until first period, and my only goal was to delay being glittered for as long as was humanly possible. It was bad enough that I'd actually agreed (under duress) to wear a cheerleading uniform to school. The last thing I wanted was to draw any more attention to my uncomfortably short skirt, the bright blue ribbon tied around my superhigh ponytail, and the fact that my current look was about as far from my trademarked antifashion combat boots as you could possibly imagine.

Somehow, I didn't think blue body glitter would do anything to de-emphasize my predicament.

"You don't stand a chance," Zee whispered, patting me consolingly on the shoulder. The good thing about having a profiler on the Squad was that she was a little more sympathetic to my obvious torment than most of the others. The bad part was that she was so perceptive that she may as well have been psychic, and the very idea of psychic cheerleaders scared the crap out of me.

"I could make a run for it," I said under my breath.

Zee shrugged. "You could try," she said, "but the twins might take it personally, and then you'd wake up tomorrow with rhinestones glued to your eyelashes."

I stared at Zee in complete horror, knowing that there was at least a ninety-nine percent chance that she'd accurately predicted the twins' most likely course of action. While I considered the inhumanity of having my eyelashes defiled in my sleep, one of the twins snuck up on me, and before I could dive-roll out of the way, she had a hold on my arm.

"Hold still and close your eyes!" Brittany ordered.

I wondered briefly if keeping my eyes open would delay the inevitable glittering, but soon found out that nothing could stand between one of the twins and adorning my face, breastbone, and arms with a substance more or less defined as powdered girliness.

"So," Brittany said, the edges of her lips pulling up into a devilish smile as she finished the job. "How's your brother doing these days?"

First glitter and now this. She was really pushing her luck. "You do realize that I could kill you, right?" I asked. "With my bare hands and very little effort."

"No killing members of the Squad." Brooke issued a drive-by order in a tone so serious that it might have been amusing were it not for the fact that one of the "hottest" girls in school was asking me about my impossible, obnoxious, and supposedly endearing younger brother. Noah considered himself a ladies' man, which basically meant that he was forever trying to charm older, unavailable girls who almost invariably had large, angry boyfriends who didn't find Noah's overtures adorable in the least.

I'd spent years trying to convince Noah that he wasn't irresistible, and for some reason, the twins—heck, the entire Squad—seemed to enjoy undoing all of my hard work. As far as I'd been able to tell, none of them (with the possible exception of Lucy, and I so wasn't ready to mentally go there) were actually interested in Noah, but they got a kick out of flirting with him, just because they knew it irritated me. As for Noah, he'd spent more time moonwalking and victory dancing in the past two weeks than he had in his entire life, which was really saying something.

"You know, he *is* kind of cute, Toby." Tiffany appeared beside her twin and gave me an impish look.

This went beyond friendly teasing, and there was no way I could let it stand. Even if we were, by some stretch of the word, friends, I had a moral obligation to discourage their feigned interest in my brother, for the good of the world as well as my own sanity. After a moment's consideration, I decided to go with the truth. "Yeah, well, he kind of wants you guys to have a naked pillow fight in our living room."

For some reason, the twins thought this was an absolute riot, which just goes to show that their mother probably dropped both of them on their heads repeatedly as small children.

"Ha-ha," I said dryly. "My brother likes naked girls. Yes, very funny."

They continued laughing and I decided it was time for a change of subject. Luckily enough, I knew exactly which direction I wanted to push this conversation. A few weeks earlier, I'd discovered something about one of our contacts in Washington that had rocked me to the core, and since then, I'd been trying to figure out which, if any, of the others knew about it. The twins were among the last on my list, and now seemed as good a time to broach the subject as any.

"Speaking of things that don't involve my little brother"—I gave them each a look that, had it been any more pointed, would have been capable of drawing blood—"we haven't heard anything from the Big Guys in a while."

"Brooke talks to them all the time," Tiffany said. "They're the ones who told us about the TCIs. Obvi."

"Plus they sent us this really cool volumizing mascara last week," Britt added. "It's made by like NASA."

I couldn't begin to fathom why NASA would be designing mascara, but didn't bother to ask Brittany if she was mixing up her acronyms. I had more important things on my mind. "Don't you guys ever wonder who the Big Guys are?" I asked.

The twins stared at me, clearly not comprehending such curiosity.

I tried to put this in terms they would understand. "For all we know, they could be really hot or something."

That got identical contemplative looks out of the two of them, until Brittany realized that our superiors in Washington were "probably like really old," and then the two of them shrugged off the entire conversation and began to apply a second coat of glitter to my body, on the off chance that my sparkle had waned during the course of our conversation.

Each and every girl on the Squad was a master of deception, but the more time I spent with them, the better I got at reading the subtleties of their body language, their tones of voice, and their patterns of behavior. For the twins, worrying about my "sparkle quotient" was more or less the norm, and every instinct I had told me that all they knew about our superiors was that they had access to cosmetic prototypes that would have made other fashionistas drool.

Like the other girls I'd spoken to, save for one, the twins didn't know anything about the man who'd been our liaison in Washington on our last mission. The only person I hadn't spoken to about it was Brooke, and that was because Brooke and I didn't talk. She issued orders. If I was in a good mood, I considered following them. Besides, I was positive that Chloe knew something she wasn't sharing, and if Chloe knew the truth, Brooke did, too.

They just didn't want the rest of the Squad to know it.

The fact that the twins were getting a little too personal with their glitter distribution kept me from dwelling on my little mystery too much. I was afraid that if I let Brittany and Tiffany continue with their dastardly glitter ways, I'd be sparkling where the sun don't shine in no time.

"Don't you two have somebody else to glitter?" I narrowed my eyes, and to my incredible relief, they stopped the glitter application to answer my question.

"Oh, no," Tiffany said seriously. "You're the only one who needs G.A."

G.A.?

"Glitter Assistance," her twin clarified.

When it came to makeup, the twins didn't trust me to know my lips from my lids. You confuse eyeliner and lip liner once, and you're branded for life.

As if they somehow knew that a brief makeup-related thought had crossed my mind, the twins whipped out tubes of lip gloss in synchronized motions, and before I could so much as threaten bodily harm, my lips were pink and shiny and tasted vaguely like strawberries.

It was times like these that I really needed to do something, anything, that made me feel like me. Not too long ago, I'd found out that I wasn't the only Squad member who'd been cheerlead-o-fied upon joining up, and I didn't want to get to the point where my cover became my identity. I was still me, and unlike Zee and Chloe, I had no desire to forget it and become somebody else.

"Anyone want to spar?" I asked. There was nothing like a good fight to make me feel like myself again. It must have had something to do with those "aggressive tendencies" my school counselors were always talking about. Luckily for me, one of the perks of being on the Squad was the amazing underground facility called the Quad. I was still finding my way around, but the week before, I'd discovered a first-class training room, with plenty of space for a little friendly hand-to-hand.

"School starts in twenty-eight minutes," Tara told me.

I think she vastly underestimated my need to hit something. Or someone.

"That gives us at least twenty minutes," I said. "Come on, who's up for it?"

I glanced at Brooke, and for a long moment, she stared back at me. I recognized the thirst in her eyes. She was a competitor, plain and simple, and as odd as it seemed, a morning fight sounded just as good to her as it did to me. When I first joined the Squad, I thought Brooke and I were complete and utter opposites. I was the anticheerleader, and she was the poster girl.

These days, I wasn't quite so sure.

"We're wearing cheerleading uniforms," Tara said, making an admirable stab at talking me out of what I'm sure she thought was a very bad idea. "And body glitter."

"I promise I won't hurt anyone's glitter," I said, my eyes still on Brooke. The last time we'd fought, she'd ended it before either of us had had much of a chance to win.

"Brooke." Chloe Larson stepped in front of Brooke, effectively blocking me from her view. "I thought we'd go over the chant order for the pep rally. I think we may want to put 'Clap Your Hands' before 'Stand Up, Up.'"

Brooke's facial expression never changed, but I could almost hear her internal sigh as she realized that neither one of us was getting a rematch this morning. "Just a sec," she told Chloe. "Lucy?"

"Yeah huh?" Lucy popped out of a nearby bathroom stall, and I blinked as the glare off her glittery chest struck me straight in the eye.

"Toby wants to spar," Brooke told her. "Make it interesting."

Lucy was little, perky, and happier than just about any person I knew. Needless to say, the happiest girl in the world wasn't exactly my first-choice punching bag. Then again, I'd never seen her fight, and if there was one thing the past few weeks had taught me, it was that underestimating any of these girls was a very, very bad idea.

"You ready?" Lucy asked me, bouncing on the balls of her feet. I nodded, and beside me, Tara sighed.

"You want me to come with?" she asked.

I shook my head. I was pretty sure I could handle Lucy, and because it was Lucy, who'd always been nice to me in her own special Lucy way and who hadn't, for instance, forced gloss upon my unwilling lips in the past five minutes, she wasn't in any real danger from me, either.

Lucy bounded back into the bathroom stall, and then returned a moment later. "So how's your day going?" she

15

asked, coming up and hooking her arm through mine. "I mean, I know it's pretty early, but so far, so good?"

I was glossed and glittered and on edge, and I had a sinking suspicion that I wasn't going to be getting any answers about our superiors any time soon, but I also had an assignment, and the thought of tailing Jacob Kann after school was enough to make up for the rest of it. With any luck, I'd actually get to break into his hotel room.

"So far, so good."

Five minutes later, we were in the training room, and Lucy was sitting on the ground doing a butterfly stretch, the soles of her feet touching each other, and her knees pushing down toward the ground.

I took a few deep breaths and warm-up kicks, and by the time Lucy bounced (literally) to her feet, I was ready to go.

We stood there for an elongated moment, looking at each other, and then Lucy flew at me. She was fast—I'd give her that much, and she knew how to put what little weight she had behind a punch. Despite the fact that I'd told myself not to underestimate her, the speed of the movement took me off guard, and she managed to catch the edge of my shoulder as I belatedly moved to dodge her blow.

Without thinking, I turned, absorbing the force and moving with it, and grabbed her arm. With a single, smooth movement on my part, Lucy was flying through the air, and I was reminding myself that I really didn't want to hurt her.

Realizing she was airborne, Lucy somehow managed to turn her flight into a technically perfect front flip, and as soon as she landed, she came at me again. For several minutes, we got stuck in that pattern—Lucy advancing on me enough to punch or kick, me dodging and using her own momentum to throw her into some kind of twisting flip. After the first time, none of her punches or kicks touched me, and even though she seemed to be having a good time, I was starting to feel kind of bad and figured it was time to end things.

As she landed from her umpteenth flip, I moved forward, kicking low with my left foot in a motion meant to sweep her feet out from underneath her. She fell, but was back on her feet instantly, and as I tried to temper my reaction to her skill level, she managed to land a solid kick to my chest.

I grunted, spun, and came disturbingly close to throwing myself into a roundhouse. Keeping my head in the game, I short-circuited the movement. My roundhouse was not a thing to be taken lightly.

"Ummm . . . Toby?" Lucy's voice was somewhat hesitant as she backed away from me slowly.

"Yes?"

"Remember how Brooke said for me to make it interesting?"

I nodded, relatively unconcerned. Lucy was good—definitely better than I'd expected, but there was a very real chance I could have taken her with my eyes closed.

"Toby?" Lucy prodded.

"I remember."

Lucy smiled tentatively. "Just checking." She moved quickly, her hands blurring with the speed at which she reached back and somehow produced two sharp, metal objects.

Throwing knives? What the . . .

And then we were fighting again, and instead of dodging

17

Lucy's punches, I was avoiding the thrusts of the knives. I grabbed hold of her left arm and twisted her wrist until she dropped the weapon, and then barely managed to duck before the knife in her right hand came whizzing at my neck.

I needed to put space in between the two of us. Fast. Without even thinking, going entirely on instinct and years of training, I flew into a series of back handsprings that took me away from her and landed just in time to see Lucy take aim and throw the final knife.

I dove down and out of the way, twisting to allow my shoulder to absorb the impact as my body hit the floor, and then I rolled on autopilot back to my feet.

Lucy smiled hopefully. "Wasn't that interesting?"

My heart was beating hard against my rib cage, and the adrenaline was flowing. I opened my mouth and then closed it again. I wasn't sure whether to be incredulous or ticked, or possibly oddly elated. On the one hand, Brooke had more or less told Lucy to throw knives at me. On the other hand, it *had* made things more interesting. I could take Lucy with my eyes closed. Lucy with knives was another story altogether.

In the end, I settled for disbelief. A month ago, Lucy and I hadn't even lived on the same plane of social existence, and now she was throwing knives at me, in the friendliest of all possible knife-throwing ways.

"Yeah, Luce," I said. "Really interesting."

Her smile brightened the second she got that I wasn't mad at her, and she immediately began babbling. "We don't use knives that much. Most of our weapons are a lot more covert, and we don't engage in much hand-to-hand contact with our marks. I mean, if cheerleaders started

18

pulling out knives, then people wouldn't see us as cheerleaders, you know?"

It occurred to me to wonder where exactly she'd managed to hide the knives. Cheerleading uniforms weren't exactly ripe with knife-shaped hiding places.

"I'm thinking of seeing if I can fit one of these things into some kind of brush or comb," Lucy continued. "Or maybe some poms. That would be awesome."

This conversation was disturbing on so many levels, but as the two of us straightened our ponytails and headed off to class, I couldn't help but think that it could be worse.

For example, I would have been far more disturbed had Lucy taken her cue from the twins and started talking about Noah.

CHAPTER 3

Code Word: Rumor Mill

"Miss Klein, how kind of you to join us." Mr. Corkin, my history teacher, flashed me an evil look as I slid into my seat. I'd somehow managed to make it through my first four periods and lunch before taking a fevered (and, I might add, futile) stab at glitter removal. As a result of that last-minute attempt, I was late to fifth hour, and Corkin, who hated me as much as I hated history, was thrilled to have a reason to engage in Toby bashing, his favorite non-Olympic sport.

Before I'd joined the Squad, he would have done more than verbally berate me for coming into class a good three minutes late, but at this school, being a varsity cheerleader or football player meant something. As sick as it was, my uniform and the insane amount of blue glitter on my chest completely insulated me against the threat of detention. Plus it really didn't hurt our cause that the vice-principal, the man in charge of discipline, was our faculty sponsor.

"Perhaps you've gone deaf as well as ill-mannered." Mr. Corkin was intent on getting a response out of me, even if it meant repeating himself. "How kind of you to join us."

Despite my Cheerleaders Get Out of Jail Free card, I didn't respond to Mr. Corkin's comment with, "How kind of you to KISS MY CHEER-SKIRT-COVERED BOOTY," which was, believe me, on the tip of my tongue. Instead, I went with a slightly more diplomatic approach.

"Body glitter emergency," I said darkly, my face completely and utterly devoid of expression. It was, all things considered, an asinine excuse, but if anyone other than me noticed that fact, they hid it well, and without a word, Mr. Corkin moved on with his lecture.

After about five minutes, I started to get twitchy, and surprisingly enough, it had nothing to do with Corkin's monotone and everything to do with the fact I wasn't used to sitting through class in my uniform. Between the spandex underwear covers ("bloomers" or "spankies" depending on your mood and which made you feel like less of a complete idiot to say) and the supershort polyester skirt/shell combo, I was in cheerleading agony. Add to that the fact that trying to scrub off the glitter had simply resulted in itchy, glittery skin, and whatever dignity I'd originally managed to hold on to during my transformation from "not" to "hot" was seriously in danger.

As class progressed, I could feel myself getting more and more wound up. I wasn't a fan of sitting still, and whatever steam I'd blown off dodging knives that morning was long gone. Even remembering the glint of steel as Lucy flung her weapon directly at my body did nothing to allay my misery.

I was beginning to wonder if this class would ever end. Then again, once class was over, it was only T-minus two hours until the final bell, the pep rally, and the official end of my life as an outsider. The majority of the student body had already accepted me as popularity royalty. Brooke's word was law, and she'd chosen me for the God Squad. I'd already moved from the fringes to the central table at lunch, and when it came to halftime performances, I was officially a veteran of butt-shaking.

But in another two hours, as I waved goodbye to my last ounce of dignity, I was going to stand up in front of the entire school and encourage the student body to put their hands together for our football team, a group of guys who, by and large, deserved a kick to their collective crotch far more than they deserved applause.

I tried not to let myself think about the fact that there was one football player who seemed to have as much derision for the whole system as I did. His name was Jack Peyton, he was tall, dark, and drop-dead gorgeous, and even though he was the school's most eligible bachelor, he accepted that position with an ironic detachment that I almost had to respect. He was smart, sarcastic, and more charming than I'd ever given him credit for. And three weeks earlier, we'd kissed.

At the time, he'd been my mark—the son of a local baddie, the head of a law firm that had its well-protected fingers in everything from terrorism to the mafia. As if that didn't complicate things enough, the discovery I'd made about our superiors, the one that I'd spent the past few weeks trying to sort out, was that Jack Peyton was almost as connected to our program as he was to our enemy. His uncle was our liaison in Washington, the Charlie to our Angels, and most of the girls on the Squad didn't have a clue. I had no idea how one Peyton had ended up at the head of what was more or less a terrorist cell, while the other headed the CIA unit designated to take that cell down, but either way, Jack was the crown prince of Evilville, and as a bonus, the ex-boyfriend of not one, but two varsity cheer-leaders. He was off-limits in every possible way, and I'd kissed him. Not, in retrospect, my best move, and the fact that I'd followed the kiss by punching him in the stomach and bolting out the door hadn't exactly shown the kind of grace under pressure you might expect from a teenage oper-ative. It definitely wasn't my finest moment, and since then, I'd been doing my best to avoid Jack. Not an easy task considering we sat at the same lunch table and shared a bus to away games.

"Pssssssst. Toby."

It took me a second to realize that the girl next to me was saying my name. Even after being on the Squad for nearly a month, I still wasn't used to the fact that people actually knew my name. I'd gone to eight schools in the past ten years, and except for the bullies that I'd been forced to take out, none of the other kids had ever paid much attention to me. I was anonymous, and I preferred to stay that way.

"Psssssst. Toby!"

Persistent, wasn't she? I cast a glance at Mr. Corkin, who was prattling on about some battle I couldn't have cared less about, and then I turned back to the girl and answered.

"Yeah?" I tried for a tone that conveyed, "Stop talking to me, and do not, under any circumstances, ask me a ques-tion about cheerleading, body glitter, or Jack Peyton."

Unfortunately, either my tones weren't very expressive, or the girl next to me really didn't excel in reading between the lines.

"Is it true that the God Squad has their own line of body glitter with Calvin Klein?"

One of the most widespread rumors when I'd made the

varsity squad was that I was Calvin Klein's love child. Proof that, as I'd long suspected, people at this school were dumb.

"Pssssst! Toby!"

Miss Persistent wasn't going to quit until I gave her an answer, and so I did. "Yes," I deadpanned, tired of shooting down ridiculous rumors. "Calvin Klein. Body glitter. Entirely true."

"That is like so fab." The girl didn't pause a second before plowing on. "So is it true that Jack Peyton is going to ask you to homecoming during the pep rally?"

"WHAT?" I'm not sure whether my response was a yelp or a yell, but whatever it was, it was loud.

"Miss Klein!" Mr. Corkin was not pleased, but I wasn't exactly in a state of mind to care.

"Would you mind terribly," he said tartly, "if I asked you to save your conversations, as stimulating as I'm sure they must be, for after class?"

"Not at all," I said through gritted teeth. I had bigger problems than Corkin, like the fact that the words *Jack* and *homecoming* had just been used in the same sentence. I wasn't going to homecoming, and I certainly wasn't going with Jack.

No way. No how.

Completely oblivious to the nature of the thoughts beating against the inside of my skull, Mr. Corkin smirked, pleased that I'd backed down for the second time in one day. And just like that, something inside of me snapped. I needed out of this class and away from the rumor mill. Most of all, I needed to wipe the cocky expression right off his history teacher face.

"Mr. Corkin?" I said, pitching my voice to mimic his

24

exactly. "Would you mind terribly if I asked you to KISS MY—"

"Miss Klein!"

Fifteen seconds later, the smirk had been firmly wiped off of Corkin's face, I was on my way to the vice-principal's office, and the rumor mill was effectively five thousand miles away.

All in all, I was pleased.

CHAPTER 4

Code Word: Detention

The vice-principal was not nearly as pleased with my performance in history class as I was.

"You've been doing so well," he told me. "I really thought the other girls were rubbing off on you. None of your teachers have complained, and you've only been sent to my office a handful of times."

It was on the tip of my tongue to tell Mr. Jacobson that the fact that I'd stayed out of trouble had less to do with the way that I'd changed and more to do with the fact that the way people treated me had changed. In the P.S. (pre-Squad) period, I'd primarily gotten into trouble for mouthing off and for beating up football players who richly deserved it, including, but not limited to, those who threatened the life of my little brother. Now the football players didn't mess with me. It was funny, they'd never been scared of the fact that I could take any of them at any time, but now that I was one of *those girls*, all it took was a warning look, and they left Noah alone.

I had to wonder if it had anything to do with the fact that being beat up by the loner girl wasn't anywhere near as humiliating as being beat up by a cheerleader. In all likelihood, it was probably more closely related to the fact that the collective feminine wiles of the Squad kept the boys at this school firmly under our (and I include myself in this group loosely) thumbs.

As for mouthing off, maybe I had changed. Not for the reasons that Mr. J thought, but maybe I'd stopped being quite so openly rebellious once I'd started to learn to keep my real thoughts and feelings (and, in some cases, my real identity) hidden behind whatever cover I was assigned.

I frowned. The idea was, to say the least, disturbing.

"I haven't changed," I told Mr. J. If I had, I certainly hadn't meant to.

"Toby, you cannot tell a teacher to . . . ahem"—Mr. J consulted the slip of paper Corkin had sent with me to the office—"kiss your posterior region. I expect you to show all of your teachers, even the ones you don't like, a certain amount of respect."

Given that this was high school, no one concerned themselves with whether or not Mr. Corkin gave me the same courtesy. Even if I'd arrived to class on time and kept my mouth shut, he would have found something to say to me. He'd hated me at first glance, judged the proverbial book by the cover, and despite the fact that the cover had since changed, his attitude toward me hadn't. He restrained himself from being too openly nasty, lest he incur the wrath of the administration, the PTA, and whoever else the Squad had in its pocket, but he still hated me.

And I had no respect for him.

I opened my mouth to explain this, perhaps explicitly, but Mr. J cut me off.

"I know," he said, "and believe me when I say that I

don't think you're entirely to blame for this situation, but we still need to do something about it."

The poor guy looked so torn. I blame the cheerleading uniform. He just couldn't give detention to a girl who had *BHS* emblazoned across her chest.

"I should give you detention," he said, sounding for all the world like a kid faced with eating the most dreaded of vegetables, "but I know how hard you girls have been working lately to get ready for the big game against Hillside this weekend, and I can only imagine how much stress you've been under."

The sad thing was, Mr. J didn't know about the true nature of the Squad. He really thought we were just cheerleaders, and this was the way he treated us. I can only conclude that he had some kind of mental illness or childhood trauma that gave him an incredible soft spot for all things cheerleadery. I made a mental note to ask Zee about it, and the moment I did, I started to wonder if the government had anything to do with the fact that the vice-principal at Bayport High had a weakness for cheerleaders. It would be just like the Guys Upstairs to handpick a vice-principal guaranteed to allow us to do whatever we wanted, or, more to the point, *needed* to do.

"If this happens again, Toby, we'll have to have a very serious talk."

He couldn't even bring himself to really properly threaten me, and this from a guy who'd never had trouble chewing me up and spitting me out before I'd ascended to the top of the social echelon.

"Just give me detention," I grumbled. I'd hated the favoritism at this school before I'd been a cheerleader, and I wasn't all that fond of it now.

"Toby, I would never ask you to skip the pep rally this afternoon over something as mild as a disagreement with a teacher." Mr. J looked shocked at the mere suggestion, as if he hadn't told me how serious my behavior was moments before.

"The pep rally," I repeated, and then the image of Jack watching as I jumped up and down and cheered my butt off popped into my head, followed directly by the words that had driven me here in the first place.

So is it true that Jack Peyton is going to ask you to homecoming during the pep rally?

"Go ahead," I told Mr. J. "Ask me to skip the pep rally. Please."

It would solve almost all of my problems. I wouldn't have to take the final step in my transformation to cheerleaderdom, I could successfully avoid Jack and any questions he may or may not have been planning to ask me that afternoon, and being in detention might even make me feel a little more like my old self. It didn't resolve the body glitter situation, but all things considered, that was probably hoping for too much.

"Toby, Friday is homecoming. It's a big game, and a big dance, and this pep rally is the start of it all. The nominations for homecoming court will be announced. I can't let you miss that."

"Sure you can," I encouraged, trying to keep the hopeful expression off my face. "I did a very bad thing. I deserve to be punished. No pep rally for me."

"No," Mr. J argued. "You didn't do anything. Not really, Toby. We both know how Mr. Corkin can be. I'll be sure to talk to him about his attitude toward you."

I'd seriously had dreams like this before. Corkin sending

me to the office only to get his butt chewed out? It was priceless. It was not, however, necessary, and avoiding the pep rally was. There was no way I could just play hooky. The Squad didn't work like that, and neither did I. But if Mr. J told me I couldn't go . . .

"It really wasn't Mr. Corkin's fault." I practically choked on the words, but I said them. "I have an attitude problem. I have no respect for authority."

I could tell just by looking at him that Mr. J wasn't buying it. He'd somehow rewritten history so that I was the victim here, and nothing I could say or do would convince him otherwise.

"I told him to kiss my a—" I said desperately.

Mr. J, darn him, started laughing before I even finished the final word.

"It's not funny. It's bad. Very bad." Even as I tried to make the argument, I couldn't help but remember the look on Corkin's face, and it took everything I had to keep from laughing myself.

"Toby, you're a good kid, and the other girls need you. It's homecoming, and I'm feeling generous. Don't bother arguing. I'm not giving you detention, and that's final. Now go back to class."

It was official. My life had done a complete one-eighty. A month ago, I couldn't have begged my way out of detention, and right now, I couldn't beg my way in.

"On second thought," Mr. J said. "Don't go back to class just yet. I think you and Mr. Corkin need a break from each other. Why don't you just take a breather?"

What kind of messed up system was this? I shouted profanities at a teacher, and as punishment, I got to skip out on the rest of the aforementioned teacher's boring lecture? How was this even possible?

You're a cheerleader, I told myself. And a spy. Anything is possible. Except, it appeared, getting out of the pep rally that afternoon. Go figure.

CHAPTER 5

Code Word: Pep Rally

"Clap your hands, everybody! Everybody, clap your hands! Let's hear it for the Lions—make some noise, you Bayport fans!"

Clap-down-clap-clap-down-clap-down-clap-down-clap-clap.

It had taken me hours to really get the clapping rhythm for this cheer. I'd finally managed to do it, but only by matching the claps (two hands hitting each other) and the downs (hands hitting your knees) with zeroes and ones respectively and converting the whole thing into binary. Twisted, I know, but that's what happens when you choose the members of your varsity cheerleading squad based on who has and hasn't hacked into the Pentagon.

"Clap your hands, everybody. Everybody, clap your hands!"

I didn't want to be here. I didn't want to be doing this, and I certainly didn't want to be smiling a big, goofy smile. Unfortunately, I didn't have much of a choice on any of the above. The others hadn't quite converted me to the way of the cheerleader, but I'd accepted the fact that when you cheered, however reluctantly, you did it like you meant it. Just because I didn't particularly want to be a cheerleader didn't mean that I wanted to be a bad one.

"Let's hear it for the Lions . . ." I executed a back handspring. It felt somehow sacrilegious to be doing any kind of flipping that didn't fall under the heading of martial arts. "Make some noise, you Bayport fans! Goooooooo Bayport!"

Finally, the cheer was over. I hadn't messed it up. I hadn't drawn any more attention to myself than was mandated by the fact that we were front and center and screaming our lungs out (or, more accurately, yelling from our diaphragms). Best of all, I hadn't made eye contact with Jack once.

"Your form on the handspring was crap," Chloe told me under her breath, smile still plastered to her face.

"Bite me, Chloe."

"Let's hear a round of applause for the heart of Bayport, the Bayport High Varsity Spirit Squad!" Mr. Jacobson had the microphone. He was absolutely brimming with pep. "Thank you, girls."

Bah. I wasn't talking to Mr. J. Was detention really so much to ask for?

While I was pondering this all-important question, a scowl settling slowly over my face, Tara came up beside me. "Smile," she said, guiding me to our seats at the very front of the bleachers.

"The cheer's over," I reminded her.

"Your job's not."

I plastered a big, cheesy smile on my face. "Happy?" I asked her.

"Ecstatic." Then she leaned forward. "If it's any consolation, it took Chloe years to learn how to tumble. She's just bitter that you can do a standing back tuck."

I hadn't even done a standing back tuck during our routine, and Chloe was punishing me for the fact that years of martial arts training had given me the ability to do one? Have I mentioned yet that she sucks?

"Cheer politics," Tara said lightly. "It happens."

"And now, please welcome this year's football captain, Chip Warner!"

The student body went crazy, except for me. I clapped, like the good little undercover agent that I was, but mentally, I replayed the many occasions upon which I'd threatened Chip with bodily harm. Good times.

"Hey, guys." Chip waited for the last hoots and hollers to settle down, and then he continued, a smile on his perfectly sculpted (and perfectly nauseating) face. "First off, I just want to thank the ladies of the varsity squad for all of their support. We love you, girls!"

"Awwwwwww."

Apparently, I'd missed the part of my cheerleading training that involved synchronized awwwwwwing. Given that pesky gag reflex of mine, this was probably a good thing.

"Next, I just want to say that the Hillside Bobcats are going DOWN!" With those words of wisdom, Chip raised both hands in the air in a V, and the crowd went crazy.

This time, I didn't clap. No one noticed, except for the only other person in the room not clapping.

Jack.

He was sitting next to the seat Chip had vacated, and having read every bit of intelligence the Squad had managed to gather on Jack, I knew quite well that he and Chip were cocaptains, and that the only reason that Chip was giving the speech was that Jack was jaded enough not to want to. He covered it well.

He glanced up and saw me looking at him. I swore under my breath, and he smiled and then smirked and then smiled again.

"Hello, Ev," he mouthed. It was his name for me, short for Everybody-Knows-Toby, which was how the girls had introduced me to him my first day as the new and "improved" Toby Klein.

I glared back at him, refusing to give in to my lips' traitorous urge to smile.

His eyes still on mine, Jack just grinned, that slow, lazy kind of grin that made me feel like I was flirting with him instead of the other way around.

Out of the corner of one eye, I saw Chloe and noticed that she, too, was looking at Jack. Chloe was one of Jack's exes. Brooke was the other. Besides me, they were the only two people who might have realized that Jack's uncle was one of the Big Guys. Coincidence? I thought not. Both of them had dated him to gain access to his father's law firm, our biggest . . . *enemy* wasn't quite the right word, but close enough. After the second breakup, Jack had developed Conditioned Cheerleading Aversion (Zee's diagnosis, not mine), and the only reason he'd shown interest in me was that I wasn't like the other girls.

For instance, none of the other girls had ever tried their darnedest to avoid him altogether. None of them rolled their eyes when he went into A-list guy mode. None of them gave as good as they got.

None of them had kissed him, punched him in the stomach, and run away.

"Thank you, Chip." Mr. J was back at the microphone. "And let me take this opportunity to say, Gooooooooooo Lions!" He cleared his throat. "And, of course, Lionesses."

Bayport was politically correct to a fault.

"I'd now like to welcome Joanne McCall, president of the Bayport High School PTA, who will read out the nominations for this year's homecoming court."

Blah, blah, blah, blah . . . wait a second. I elbowed Tara. "Check it out," I said softly. "It's the nauseatingly reminiscent mom from the mall."

My very first day on the Squad, Tara had taken me to the mall to practice my spy skills, and some random mom had practically stalked us, chattering away about how exciting it was to be young and a cheerleader. Apparently, brownnosing parents weren't all that unusual, and I'd forgotten about it (or at least tried to cleanse my mind of the way the woman had violated my personal space).

It just figured that the nauseatingly reminiscent mom was the president of the PTA.

"I cannot tell you all how pleased I am to be here," the NRM said. "These high school years are some of the most exciting and precious years of your lives, and I'm happy to have the chance to share them with you. As I'm sure most of you already know, the homecoming court consists of the queen and king, their junior and senior attendants, and the underclassman homecoming princess and sophomore attendant."

Raise your hand if you're surprised that Bayport is the kind of school that has a homecoming princess. Anyone? Anyone?

"Each year, four seniors, three juniors, and two underclassmen are nominated by the students and faculty to run for the honor of being the homecoming queen."

Did this have to take so freaking long? Who cared about the details of the process? Wouldn't it be easier for everyone to just fall down and worship Brooke now?

"The girl with the most votes will be named queen at the official homecoming game, and the remaining junior and senior nominees will be named her attendants. Additionally, the sophomore with the most number of votes will be named the homecoming princess."

Being a logical person, I could see the flaw in this system. As a nominee for queen, if the "princess" got enough votes, she could actually beat a senior out for that coveted spot, in which case I could only assume that the runner-up underclassman would get the princess title. It would have made a lot more sense if they stipulated that the queen be a senior, but this didn't seem to strike anyone else as off—either because the student body knew as well as I did that the race for queen was as good as over and Brooke had as good as won, or because I was the only person at this school afflicted with homecoming-related logic.

I braved a glance at Jack, expecting him to look every bit as tortured as I felt, but instead, he was smiling. Broadly.

"The senior nominees for homecoming queen are . . . " Mrs. McCall paused dramatically, as if there was anyone in the room who hadn't figured out exactly whose names would be on that ballot. "Brooke Camden, Chloe Larson, Zee Kim, and Bubbles Lane."

The four senior members of the Squad. Color me shocked.

Across the room, Jack's grin grew bigger and wickeder by the second. Without a word, he simply pointed in my general direction. I turned around and glanced over my shoulder. Nothing.

"The junior nominees are Tara Leery, Lucy Wheeler, and Tiffany and Brittany Sheffield."

Okay, was I the only one in the entire school who realized that Tiffany and Brittany were actually two separate people and that, therefore, there were four junior girls nominated for homecoming court and not just three? Sometimes, the mental math at this place was depressing.

"The underclassmen nominees are . . ."

Across the room, Jack's grin had settled down to a smirk, and he pointed again. A second too late, I realized that he wasn't pointing behind me.

He was pointing at me.

"April Manning and Toby Klein."

Not to sound like an acronym-loving cheerleader/spy, but OMG with a side of WTF.

"You have got to be kidding me," I muttered under my breath. Now Jack's smile made sense. He knew this was going to happen. Everyone but me had realized it. I'd said it myself—there wasn't anyone in this room who didn't know whose names were going to be on those ballots. The varsity cheerleaders were called the God Squad for a reason. And yet, somehow, it hadn't occurred to me that there were exactly two sophomores on the Squad and exactly two sophomore nominees for homecoming queen.

Now whose mental math was depressing?

"I hate my life."

Tara and Chloe both elbowed me in the stomach at the same time.

"Ouch," I hissed. "I still hate my . . ."

This time, I saw the blows coming and dodged them. Oblivious to the violence amongst the cheerleaders, the rest of the school listened as the nominees for homecoming

king—Chip, Jack, and a handful of other football players—
were read off. It didn't take me long to figure out that there
was no such thing as a homecoming prince.

Thank God.

"Good luck, boys and girls, and remember, this is a very
special time in your lives."

Yeah, I thought, a very special time for my life to suck.
I'd come to terms with the cheerleader thing. Scratch that,
I'd *almost* come to terms with the cheerleader thing, but I
most certainly did not sign on for homecoming princess. I
had a healthy disdain for things like dances and popularity.
I hated dresses and tiaras, and I wasn't even ready to accept
the fact that people at this school even knew my name, let
alone that it would be plastered on hundreds of ballots.

Life as I knew it was over. Again. And this time, things
were going to get ugly.

CHAPTER 6

Code Word: Hottie

"We're strong! We're tough! Bayport Lions—stand up, up!"

We were closing out the pep rally with another cheer, and as the student body rose to their feet at our command, I couldn't help but note the fact that I was *this* close to up-upchucking all over my Asics cheer shoes.

"We're strong! We're tough! Bayport Lions—stand up, up!"

Technically, this was a chant, not a cheer, which meant that we repeated the words and motions indefinitely until Brooke called last time. I was starting to doubt that Brooke would ever put me out of my misery, when she finally yelled those two, wonderful words.

"Last time!"

I hit the final pose, my arms in a high V and my mind in overdrive. In approximately thirty-five seconds, this pep rally would be over, and students would start pouring out every available exit. My mission was clear: I had to get out of Dodge before Dodge's Most Eligible Bachelor could so much as smirk the words *homecoming princess* at me, or ask me to the dance. After I managed to finagle my way out of the gym unnoticed, I was going to sneak down to the Quad, drown my sorrows in whatever fruity juice-like beverage lived in the fridge, and wait for Tara to come and tell me it was time to do something that didn't involve cheering or homecoming or pretending that Jack and I had never kissed.

At this point, a little espionage sounded like heaven.

Ultimately, however, things did not go exactly as planned. The moment the assembly officially ended, people rushed the gym floor, including three individuals who, for one reason or another, felt that they just had to talk to me.

The first of the three was Noah. "To-by, To-by, To-by."

My brother was an idiot. Unfortunately, he was also extraordinarily loud, and his voice carried. I spent one moment vehemently hoping that his chant wouldn't catch on, and the next plotting his immediate and violent demise.

"My sister, the homecoming princess." Noah batted his eyelashes at me. "Our little girl, all grown-up and . . ."

I took a step forward, and Noah, smart boy that he was, took a step back.

"Shutting mouth now," he volunteered.

I gave him a look that simultaneously commended his mouth-shutting decision and warned him that I wasn't in the mood to be teased.

"Hi Noah!" two voices chorused at once.

I turned to glare the twins into oblivion, but somewhere between Noah's "helllllloooooooo, ladies" and the twins' giggled response, I was waylaid by a woman with no respect for personal space and a huge smile on her Botox-ed face.

"Toby. It *is* Toby, isn't it?" Mrs. McCall, PTA president and nauseatingly reminiscent mom, came up and put a hand on my shoulder.

"Yup." I stuck to one-word answers, hoping she'd get the drift.

"I just wanted to congratulate you. Homecoming court—how exciting! Of course, it can't be that much of a surprise . . ."

If she only knew.

"You girls are just so lucky." She squeezed my shoulder. "These are such—"

"Precious times," I finished. "Yeah, I know, but right now, I've really got to—"

I didn't escape then, because in a move too smooth and quick for the human mind to follow or comprehend it, the NRM had been replaced with a JVB—a junior-varsity beeyotch.

"You must think you're pretty great." Hayley Hoffman was smiling, but she was not happy. "You think that just because you're varsity, it's okay to walk all over the rest of us."

Coming from her, the accusation was laughable. Hayley was a lifelong cheerleader and a supremely hideous person. She preyed on the weak, drank tears for breakfast, and would have sacrificed her own child on the altar of popularity. The fact that she hadn't made the varsity squad had a little to do with her lack of loyalty, and a lot to do with the fact that I'd convinced the others to vote in April instead.

Hayley still hadn't forgiven me for making the God Squad. From her perspective, I'd stolen her spot and everything that came with it, including a nomination for homecoming queen.

"Do you honestly think you deserve to be nominated?" Hayley asked. "Do you think that's fair?"

"No," I said, looking her directly in the eyes. "It's not fair."

If life were fair, the word *makeover* would never have been invented, I wouldn't have had the world's biggest spankie pants wedgie, and the words *hacker* and *homecoming princess* would have had no logical connection whatsoever. Life wasn't fair. It was twisted.

"You don't belong on varsity," Hayley said, "and you sure as hell don't belong on the homecoming court." The *and I will make you pay* went unspoken, but I was very good at reading between the mean-girl lines.

After one last glare, Hayley turned and flounced back to her sidekicks. Once upon a time, April had been one of them, but now that April had made the Squad, she and Hayley were hanging out less and less, and Hayley had already found a handful of suitable replacements—mostly other JV cheerleaders and sophomore populars who hadn't made the varsity cut that fall.

By the time I'd dealt with (read: tried to ignore) the trifecta of horror that was the Noah–NRM–Hayley onslaught, the entire student body was standing in between me and the exit, and there was no way out.

"Fancy meeting you here." Jack spoke into the back of my head, but I knew it was him.

Darn Noah. Darn the PTA president. Darn Hayley Hoffman.

"Aren't you going to say something, Ev?"

I muttered an expletive under my breath, and Jack smiled.

"That's my girl."

"I'm not your girl," I said sharply.

He stepped closer, until the rest of the crowd felt miles away by comparison. "You could be."

There were times when I almost couldn't restrain myself

around him, times when I wanted to kiss him again so badly that my lips literally hurt. This wasn't one of them. He was being suave and smooth, and I wasn't falling for it.

"Yeah," I said, "and I could also tattoo an anorexic pterodactyl on my navel, but I'm not planning to do that, either."

"Anorexic pterodactyl." He repeated my words, and the self-assured smirk on his face was replaced with repressed amusement. "Sounds more like a butt tattoo to me."

It was comments like that one that did me in. He could wax poetic about me being his girl or how beautiful I was or whatever from now until graduation, and it wouldn't inspire anything in me other than the desire to spell out for him just how much of a tool I thought he was. But the moment he started snarking or quipping or admiring my snarky quippiness, I was a goner.

"I'll make you a deal, Ev. You go to homecoming with me, and I'll save you from having to go to the God Squad after-party."

He knew how to sweet-talk a girl. He *really* knew how to sweet-talk a girl.

I glanced past his shoulder, trying to look away from the half grin on his lips, and I made eye contact with Tara. If I'd seen any of the other cheerleaders, it would have been different. Brooke and Chloe were a tad too possessive, and the rest of the girls were way too gung ho on the Jack/Toby relationship. As a general rule, Tara tried to remain more neutral. Her face was clear of any obvious expression, but for some reason, I knew what she was thinking.

Squad-wise, I should say yes. If there really was something big going down in Bayport, Peyton, Kaufman, and

Gray, nefarious law firm that it was, probably had a hand in it. For whatever reason, the Big Guys either didn't know about the familial connection within their ranks (unlikely, given the fact that they were *the Big Guys*), or they couldn't/wouldn't utilize it. As a result, the only way our operation could gain access to Peyton was through Jack.

"No." My mouth made the decision before my head did, but I didn't regret it. I didn't want to like Jack, but even if I'd actually wanted to accept his offer, how could I? I had little to no tolerance for BS, and I wasn't going to use him to get to his father again, not if there were real feelings involved.

Which, I still maintained, there weren't.

"Okay, allow me to rephrase that." Jack's half grin turned into a full smirk. "If you go to homecoming with me, I will refrain from endorsing your candidacy for homecoming queen."

I stared at him.

"Think about it, Ev. All it takes is one word from me, and you could end up as the first underclassman homecoming queen in Bayport's history. At the very least, you'd be guaranteed princess, but if the seniors split enough votes, you could win the whole shebang. Wouldn't that be wonderful?"

Oh, he was good. He was very, very good.

There was no way to get my name off that ballot, and I could only hope that April's well-established popularity would guarantee that she got more votes than me and therefore won the princess title. But if Jack was serious, and he started telling people to vote for me . . .

Not good. So not good.

"You wouldn't," I said.

Jack leaned forward, until our foreheads were almost touching. "Wouldn't I?"

Damn it, I thought. He totally would.

"Won't the senior members of the squad be thrilled if you win?"

Okay, now he was just gloating. If I somehow managed to defy tradition and win queen as a sophomore, I was a dead girl. Brooke and Chloe would beat me to a pulp with their bare hands, and who knew what kind of psychological torture Zee could heap upon me if she really tried? His plan was evil, and it was genius, and given his background, neither one of those things should have surprised me.

"I hate you." I glared at Jack.

He moved forward again, until there was virtually no space between his lips and mine. "Right back at ya, Ev."

For a split second, I was terrified that he would kiss me right there, in front of everyone, but at the last instant (and right before I either grabbed him, flipped him, and hurled him to the ground or pinned him to the wall and kissed him so hard it hurt), he pulled back.

"It's a date." He smiled again, and then walked away, leaving me in his wake trying to figure out what the hell had just happened.

Less than an hour ago, all I'd wanted was detention. Now, I was nominated for homecoming court and going to the big dance with the hottest guy in school. Somewhere out there, God was laughing at me. I was sure of it.

CHAPTER 7
Code Word: Smile

"Go ahead," I told Tara. "Ask me what happened."

She arched one perfectly plucked eyebrow at me. "What happened?"

There was something in the tone of her voice, some trick to the words that made me narrow my eyes. "You already know."

She smiled slightly and merged onto the highway. I'd finally made it out of the gym, and now the two of us were on our way to the Marymount Hotel, where our mark, Jacob Kann, had checked in earlier that week. We'd picked up bugs and tracking chips from the guidepost, our loading center, and then—thankfully—the two of us had hightailed it out of there before any of the others had a chance to ask a single question about my interaction with Jack.

About that time, I realized how strange it was that none of the others had managed to get a question in. These were girls who were trained to get information out of people. Plus they single-handedly ran our school's rumor mill. So why hadn't they asked about Jack?

The answer was simple. "The others already know, too, don't they?"

How was that even possible? The gym had been crowded and noisy, and even Tara had been too far away to hear our exchange. Jack and I had kept our voices low. And yet . . .

"There's a slight chance that I read lips," Tara admitted.

Well, that answered that question.

"And the others?" Somehow, I couldn't imagine Tara ratting me out.

Tara sighed. "I'm not entirely sure, but if I had to venture a guess, I'd say there's a very good chance it has something to do with your body language and Zee's ability to read people."

And there you had it. Between a linguistics expert and a profiler who could read people like one of those *See Spot Run* books, I had no hope for keeping any aspect of my personal life private.

"I don't like him," I told Tara.

She remained silent, but allowed the edges of her lips to twitch slightly.

"You suck." I wasn't feeling very forgiving of twitchy lips and half smiles.

"It's not that bad, Toby," she said. "If it wasn't Jack, it would be somebody else. You knew coming into this what it would entail. When you become one of *those girls, those guys* start asking you out, and to stay one of *those girls*, you have to say yes."

The idea of saying yes to Chip or any of his followers (who I liked to think of as Chiplings) made me want to swallow my tongue in a fit of loathing. In comparison, going to homecoming with Jack was significantly less nauseating.

"And for all we know," Tara said, continuing her logical assessment of my situation, "Peyton might not have anything to do with the TCI influx, in which case, your date with Jack can be just that: a date."

I had to marvel at the fact that Tara was more or less lifting my objections to the homecoming situation right out of my head. It was scary how well she knew me—and my thought process. Being on the Squad was a lot like going to summer camp—after a few weeks, you start to feel like you've known the other campers for years. The ten of us spent so much time together—mornings before school, lunch, practice (of both the cheerleading and operative varieties) after school. The Squad wasn't just an activity. It was a way of life.

"Toby?" In response to Tara's prodding, I shrugged. A large part of me still wasn't sure how I felt about the fact that I'd gone from being a loner to spending most of my waking hours around nine other girls. I also wasn't sure how I felt about how I felt about it, because I probably should have hated it more than I did.

"You want the hotel room or the car?" I asked Tara, changing the subject. Our plan of action was pretty simple. We needed to break into Jacob's hotel room to plant a series of bugs so that we could monitor his phone and in-room conversations, and we needed to plant a tracking device on his car so that we could track his location, and, if necessary, tail him tomorrow.

"I'll take point on the room," Tara said. "You can come with, though."

I knew instinctively that coming from Tara, "you can come with" translated directly to "I'll show you general procedure for breaking into hotel rooms." If she'd been any of the other girls, she probably would have come out and said it, but Tara was nothing if not subtle.

"And I'll take point on the car?" I was relatively new to the spy gig, but planting a microtracker on the bottom of a Bentley with license plate number Z1X459 seemed pretty straightforward, and I was a big fan of learning by doing. I'd spent enough time in the past couple of weeks training. I was ready for some real action.

"You'll take point on the car," Tara confirmed as she pulled into a Taco Bell parking lot across the street from the hotel. She was careful to park the car so that it was obscured from the view of anyone inside the restaurant by a conveniently placed drive-through menu, and without pausing, the two of us slipped out of the car. Right before I closed the door, I remembered to pick up the tracking device. I moved to put it in my pocket before I remembered that my cheerleading uniform didn't have pockets, and then, only mildly mortified, I slipped it into my bra.

"Someone's been practicing." Tara's eyes danced with barely restrained mirth.

"Shut up."

Sticking things inside my bra made me feel like a stripper, but after a couple of tutorials from Bubbles, I could finally manage a pseudostealth bra tuck without looking like I was groping myself. All things considered, that was a definite plus, even if I didn't actually feel less conspicuous.

As we crossed the street and headed for the hotel, something occurred to me. "Should we have changed out of our uniforms?" I asked. "If we get caught, the ginormous BHS on our chests will make it pretty easy for someone to track us down."

"We won't get caught," Tara said, "and all anyone will remember was that we were cheerleaders."

That was the thing about the uniforms—people never looked past them. Anyone who saw us would just remember seeing two cheerleaders. They'd probably think we were hot, but our faces and our identifying features wouldn't be nearly as salient in their minds as the length of our skirts, and even if they did remember seeing two cheerleaders, no one in their right minds would see us as any kind of threat.

"Besides," Tara added, "we won't be wearing the uniforms for long."

I didn't exactly follow her logic there, but Tara didn't give me the chance to ask any more questions.

"Whatever you do," she said, as the two of us crossed the hotel parking lot and entered the lobby. "Smile."

I followed Tara through the lobby and into the elevator, a smile plastered to my face. She hit the fourth floor, and then when a man and a woman hopped on at the last second, she hit several more buttons.

The couple looked at us oddly, but we just stared back, wide-eyed. After a few moments, the man's expression turned from questioning to something slightly more lascivious, but a sharp elbow to his gut (his wife's doing, not mine) snapped him out of it. A few seconds after that lovely exchange, the elevator stopped on the fourth floor, but following Tara's lead, I stayed put. The door closed. The couple got off at the sixth floor, and we rode the elevator up to the seventh.

I was a quick enough study that I didn't have to ask Tara what the deal was with our extracurricular elevator riding.

Stealth was the name of the game. Even though we existed beneath the veil of the cheerleading stereotype, getting off on Jacob Kann's floor in front of witnesses might have been pushing things, especially if the worst happened and someone figured out that we'd broken into the room.

We took the stairs down to the fourth floor, and once there, Tara zeroed in on a maid cart. She glanced around for the cart's owner, and seeing that he was suitably occupied, Tara grabbed two towels and a trash bag off the cart, and then unceremoniously jerked me back into the stairwell.

"Tell me if anyone's coming," she said, and before I knew what was happening, she'd wrapped one of the towels around her body, and underneath the towel, she began taking off her clothes.

Within seconds, Tara had stripped completely and the only thing standing in between her and being naked was the skimpy hotel towel. She folded her uniform, stuck it in the trash bag, and stashed the bag just out of sight, behind a potted plant.

"Your turn," she said.

"My what?" I narrowed my eyes at her. "Because if you're saying what I think you're saying, you might want to invest in some kind of straitjacket. Maybe a padded cell. Some electroshock therapy . . ."

"You can stay here if you really want to," Tara said sweetly, "but I thought you might want to take a quick stab at his computer."

She was playing dirty, and she knew it. A guy with terrorist connections up to no good probably had some hard-core security on his laptop, and there was absolutely nothing I loved more in this world than poking around in systems specifically designed to keep me out.

Tara handed me a towel, and I flashed back to her telling me that we wouldn't be wearing our uniforms for long.

"Is there a reason we have to do this naked?" I grumbled.

Tara shrugged. "The other options are hacking into the hotel computer system and programming our own cards. . . ."

Ooooh, that sounded like fun.

"Which we would have had to do from Chloe's lab, where our keycard programming equipment is—"

Drat.

"And finding a way into one of the other rooms, going out the window, and crawling on a fourth-story ledge over to Jacob's room."

I glanced at the towel and then back at Tara. "Let's do that one."

She rolled her eyes. "Our intel says the maid for this floor is a guy," she said. "I guarantee you he has keys to all of the rooms."

The *and I guarantee you he won't be able to deny two towel-clad cheerleaders their heart's desire* went unspoken. I may have been new at this, but I wasn't stupid. I saw where the whole towel thing was going.

"Are we sure Kann isn't in his room?" I asked, making one last effort at avoiding the inevitable.

Tara smiled. "He's in the hotel bar. We passed him on the way in, and he'd just ordered a fresh drink."

Sometimes, the observation skills of cheerleaders amazed me. These very skills also tended to force me to do things that I really didn't want to do, like strip in the stairwell of a local hotel, but there are some forms of logic that you just can't argue with.

"For the record," I said, resigning myself to my fate and wrapping the towel around my body, "when I said I'd rather walk around naked than wear this stupid uniform, I was being facetious."

CHAPTER 8

Code Word: Come Hither

Getting into the room was a snap. Julius, the male house-keeper, took one look at our towels and lost any and all verbal ability he might have once had. Ever seen one of those cartoons where the guy's eyes literally pop out of his sockets, and he goes, "Owwwwooooooga, owwwwoooooooga"? That was Julius, except for the fact that the poor guy couldn't even manage a sound. Luckily, despite the fact that his mouth didn't seem to be working, his all-access keycard proved itself fully functional. He opened the door to Kann's room, and gestured incomprehensibly with one hand.

"Thanks," Tara and I chorused in unison. I can only conclude that as the door closed behind us, poor Julius in all likelihood fainted dead away on the floor.

Pushing thoughts of unconscious housekeeping staff out of my head, I glanced around the room. It was a pretty sweet setup: foyer, bedroom with king-sized bed, bathroom with enormous Jacuzzi, and a fully stocked bar. Apparently, having parents who ran their own mafialike operation really paid off.

Beside me, Tara surveyed the room. I got the distinct feeling that her assessment had less to do with how posh the accommodations were, and more to do with identifying secondary exits and analyzing in-room acoustics.

"The window would suffice in a pinch," Tara said finally, "but if by any chance Kann does happen to catch us here, our best bet is probably to pretend we saw him at the bar and decided to seduce him."

"WHAT?"

"We won't actually seduce him," she assured me. I was less than comforted. The words *come hither* weren't even in my vocabulary, and I had no interest whatsoever in playing the seduction card to get out of a mess, even if there was nothing physical involved. Ew.

Instead of elaborating on the nonseduction and comforting me further, Tara began a careful sweep of the room, looking for any security devices or wires that might already be in place. "This room's clean," she said, and in a movement so casual I barely even noticed it, she pulled a listening device out of her bra and placed it underneath the desk.

About that time, I realized that Tara wasn't actually wearing a bra, and I spent a good forty-five seconds wondering how she'd managed to keep the bugs in place on her chest. Since I wasn't quite up to her level, I'd opted for actually holding on to the tracking chip. It may not have been stealth, but it was secure.

Tara moved quickly and efficiently, violating several laws of boob physics as she bugged the bathroom and moved toward the telephone. After fiddling with the receiver for a moment, she frowned.

"What?" I said.

She didn't reply. Instead, she pulled a bobby pin out of her ponytail, and with a few highly precise movements, she removed a small, round chip from the phone.

"The phone's already wired?" I mouthed.

Tara nodded and began resweeping the rest of the room, making doubly sure that she hadn't missed any other listening devices the first time. Finally, she spoke. "We aren't the only ones keeping track of Jacob Kann."

"One of the other TCIs?" I guessed. It wasn't that much of a stretch to think that one minor-league bad guy might be bugging another. Were I a bad guy, I would have wanted to keep an eye on the competition, too. The real question was, competition for what?

"We'll bring the bug back to the lab," Tara said. "We'll be able to see if it matches anything in our files, trace its origin. Plus Chloe can continue to feed them audio tracks so that they don't realize we've disabled it."

As much as I hated to admit it, Chloe did have her uses.

Tara carefully traded the bug she'd found for one of our own, and I scanned the room again until I found what I was looking for: a fifteen-inch Mac laptop. Excellent.

Waltzing over to it, I could already feel the juices starting to flow. I booted up the computer, and in under three minutes, I guessed Kann's log-on password using nothing more than the information I'd read in his file and my own code-savvy mind. Most people choose passwords that mean something to them, and Kann wasn't an exception, though at least he mixed things up a bit. He probably thought he was pretty swift, using his middle name *backward*, followed by the year he was born.

Simpleton.

Ready to really dig my teeth into something juicy, I searched the hard drive for compressed or encrypted files, and while the computer made happy thinking noises, I leaned back in my chair.

"I'm going to go grab our clothes." Tara was finished with the bug and already thinking about our exit, which, it appeared, would be clothed.

Five minutes earlier, those words would have been music to my ears. Now, I was too deep in Happy Hacker Land to care.

It quickly became apparent that Jacob Kann didn't have much of interest on his computer. All of his files were boring (also known as not encrypted). That said, just because there wasn't anything fun for me to play with on his computer didn't mean that there wasn't any valuable information there; it just meant that nothing he had would be much of a challenge on the decoding front.

Still hoping to come up with something cool, I launched Kann's internet browser, and while it booted up, I reached up and undid the clasp around my neck. The twins were big on accessories, an obsession I would have lamented were it not for the fact that all Squad accessories came equipped with something extra. This particular necklace doubled as a portable hard drive with a ridiculously large amount of memory. I slid the charm off the chain and pressed gently on one side, revealing a USB plug. I inserted it into Kann's computer, and with a few more commands, the computer began copying the entire contents of its hard drive to mine.

Meanwhile, the internet was up and running, so I checked our mark's browsing history, which led me directly to his primary email account. He had his computer set to remember his username, and the password was—you guessed it—his middle name backward, followed by the year he was born.

Seriously, I thought, did this guy flunk out of wannabe terrorist school? What kind of TCI used the same password for all of his accounts? I knew fourth graders who realized that was a bad idea.

Not that I was complaining, only I kind of wanted to, because when it came to hacking, I lived for the challenge, and this was kid stuff.

I'd just opened Kann's inbox when Tara knocked at the door. I probably would have been more paranoid about whether or not it was indeed Tara, except for the fact that she knocked to the rhythm of "Clap Your Hands." Smart girl.

After setting Kann's inbox, sent mail, and address book to copy over to my drive, I got up and walked over to the door. I peeked out the peephole, just to be on the safe side, and then let Tara in.

"Finished?" she asked me.

I glanced back over at the laptop. "Five minutes, tops."

"We only have three."

Get in and get out—that was the Squad motto, and there was a decent chance that we'd already been here too long.

"Three minutes," I agreed. "Can I have my clothes?"

Tara tossed them to me, and content that the computer was doing its thing, I went to the bathroom to change. I'd just zipped my skirt up the side and stuck the tracking chip back in my bra when I heard the door to the room slam open and then slam shut.

Uh-oh, I thought. Tara didn't slam doors. Ever. And the sound of the slamming did not in any way sound like one of our cheers. No matter which way I approached the situation, one thing was clear: there was somebody else in the room, and that was a very, very bad thing.

Moving as silently as I could, I leapt into the Jacuzzi and pressed myself against the bottom, using the side to obscure myself from view as best I could. I spent exactly three seconds seriously hoping that Kann—assuming that he was the one who'd crashed our spy party—wouldn't come into the bathroom, and another two hoping that Tara had opted for hiding herself over attempting to seduce our mark.

Despite the fact that their threat levels weren't that high, the TCIs were on the Watch List for a reason. Jacob Kann was dangerous, and as I thought of my partner out there with him, I had to push down the urge to go charging out of the bathroom, half-dressed, and take him down. Only the incessant training that had been drilled into my head over the past month—*do not physically engage a mark unless specifically instructed to do so; protect your cover and trust your partner to protect herself*—kept me from doing just that, and the training only held me off for an additional six seconds. Luckily, in that time, Jacob Kann muttered several curses about females under his breath, grabbed what sounded like a set of keys off of a dresser, and stomped back out the door.

Cautiously, I stuck my head out of the bathroom and saw Tara maneuvering back through the window.

"Hang from the ledge?" I asked her.

"Dove into the bathtub?" she returned.

I threw my top on instead of responding, and she grabbed my hard drive out of the computer. "Lucky for us, Kann is oblivious," she said, tossing it to me with one hand

and hitting the computer's power button with the other. "Ready to run?"

I caught the hard drive and slipped it back onto the chain around my neck. "Run?"

Tara shrugged, seemingly nonplussed by our brush with getting busted. "He came up here to pick up his car keys," she said, "and we still need to tag his car." With that, she ducked back out the window, and I followed, a little bewildered, but in too much of a hurry to ask.

"Fire escape," I noted as we started taking the stairs down two at a time.

"Leads directly to the parking lot."

"Convenient," I said.

"Fast," Tara said, her tone completely conversational. "We may have to jump the last flight if we want to beat Kann to his car."

"Like I said," I told her. "Convenient."

After that, we just ran. Most people vastly underestimate the amount of conditioning done by the average cheerleader. I was in the best shape of my life, and it wasn't because of the spy half of our gig. Moving in perfect synchrony, Tara and I reached the top of the last flight, and in the interest of saving time, we flipped ourselves off the side, braced and ready for impact. Like the good cheer girls we were, we stuck our landings. I met Tara's eyes for a split second, and she nodded toward my chest—and the tracking chip that was somehow, miraculously, still in my bra.

"You go," she said. "I'll run interference if you need more time."

She was the senior partner, and that was an order. I didn't question it, I didn't resent it. I just followed it. I slipped the chip out of my bra, and still moving at warp speed, scanned the parking lot and zeroed in on covered parking. Given his luxury digs, our mark definitely seemed the type to shell out a few extra bucks in order to park in the shade. After that, the Bentley wasn't hard to find.

Within seconds, I was under the car, fastening the chip into place. Working with the last of my momentum, I rolled out the other side just as Tara intercepted our mark several cars down.

"Have you seen a blue ribbon?" I heard her ask, and even from under the car, I could make out the sexy pout in her voice. "My friend seems to have lost hers."

Realizing that Tara had given me the perfect excuse for being on the ground near Kann's car, which probably would have appeared somewhat sketchy in most situations, I ripped the ribbon out of my hair and then popped to my feet.

"Found it!" I held the ribbon up triumphantly and hoped that it never occurred to Kann that I might have been up to something other than ribbon chasing.

One look at our mark's face told me that he wasn't the type to go gaga for cheerleaders. In fact, all evidence suggested that he was the type to roll his eyes and dismiss their missing ribbons out of hand.

Perfect.

I started walking away from Kann's car, and he brushed past me to get to the driver's-side door. My back to the car, I walked toward Tara. Behind me, I could hear Kann's keyless entry beeping, and I glanced over my shoulder to see him reaching for the door handle.

And in that moment, that single quarter of a second before Kann pulled the door open, I remember wondering why I'd looked back. And then the moment was over, Kann opened the door, and with a sonic boom, the entire thing exploded into flames.

Tara reacted faster than I did. She dove on top of me, forcing me to the ground and out of the way of flying debris. My head hit the pavement, and the last thing I remember thinking before losing consciousness was that if Tara had been a second slower, or if I'd been any closer to the car, I'd be dead.

CHAPTER 9

Code Word: Naked

Jack is standing next to me. My hands are sweating. I think he's asking me to dance, but there isn't any noise coming out of his moving mouth, and really, he should know better than to make any such requests. I don't dance.

The world around me jumps violently, and when it finally stands still again, I'm dancing, and I don't understand why. As we've already established, I don't dance. And yet . . .

My body is moving faster than I can mentally keep track of the motions. I have no control over the spastic, sensual movements, and Jack's just standing there, looking at me, and all of a sudden, I'm wearing my cheerleading uniform, and Jack is Lucy, and she has a giant fish in each hand.

No, not fish. She has knives. Or is that dynamite? Wait, it's Chinese throwing stars. Definitely Chinese throwing stars. She throws them at me, and all of a sudden, the stars are fish, and I'm not wearing anything but a towel. And then Lucy is Jack again, and the battle star fish have exploded into confetti.

"And this year's homecoming queen is . . ." The voice on the loudspeakers sounds suspiciously like Ryan Seacrest. The words echo in my head—tiny, audible portents of doom.

Jack stares at me with an ironic smile on his face. My heart thumps viciously in my chest, and I wish to God I was still dancing, because even that was better than this.

"Toby Klein!"

It takes me a moment to process that they've said my name and another to realize what it means. No. Oh, no.

All eyes are on me, and when I look down to avoid their stares, I realize that I have much bigger problems than any tiaras in my immediate future.

The towel is gone, I'm naked, and Jack is staring at me. Again.

"Toby." Tara's voice broke into my mind, and it was a double-edged sword. On the one hand, as consciousness seeped slowly back into my body, I realized that I had a headache roughly the size of North America. On the other, however, waking up made me realize that the whole thing with the nakedness and Jack and being the homecoming queen was just a nightmare, and that was a Very Good Thing.

"Ow." I put my thoughts into words as coherently as I could.

"I know," Tara said. "You took a pretty hard hit to the head. We need to get it checked out."

I blinked several times and then set about trying to figure out where I was and what Tara was talking about. I'd just realized that I was in the backseat of Tara's car when her words finally triggered something in my mind.

"Hit to the head. As in my head and the ground? Or my head and flying debris? Because the car . . ." I trailed off. "Oh, God, the car."

"You're okay," Tara said, her voice low and smooth. "You're going to be fine."

I sat up, slowly, and Tara leaned toward me. She took my head in her hands, and peered carefully at my eyes.

"Your pupils aren't dilated," she said. "Can you track my finger?"

I followed her French-manicured index finger as it zipped back and forth.

"Headache?" she questioned.

I gave her a look that I hoped conveyed a properly large amount of "duh."

Tara was not the least bit deterred by my response. "Nausea?"

"No."

"You probably don't have a concussion," Tara told me, "but procedure says we have to get you checked out, just to be sure."

"Better safe than sorry?" I asked, a single note of sarcasm creeping into my voice. I'd known logically that spying was a dangerous gig, but the fact that there were procedures for stuff like this kind of hit that message home.

"More or less," Tara replied.

"Makes sense," I said. "I mean, I'm guessing the government likes to cover all their bases when their top-secret underage teenage agents almost get *blown to freaking pieces!*"

"Drama queen."

I never thought I'd live to see the day when a cheerleader would call me a drama queen.

"I could have been killed!"

Stupid Big Guys. Stupid bomber. Stupid Jack's uncle.

This time, Tara just mouthed the words. "Drama. Queen."

"Exploding car," I countered. About that time, it occurred

to me to ask the question that my subconscious was deliberately skirting. "Jacob Kann?"

Tara shook her head.

"Our mark is dead." I said the words out loud, but they still didn't feel real. "Somebody killed him."

"We'll find out who," Tara said. "And why."

I was in shock, and her words were strangely comforting. Jacob Kann hadn't exactly been one of the good guys. In fact, there was a very good chance that he was one of the bad guys, but I felt oddly compelled to avenge his death, to find the person who planted that bomb and to make sure they couldn't ever do it again.

"The Big Guys are sending in a special team," Tara told me. "Half to run interference with the local law enforcement, and half to speed up the forensics end of the investigation. We should know more about the explosives used by tomorrow."

I rubbed the side of my head and was immediately rewarded with a sharp, throbbing pain.

"Don't touch it," Tara said. "I stopped the bleeding, but it's going to be a heck of a bruise."

"Stopped the bleeding?" That sounded serious. "How long was I out for?"

"Five minutes," Tara said. "I got you to the car and left ASAP, drove a couple miles away, and once we'd cleared the scene and I'd called in the situation, I pulled over to try to wake you up." She paused and handed me a bottle of something that looked like body splash. I smelled it and my eyes immediately began tearing.

"It's good for bringing people back," she said. "Don't ask what's in it."

I accepted her advice.

"You going to be okay to ride the rest of the way to the emergency room?"

I stared at Tara. "Emergency room?"

"Protocol."

"Yeah, we already covered that, but I just figured . . . I mean, don't we have our own doctor? Or some kind of top-secret medical base or something?"

"Absolutely," Tara said, arching an eyebrow at me. "It's under a volcano and run by a mad scientist."

I gave her a look. "We have a helipad," I told her. "I don't think a med center is that much more ridiculous."

She shrugged, conceding the point. "We have somewhere we can go if things are serious. If not, we hit up the ER."

My super spy senses told me that I wasn't going to get any more information out of her about the top-secret place we could go for "serious" injuries, and I didn't really feel compelled to dwell on the fact that my current injuries could have easily been more severe.

"So," I said. "About that emergency room."

Ten minutes later, we arrived at the Bayport Hospital ER.

The woman at the front desk asked me the nature of my injury. Tara responded before I had the chance. "We dropped her."

The woman clucked her tongue. "You girls," she said. "I swear, you're in here more than the football players."

It took every ounce of subtlety I had to refrain from gawking at Tara's audacity. She was trying to pass off my near-concussion as the result of a cheer injury?

"Well, cheerleading is the second most dangerous sport in America," Tara said.

The woman smiled. "Right after polo," she said. Clearly, she'd somehow heard this spiel often enough that she'd come to believe it was true. I sincerely hoped that my health was not in any way in her hands.

"You girls sit down," the woman said. "I'll sneak you in just as soon as a room opens up."

"Thanks, Nora," Tara said. Then she hooked her arm through mine and prodded me toward the waiting room.

"Second most dangerous sport in America?" I asked under my breath, my tone incredulous. "Where do you guys get this stuff?"

"Oh," Tara said as we sat down. "That's actually true."

"Yeah, right."

"Seriously," Tara said. "Cheerleaders sustain more debilitating injuries than almost any other kind of athlete."

I opened my mouth and then closed it again, completely unsure how to respond to Tara's claim.

"Really, Toby. Everyone on the Squad has gotten to know Nora really well, and it's not because of our *extracurricular* activities. It's because cheerleading is hard on your body. People get dropped. Ankles get twisted. Teeth get knocked out. It happens."

"And when something 'happens'—" I made liberal use of air quotes.

"We come here," Tara finished for me.

"And so when something . . . *extracurricular* happens . . ."

Tara nodded. "We come here."

I added this entire conversation to my list of reasons why cheerleaders were actually freakishly suited to life as

69

operatives. Our cover even worked to explain injuries incurred in the line of duty.

For a little while, Tara and I were silent, but I finally had to ask. "So what have you come in here for?"

"Last time, it was a fractured pelvis."

"Ouch. Somebody drop you?"

"Nope. Herkie."

I tried to figure out how exactly one could fracture a pelvis doing a cheer jump, but Tara just shook her head, a wry smile on her face. "Don't ask."

We fell back into silence then, and I made a mental list of questions I'd ask my partner once I was in the clear to talk about the more classified aspects of our lives, starting with whether or not she'd ever been injured as an operative, and concluding with how exactly she'd managed to get me from the parking lot to her car, presumably without anyone noticing.

"Toby?"

Tara nudged me when Nora called my name. "Let's go."

By the time we were situated in a small exam room, I was half-convinced that I was still dreaming. Just to make sure that I was awake, I looked down to confirm that my clothes had not suddenly disappeared.

Still there.

Tara took a seat on the exam table and I did the same. After a moment, she took an iPod out of her backpack and offered me one earpiece.

"Nora's great about getting us in quickly," she said, "but the doctors usually take forever."

I accepted the earpiece somewhat suspiciously. On the whole, I had not been impressed by the musical preferences of my cheerleading cohorts, and there was at least a five percent chance that she'd make me listen to the words to some new cheer we were getting ready to learn.

Instead, I watched as Tara hit several buttons, and a few seconds later, Brooke's voice came through our earpieces, loud and clear.

"Took you guys long enough. How's the security reading on your communicator, Tare?"

"There was a wait," Tara explained. "And it's good."

I processed this conversation and then spoke up myself. I had no idea where the microphone was on this not-really-an-iPod, but I decided to go on the assumption that Brooke would hear my words.

"Yes, I'm okay, Brooke. Thank you for asking. Your concern is sweet, but really, you don't need to worry about little old me."

"If you weren't okay," Brooke said, "you wouldn't be in the emergency room."

Her logic seemed counterintuitive, but given the conversation I'd had earlier with Tara about how procedure was different for serious injuries, Brooke's words made sense.

"So what's up?" Tara asked, careful to keep our side of the conversation generic and innocuous enough that if the doctor walked in, he wouldn't notice anything out of the norm.

"No word yet from the special unit the Big Guys sent in to check out the blast," Brooke informed us.

"I can't believe they wouldn't even let me look at it!" That was Lucy, speaking from somewhere in the background. "Totally unfair."

There were few things our weapons expert loved more than a good explosion.

71

"Sorry, Luce," Brooke said. "I tried."

I thought I heard a note of strain in Brooke's voice and inferred that trying—and failing—wasn't something Brooke was overly fond of. If she'd tried to get Lucy in on the explosion recon and hadn't been able to, that meant that the Big Guys had forbidden it, which meant that maybe Brooke wasn't exactly as in charge of this mission as she had been this morning.

Knowing her as I did, I could imagine just how well that was going over.

"So how did everyone else's thing go?" Tara asked, still keeping with the quality vagueness.

"You know how when you called in Toby's injury, you mentioned that you'd found a chip in Kann's phone?" Brooke asked.

I just loved it when people talked about me like I wasn't even on the secured, high-tech line.

"Were there more?" Tara asked, her voice even and measured.

I could practically hear Brooke nodding her ponytailed head. "Two of the other phones were also already bugged— Amelia Juarez's and Anthony Connors-Wright's."

"And the third?" I asked, screening my words to make sure they would be opaque to potential eavesdroppers.

"Hector Hassan's phone was not bugged," Brooke said. "We haven't gotten anything significant from the audio yet, but if Amelia, Jacob, and Anthony were all bugged and Hector wasn't—"

"Then chances are, he's the one who . . ." I tried to censor myself. "Did the phone thing to the others."

"That's the current theory," Brooke said. Then there was

a long, significant pause, and I got the distinct feeling that I was missing something. It fell into place the second that the doctor stepped into the room.

If Hassan was the one who'd bugged Jacob Kann's phone, then there was at least a chance that he was the one who'd planted the bomb. I was suddenly overcome with an urge to jump off the exam table and rush out to kick some TCI a-s-s. Because as it turned out, almost getting blown up? Not nearly as much of a deterrent as one might think.

"Toby Klein?" the doctor said.

I nodded, and Tara subtly hit the pause button, ending our communication with Brooke, before gently taking the earpiece from my ear.

"Sorry," she said. "We were in the middle of a song."

The doctor nodded and approached me. "What seems to be the problem?"

"I . . . uhhhh . . . got dropped." I still couldn't believe that anyone would buy that excuse.

"Prep or full extension?" the doctor asked.

I was somewhat disturbed by the fact that this doctor knew cheerleading terms that I didn't.

Seeing my confusion, the doctor grinned. "You must be new," he said. "Let me ask it this way—how high up were you?"

I tried to gauge the right way to answer that question. "Kinda high up?" I answered. "I think I hit pretty hard. I blacked out for a few minutes."

The doctor shook his head and then took a closer look at the cut on the side of my head. "It's not deep," he said. His gentle tone lulled me into a false sense of security, and then his fingers prodded my bruise. "Does this hurt?"

I yelped and let loose an impressive string of expletives.

"Okay," the doctor inferred, seemingly bemused, "that hurts."

He pulled a light out from the front pocket of his lab coat and shined it in my eyes. He continued examining me as he ran through a list of questions, some of which Tara had asked me earlier, and some of which she hadn't. In the end, he said that he didn't think I had a concussion and that an MRI wouldn't be necessary this time.

"You got off easy," he told me. "If you'll take my advice—and they never do—you'll get out of this game while you still can."

I had to remind myself that he was talking about the cheerleading aspect of it. He had no idea what we were really up to. Either way, there was exactly zero chance of me quitting. If anything, recent events had caused some perverse part of me to want to throw myself into this mission more.

Seeing the refusal to quit in my eyes, the doctor sighed. "I have three daughters," he said. "The oldest one is five. If she wants to play football when she's in high school, I'll buy her the jersey, but the second the word *cheer* leaves her mouth, I'm locking her in her room until she's thirty. It's just too dangerous."

And with that, he was gone.

I turned to Tara. "And you said *I* was a drama queen."

Tara grinned. "Let's go," she said. "I think you have something Brooke will be very, very happy to see."

Tara's words registered, and after a few seconds, my hand flew to my throat. My necklace was still there, and the charm appeared to be in one piece. Until that moment, I'd completely forgotten that I was wearing the contents of the late Jacob Kann's laptop around my neck.

I smiled, thinking how satisfying it would be to hand the data stick to Brooke all gloatylike, and echoed Tara's words. "Let's go."

And then, because a full fourth of my brain had become dedicated to cheers, I rephrased my words with but a hint of irony in my voice. "L-e-t-s-g-o, let's go, let's go, l-e-t-s-g-o . . ."

Tara grinned. "Let's go!"

CHAPTER 10
Code Word: Prezzies

By the time Tara and I got back to the Quad, my mood had improved significantly. You know your life is bordering on the absurd when a day you almost get blown up, but *don't* have a concussion, is a good day. I think it's safe to conclude that I was pretty much in happy denial land. All I could think about was that, despite our mission's disastrous ending, I'd managed to do something that none of the other girls had.

I'd gotten computer intel. If any of Jacob Kann's lovely, unencrypted files contained information about what he was doing in Bayport, that would be huge. Now more than ever, we needed to find out why the TCIs were here, because with Kann's death, one thing had become crystal clear.

Whatever it was that had brought the TCIs to Bayport was worth killing for.

"Toby, OMG, are you okay?" Lucy greeted me with a huge hug and a mouthful of high-speed babble. "We were like so worried about you! I mean, I know you were standing far enough away from the blast that the resulting heat wave shouldn't have affected you, but flying debris can be so totally deadly and stuff!"

"I'm fine," I assured her. "Really, Luce."

Tara rolled her eyes, probably at the fact that I'd gone from Drama Queen mode to downplaying the whole thing. All it took was a little sympathy.

"Do you think the cut will heal before homecoming?" Lucy was wide-eyed at the prospect. I brightened slightly at her question. Would this negatively affect my chances for homecoming princess?

Please, I thought, let this negatively affect my chances for homecoming princess!

"Don't worry, Toby. We've got you covered." Brittany handed me a small gift bag, and then Tiffany handed me a slightly larger one.

"Oooohhhhh," Bubbles said appreciatively. "Prezzies!"

I was somewhat skeptical of anything that involved the twins handing me packages. Somehow, I doubted there was chocolate inside.

"The blue one has a new liquid base in it," Tiffany said. "It's totally safe to use on wounds, and it's got this poly-microfiber thingy in it that completely camouflages even the worst bruises."

Oh, goody! Makeup.

"What's the pink one have in it?" I was almost afraid to ask.

Brittany reached a hand out to touch my hair. "Proto-type conditioner," she said. "Explosions wreak havoc on your hair's moisture levels."

I almost got blown up, and the twins were worried about the effect it would have on my hair. Why was I not surprised?

"Good. You're back." Brooke pushed through the others

to stand directly in front of Tara and me. "You two ready to give us the full rundown on your recon?" Her gaze lingered on my bruised temple for just a moment, and I thought I saw something that might have been worry behind her eyes. Then again, it also might have been unadulterated disdain. I'm always mixing those two up.

"We're ready," Tara said. Then she looked at me, and the edges of her lips turned up slightly. "Let's go."

The look in her eyes, in combination with the tone in her voice on those last two words, had me fighting an insane urge to giggle, even though our "let's go" joke wasn't objectively funny at all. I blame the fact that, between the body glitter, the pep rally, and nearly being decapitated by flying debris, it had been a pretty stressful day.

Not saying a word, and somehow managing to keep my stress-induced giggle impulse to myself, I followed the others to our conference table and sat docilely while Tara began calmly and methodically walking the others through our mission.

"Your potentially hostile target almost caught you guys casing his room?" Brooke asked.

Tara inclined her head slightly, acceding the point, but the look in her eyes was pure steel. "He didn't catch us."

"Get in and get out," Brooke said. "You were supposed to get in and get out."

Personally, I thought she was blowing this a little bit out of proportion. She hadn't been the least bit concerned about the fact that I'd almost been blown to Toby bits, but she was upset that we'd overstayed our welcome in Kann's room?

"He didn't catch us." I backed Tara up, even though

there was a distinct chance that she would have preferred that I keep my mouth closed.

"He could have," Brooke countered tersely.

"He's dead," I told her.

Even Brooke couldn't argue with that.

"And besides," I added, reaching back to unclasp my necklace. "If we'd gotten in and out more quickly, I wouldn't have been able to get this." I slipped the charm off the chain and threw it to her. Moving on reflex, Brooke caught it.

"The contents of his hard drive." I smiled brightly, looking every inch the cheerleader. "And his email."

Brooke became very still, her eyes locked on mine. "Seriously?"

I nodded.

She smiled. "Sweet." And then, without a word, she tossed the data stick to Chloe, who caught it just as easily as Brooke had a moment before.

"Think you can have the data sorted by morning?" Brooke asked her.

Chloe grinned. "Natch."

A few seconds later, I came to the realization that Brooke had put Chloe in charge of looking for meaningful data on *my* disk, and I actually managed to stop gloating long enough to protest.

"I can do it."

Brooke didn't pause a beat. "You can go home," she corrected. "And rest. Right after you talk to Zee and convince her that you're not traumatized for life." Even though Brooke clearly considered this an order, there was something almost gentle in her voice. In fact, of all the words she'd ever spoken to me, these were the only ones that didn't sound like some variation of *You are a retarded cheerleader. You are a cheertard.*

While I was still processing her tone, she turned to the others. "We've got intel coming in on the other three TCIs. We'll split up and sort through the audio feed and GPS data on their movements since we planted the chips. If Chloe can pull something meaningful off of Kann's hard drive, we can backtrack and download any info the Big Guys have on phone records to cross-reference any common contacts here in Bayport. With any luck, we may be able to identify the threat before the Big Guys do, in which case, we may actually be able to keep this case a Squad operation."

I didn't need Zee's PhD to read the look in Brooke's eyes. She didn't want to hand this case over. For that matter, neither did I. Somebody had made me bleed, and that same somebody had killed my mark. That made this personal, and Brooke seemed to regard it as the same. This was officially one of those times when Her Royal Highness, the cheerleading captain, was a person I almost liked and borderline understood.

"Go home," Brooke repeated her earlier order to me. I didn't like it any more this time than I had before. I'd earned the right to be here. There was data to be processed, feeds to listen to, and she expected me to go home? Forget what I said about understanding her. She was clearly wacky.

"There is no way I'm—"

"Home," Brooke said, and the bossy, I-Rule-the-World tone was back in her voice. "We'll debrief you tomorrow."

I looked at Tara, hoping she'd back me up, but she rolled

her eyes. "You were nearly concussed," she said. "One night off won't kill you, and rest would probably be a good idea."

Traitor.

"What do you expect me to do at home? Sit around and wonder what you guys are doing here?"

"What did you do before you joined the Squad?" Tara asked in what I hated to admit was a completely reasonable manner.

"Yeah," Tiffany piped up. "We always sort of wondered that. Because, I mean, you like didn't really have any friends, and you didn't really seem like you did anything, and . . ."

Her twin elbowed her, and Tiffany, amazingly enough, shut her mouth. I was temporarily grateful to Brittany, until she came up with a suggestion for how I should spend my newfound downtime. "Do that deep moisturizing conditioner treatment we gave you." She narrowed her eyes at me. "Besides the fact that explosions dry out your hair, we've totally been meaning to talk to you about volume and bounce."

Needless to say, that was a conversation that I would willingly have right after I volunteered to dance in the *Nutcracker* and legally change my name to Buttercup Posy-Pants.

"If you want," Tiffany offered brightly. "We could come over and help you."

Translation: We can come over and torture you. And then they'd follow the hair treatment by faux flirting with Noah, and I'd end up actually concussing myself by banging my head repeatedly against the closest wall.

"You stay," I told the twins, shooting Brooke an aggrieved look. She smiled smugly back, and I realized I was being manipulated by the master. And her minions.

"Fine," I said. "I'll go, but if anything needs decoding—*anything*—you call me. Deal?"

Brooke inclined her head slightly, and I got the feeling that that was as much of an answer as I was going to get.

"I'll walk you out," Zee volunteered. Tara opened her mouth and then closed it again. She'd probably been on the verge of making the same offer, but Brooke shook her head slightly, and Tara remained silent. With one last nod at all of the others, Zee and I made our exit, and for a little while, we walked in silence.

"Chip asked Brooke to homecoming," Zee volunteered finally. She was always the first one to know school gossip. "And Marty Bregman asked Chloe, but she turned him down, of course."

I didn't even know who Marty Bregman was.

"That's the point," Zee said, lifting the thought from my head. "You don't know who Marty is. If he mattered, you would, hence Chloe politely declining."

Somehow, I seriously doubted that Chloe's decline was anywhere near polite. She had a chip on her shoulder, and the fact that Brooke had an A-list date couldn't have been sitting well with her.

"Who are you going with?" I wasn't exactly an expert at girl talk, but I was pretty sure that according to Girl Law, this was the question I was supposed to ask the Gossip Queen next.

"Aaron Lykeman," Zee said.

That name I knew—vaguely. He was a football player and one of the Chiplings.

"Any other gossip?" I asked. To me, rumor was still a four-letter word, but as long as Zee was talking about other people, I didn't have to worry about her going all Freud on me.

"Not really," Zee said. Apparently, there was a first time for everything. "I actually wanted to talk to you about Brooke."

Say what?

"I know she can seem kind of intense," Zee said, "and I know you think she's bossy, but Brooke's under a lot of pressure right now."

The last time Zee had pulled me over for a heart-to-heart, it was about Chloe. This time, it was Brooke. I was starting to wonder if our resident profiler's mission in life was to make me understand the psychological complexities of bitchiness.

"Pressure?" I tried to sort it out in my own mind before Zee could throw herself into full-on wisdom-imparting mode. "Well, there was an explosion," I mused. "And it sounds like the Big Guys Upstairs are kind of breathing down her neck about it."

"And," Zee added, "homecoming's this weekend."

As if I needed reminding.

"As far as Brooke's concerned, she can't afford to lose this case, and she can't afford to lose that crown." Zee gave me a look, willing me to understand her.

I tried to oblige. Apparently, Brooke was stressing about whether or not she'd win a title everyone already knew was hers. And this was supposed to make me feel sorry for her how?

"As far as Brooke's mother is concerned, losing out on queen and losing a case to the Big Guys are equally unacceptable outcomes." Zee paused. "She's really leaning on Brooke right now."

Ahhhh . . . the infamous Mrs. Camden. All I knew about her was that she'd trained Brooke for the Squad program from the cradle. From the tone in Zee's voice, it sounded like she was pretty hard-core about it, even now.

"Brooke's mom can be . . . intense."

At this point, I was used to Brooke being Brooke. A few weeks ago, I probably would have told her to stick her pom-poms where the sun don't shine if she'd even thought about pulling me off a case, however briefly. All things considered, my response to Brooke's "request" was looking downright reasonable, and Zee's info-dumping seemed less than necessary.

"Anything else to share, O Wise One?" I asked.

"Actually," Zee said. "Now it's your turn to share."

I stared at her dumbly.

"You're tough, Toby, but you also saw somebody die today." Zee carefully measured my response. "That's a hard pill for anyone to swallow."

"Technically, I didn't see him die." I shrugged the words off, even as I said them. "I was sort of unconscious at the time."

"Uh-huh." Zee was less than persuaded by my response.

"It doesn't seem real." I tried for honesty over technicalities this time. "This whole thing—what we do, who we are—it's all just so surreal that I can't quite wrap my mind around the fact that today actually happened."

"Believe it or not," Zee said, "that might be a good thing."

And here I'd thought denial was a psychological no-no.

"What we do *is* surreal," Zee said. "It's unbelievable, and there would probably be something wrong with you if you didn't have a hard time processing this. I just need to know—are you having second thoughts?"

"Second thoughts? About the Squad?"

She nodded.

"I'm starting to think the CIA is seriously deranged for letting us do this," I told her, "but that doesn't mean that I don't want to do it." I paused. "Actually, the fact that we probably *shouldn't* be doing this kind of makes me want to do it more."

Zee snorted. "Adrenaline junkie," she accused.

"Maybe," I said.

"Or maybe," Zee filled in, "the fact that the danger is real is making you realize that the good we do is real, too."

I didn't reply. Zee was the PhD, not me, and I wasn't all that curious as to why nearly having my head taken off by flying debris was more of a turn-on to the spy gig than a turn-off.

"You'll call if you need to talk?" Zee asked.

I nodded. "Sure."

"Cool."

"That it?"

Zee grinned. "Unless you want to talk about your feelings for Jack?"

I glared at her.

"Didn't think so."

CHAPTER 11

Code Word: The Fam

For the first time since I'd joined the Squad, I walked through my front door before eight o'clock at night. The first couple of weeks, I kept thinking that my mother would at least ask why we were having such long practices, but apparently, unbeknownst to me, she'd caught a documentary on competitive cheerleading, and she didn't seem to think that the hours I was keeping were all that unusual.

Then again, there was very little that did strike my mom as unusual. She was the kind of person who could walk into a room and discover that it was filled with penguins, and she would just shrug it off like it was nothing. She wasn't at all oblivious; she noticed everything, took note, and filed it away for future reference, but nothing fazed her. Nothing. My dad was the exact opposite. Most days, he was so caught up in equations and theorems that the mere existence of nonnumeric entities in the world took him by surprise.

"You're home for dinner," my mom commented the second she set eyes on me. "Help me set the table."

See? No questions as to why I was home for dinner, or, for that matter, how I'd gotten the cut on the side of my head. She definitely noticed it, and the look in her eyes told me that she wanted me to know she'd noticed it, but she didn't spare it so much as an additional comment.

I set the table for four, and at the last minute, my mom had me add a place setting, which could only mean one of two things. The first option was that my dad had brought someone home with him from work. The second was that one of Noah's friends had tagged along after school. I spent a single moment devoutly praying that it was the first option. I would rather listen to multiple socially awkward physicists wax poetic about string theory than suffer the company of the freshman goof squad.

"Mom?"

"Yes, dear?"

"Who's the fifth setting for?"

"Noah's friend Chuck."

Today was just really not my day. Chuck had an unhealthy Toby obsession. He'd had the aforementioned obsession since the pre-Squad days, and needless to say, my becoming the stereotypical teen boy's dream overnight hadn't done much to dissuade him.

Long story short, I wasn't looking forward to dinner.

By the time Chuck and Noah slid into their seats at the table, I had a very simple plan. I was going to eat quickly. I was going to glare at anyone who tried to talk to me, and I was going to thoroughly pretend that there wasn't still blue body glitter on my chest. It wasn't a foolproof plan, but it was functional, and after the day I'd had, I wasn't sure I could hope for much more than that.

"Hey, Tobe." Noah greeted me cheerfully. In fact, he sounded just happy enough to sketch me out. If he was happy, he was up to something.

"Mmvvmmmesh," Chuck mumbled. I was about ninety percent sure that he was trying to say hello, but decided to ignore his mumbling altogether. It was kinder that way. Really.

"So," my mom said, taking her seat next to my dad, whose eyes were glossed over in that "I'm working out a new theory of black holes" kind of way. "Anything interesting happen at school today?"

I shot darts at Noah with my eyes and hoped the threat of violence was coming across clearly enough. The last thing I needed was for my brother to advertise the fact that I'd been nominated to homecoming court.

"Some of the girls who dig me got nominated for homecoming queen," Noah said, heeding my warning and choosing to talk about the other nominees instead. "But, of course, the real competition will be which one of the lovely ladies gets to go as my date. I can only hope there will be no bloodshed and a minimum of tears."

Now do you see why the twins really didn't need to encourage him? Noah was basically a puppy, the kind who's always chewing on shoes and jumping up on people and wanting them to rub his belly (metaphorically speaking, I hope). My brother was one hundred percent unabashed energy, and for reasons that continue to elude me to this day, he was confident in his appeal to the fairer sex, even though he'd never actually succeeded in convincing a girl to go out with him.

"Toe." Chuck tried to say something, but didn't quite

succeed. To put things mildly, good old Chuck didn't exactly have Noah's confidence.

"Toe?" my mom prodded.

"Toby got nominated, too," Chuck blurted out, and I realized that I'd been wasting my dart eyes on the wrong freshman.

"Nominated for what?" my father asked, just now tuning in to the conversation.

"Homecoming court," my mom said, her voice devoid of any emotion resembling surprise, shock, or outrage.

"What?" my dad repeated, wrinkling his forehead and blinking several times.

"Homecoming court," Noah repeated, flashing me a victorious grin. "I'm her campaign manager."

"No, you're not," I told him, my voice and my expression equally dark.

Noah leaned in and spoke in a stage whisper. "We're going to have to work on your people skills."

Noah wasn't actually a ladies' man, and he didn't have my aptitudes for physical competition or mathematical thinking, but when it came to being able to press my buttons, he was nothing short of a prodigy.

In fact, that was the one thing that Noah and the twins had in common.

In order to survive the rest of the cozy family dinner, I checked out mentally and let my mind wander. I ran Jacob Kann's file over and over again in my mind, and then walked back through our mission, step by step, looking for anything we might have missed the first time around, any clue that Kann's hours were, from the moment we stepped into his hotel room, severely numbered.

I started with what I knew about him personally. Jacob Kann was single, young, and wanted to prove himself to his mafiaesque family with some insanely big gesture, like bringing in a ton of money from some well-connected terrorist groups. He'd been in Bayport for two days. When we'd arrived at the hotel, he'd been hanging out in the bar, and while we were casing his hotel room, he'd come storming in, obviously in a bad mood.

I let my mind dwell there for a moment, trying to create possible scenarios in my mind. Why had Kann left his car keys in his room? Had he just forgotten them, or had he not planned on needing them at all? Why had he suddenly been in such a hurry to leave the hotel bar?

And, I thought, my mind pulling up a question that hadn't occurred to me until that moment, why was he in the hotel bar in the first place? His room, the very definition of lush, had come equipped with its own bar. So why was he drinking in the lobby? Was he meeting someone? Hoping to pick up some girls? Had he left because a woman had rejected him? Or because a meeting had gone sour?

There were too many possibilities, too many questions that we might not ever get the answers to. One thing was for sure. Jacob Kann wasn't going to be answering them any time soon.

I switched the scene in my mind and concentrated on the few seconds that I'd been under Kann's car. Had I seen anything out of the ordinary? Had the bomb been there, staring me in the face the whole time? How had it been triggered to explode when Kann opened the door? And why did someone want him dead in the first place?

Then there was the bug in Kann's phone. Was Hector Hassan—the only TCI who hadn't been bugged himself—

really the one responsible for bugging the others? And if he was, did that mean that he'd been the one to plant the bomb? Or had that been someone else altogether?

Occam's razor, I thought. With a physicist for a father, I'd heard enough bouts of random science babble to know exactly what Occam's razor—a scientific and philosophical principle—said. Given two equally plausible explanations, the simplest one is most often correct. In this case, the simplest explanation was that the person who'd bugged Jacob Kann and the person who'd planted the bomb were one and the same. Someone was keeping tabs on three out of the four TCIs, and for whatever reason, that someone had wanted one of them dead.

But why? And who? Why were the TCIs here? What were they after? And why kill Kann and not the others? For that matter, why bug only three out of the four?

"I really think you're on the right track here, Toby." Noah's voice cut into my thoughts. "Going to homecoming with Jack Peyton will do wonders for your image. It just screams homecoming quee—"

Noah didn't get to finish his sentence before I closed my fingers around his throat, cutting off the words.

"Toby," my mother said mildly, "don't strangle your brother."

I let go of Noah's throat, and he dared a taunting grin.

If Noah knew that I was going to homecoming with Jack, there was a decent chance that the entire school knew. I hated it that my business was automatically everyone else's, just because I sat at the "right" table at lunch. And how in the world had the news spread so fast?

Thinking about Jack and homecoming made me consider that perhaps Occam's razor wasn't the principle of reasoning to use to figure out what had happened this afternoon. In a single day, I'd been nominated for homecoming queen and had a simple surveillance maneuver end with a sonic boom. Maybe this whole situation boiled down to a different kind of philosophy: Murphy's Law.

Anything that can go wrong will.

CHAPTER 12
Code Word: Hair Products

An hour and a half later, I was sitting on my bathroom floor, trying to decipher the instructions Brittany and Tiffany had left me regarding my conditioning regime. Between their use of nonwords like *fantabulous* and *bodylicious*, their proclivities toward measuring time relative to teen television, and my subpar hair vocabulary, decoding the note they'd left me was easier said than done.

I turned the bottle over in my hands, hoping for instructions. No such luck. The fact that the superconditioner was in an unmarked container didn't surprise me. Half of the twins' hair products were acquired on some kind of beauty black market that I tried not to ask too many questions about. Really, it was better that I didn't know.

"Okay," I told myself by way of a pep talk. "You can do this." I'd been drafted for the Squad because of my ability to deal with codes of both the electronic and written variety. Pseudo-incomprehensible conditioning instructions should have been a piece of cake.

After about five more minutes, I gave up hope of deciphering the third line of the instructions and decided that my best bet was to wet my hair, slap the goop on it, leave it there for "three episodes of *Laguna Beach* on DVD," and then rinse it out.

I stood up, stuck my head in the sink and turned on the faucet. The water was warm on my head, and as I soaked my hair, I couldn't help but think that it didn't feel like my hair. It was soft and smelled like flowers instead of generic all-in-one shampoo/conditioner. In short, this really wasn't my hair, despite the seemingly contradictory fact that it happened to be growing out of my head.

Once my hair was soaked, I turned off the faucet, sat back down, and counted backward from three as I unscrewed the top to the bottle.

"Three, two, one . . . here goes nothing."

The conditioner smelled strongly of mint, and just breathing it in had me blinking back tears. That was some potent stuff. I briefly considered the possibility that the twins were experimenting on me, and then decided against it. Of all of the cheerleaders, I was the one most likely to voluntarily shave my head, and the twins were responsible for making sure that I didn't commit hair felonies. Anything they gave me was guaranteed to make me girlier and more starletesque, so the chances of the two of them experimenting on me were really slim to none.

Desperate to protect myself from the scent of the treatment, I wrapped a towel around my head and went back into my room in search of a distraction. Out of habit, I ended up at my computer, but instead of launching an internet browser, I pulled up a Word document I'd been working on for the last few weeks and added a new line of text.

The twins don't know anything.

"And," I said under my breath, unable to ignore the tingling in my nostrils, "they might be trying to kill me."

As I skimmed the rest of the file, I wondered why I was even reading it again. I knew what it said. I'd written every word myself, and I thought about it almost every day. This document—not even a half-page long—contained everything I'd managed to find out about Jack's uncle. His name was Alan Peyton. He'd grown up in Bayport and was a year older than Jack's dad. He wasn't listed in any of the Peyton firm's official annual reports. Chloe acted sketchy when I hinted that I'd figured something out. None of the other girls had reacted at all.

And that was it. Given that I was part of an elite operative team, I probably should have been able to find out more, but short of hacking into the Big Guys' mainframe (which I was pretty sure would be frowned upon), there wasn't much I could do besides talk to the others and run a Google search on the name. It wasn't like I *needed* to know; I just wanted to. I wasn't concerned about the connection. If I'd figured it out, there was pretty much zero chance that it had somehow evaded the CIA's notice. I mean, good old Uncle Alan left messages on the firm's answering machines. That wasn't exactly lying low.

Since I wasn't worried about the connection, I could only conclude that my fascination with it was based on two things. The first was the fact that I viewed the world in terms of patterns, and the inner workings of this particular family tree didn't fit any I'd ever seen. This whole situation just did not compute. If Jack's dad had been older, and the uncle had been younger, then maybe I could have made sense of it, but I just couldn't figure out why the heir to the family business would dedicate his life to tearing it down.

The second factor in my fascination, as much as I hated to admit it, had to do with Jack, and the way that on some level, I couldn't help but wonder where he would fall on the family tree. Figure out the pattern, figure out Jack.

I'd officially spent way too much time around Zee, because before I'd joined the Squad, I hadn't analyzed my own motives nearly this much. I shut the Word document and pushed all thoughts of Jack out of my mind.

Great, I thought, now I need a distraction from my distraction. I got up from my desk and started looking for something that wouldn't have me analyzing my subconscious desires, and I found it under my bed.

It was a plain, vanilla-colored notebook, with no title and no decoration on the cover. Of everything that the Squad had given me, this book was the lone item that wasn't sparkly, lacy, or ridiculously brightly colored. For the first time since Lucy had handed it to me, I opened the book.

It was supposed to be some kind of history of the Squad program, but since Lucy had provided me with the Cliffs-Notes version, I'd never read it for myself. As I flipped through the pages, I smiled. If I'd realized the book was written in code, I probably would have paid a lot more attention to it a lot earlier.

On the surface, the scrapbook seemed straightforward enough: pictures and pieces of fabric and neatly written paragraphs about games, halftime routines, and private jokes. It was at least twenty-five or thirty years old, and as I flipped the pages, I couldn't help but notice how cheer fashions had changed over the years. The skirts were significantly shorter now, and half of our tops revealed midriff. Our plethora of cheer uniforms (because we wore our uniforms every game day and couldn't repeat outfits in a given week) boasted more eclectic styles, too.

I paused, wondering if Zee could somehow reverse the fashion programming the twins had obviously crammed into my head somewhere along the way.

"Look at the code," I told myself sternly. "Not the clothes."

I scanned through all of the written material, looking for letters that were bolded or tilted or written in a slightly different script than the others. That was the Squad low-maintenance encoding technique of choice.

I found nothing.

Okay, I thought. This could get interesting.

I tried looking for words that felt out of place in context with the others on the page. If I could identify at least one word that had been chosen for a property other than its meaning, I might be able to pick up on some pattern or trick to it. The third letter of the third word on the third page, combined with the fourth letter on the fourth page, or something like that.

Ten minutes later, all I'd managed to pull from the book using that method was *sweet taco*, which I seriously doubted had any meaning relevant to the history of the Squad program.

I went through all of the numbers mentioned, and substituted in their alphabet and reverse alphabet correlates, but came up with nothing but garbage.

"Hmmmmm." I actually made the sound out loud, knowing that it was ridiculous to do so and not really caring.

There was a chance that the code required a second text. Most good codes did. That way, you couldn't decode one unless you had both, decreasing the likelihood that someone who wasn't supposed to would break it. But, I told myself, I was *supposed* to be able to break this one. Lucy had given it to me. If I'd needed a second source to sort out the code, she would have said something, or at the very least given me the second source in one form or another.

Since the only thing other than the book that Lucy had given me in recent memory was a throwing knife barreling toward my face, I dismissed my "multiple sources" theory and flipped through the pages again. Absentmindedly, I reached up and touched the towel around my head, and in the back of my mind, I wondered how much longer I was supposed to leave the conditioner in.

How long were *Laguna Beach* episodes anyway?

As I mussed with the towel, a single piece of hair fell out of its hold, and a drop of water fell onto the book. I haphazardly shoved the hair back under the towel, and stared at the wet mark, half expecting for some cheerleading or espionage deity to descend from the heavens and smite me for desecrating ye olde sacred history of the Squad.

The drop dried soon enough though, and I escaped any smitings that might have been heading my way.

And then, just like that, I knew.

"It's not encoded," I murmured. "It's invisible."

The girls on the Squad were almost as fond of invisible ink as they were of sparkly gel pens. I just had to figure out what the trigger to visibility was, and then I'd be set. It obviously wasn't water, which was the only trigger I'd run across before. A specific chemical combination was possible, but unless it was the chemicals involved in powdered

98

blush or something like that, it didn't seem entirely likely. That left heat and light.

I grabbed the lamp off my desk, and positioned it so that I could hold a single page of the book directly above the lightbulb. At first, nothing happened, but then, as the pages heated up, the words written behind the visible script popped to the surface, and I read.

And read.

And read.

For the most part, there was nothing that I hadn't been told before. The program had been created because, at the height of the Cold War, the government had secretly decided to begin training younger and younger agents, and while select boarding schools and military academies provided male trainees, they'd had difficulty locating a group of females who consistently and predictably fulfilled their requirements. The special task force assigned to recruitment was looking for girls who were beautiful and able to use their looks to their advantage, girls who were smart but didn't seem on the surface to be much of a mental threat. Girls who were athletic, manipulative, and capable of keeping their true identity a secret.

And somewhere along the way, someone had suggested cheerleaders.

It was a miracle that person hadn't been laughed right out of Washington, but they hadn't been, and a handful of pilot programs were started at select schools across the country. Trainees were chosen based on a complex algorithm of requirements, ranging from IQ to athletic prowess and psychological fitness. Upon graduation, they were given tests and some of the girls were offered positions at

Quantico or within the CIA, Secret Service, or some kind of covert ops division I didn't quite understand.

Caught up in what I was reading, I turned the page, but didn't pay enough attention to what I was doing, and was soon bombarded with the smell of scorching paper. I jumped, pulling the book back, and considered the notion that perhaps people should refrain from giving me things that they didn't want wet, burned, or otherwise destroyed.

Even though the pages hadn't caught on fire (yet), I blew on them for good measure and then plopped down on the floor.

What had I been looking for in the book? The question hit me as I blew. I knew how the program had started, I knew that if I kept on reading, I'd get to the part of the history where the program was disbanded in the early nineties, with the exception of a single Squad, located conveniently near a law firm that the government wanted to keep a particularly close eye on. Our Squad was operational, far more so than any of our predecessors, and when we graduated, we didn't have to deal with more training; we got our choice of assignments.

Even though the invisible letters were once again hidden from my eyes, I glanced down at the book, as if the pages themselves should somehow provide the answers to whatever questions I couldn't quite bring myself to ask. What was I thinking? Did I really expect the book to have anything to say about my current predicament? Like maybe a previous Squad member had written down everything she'd learned the hard way about dating the heir to an evil empire. Or maybe I subconsciously thought that the book held the secrets to making a homecoming nomination disappear, or the answer to the many questions about our case that I'd asked myself at dinner. Better yet, I might have even expected it to contain some insight on how exactly somebody could go from Son of Evil to Force of Good overnight.

At this point, I'd even settle for something that advised me on how best to procure detention.

Yeah, right.

I stared down at the picture on the page in front of me, and I couldn't help but wonder who the smiling girls in this book, the original Squad trainees, had really been. The captions only included their initials, and the pictures made them look more or less like either Marcia Brady or Farrah Fawcett clones, depending on the angle. Same smiles, same hair, flipped out at the ends, same self-confident looks in each of their eyes.

Was "KM" really just a cheerleader? What about JP or MC or the other girls on the page? Were they the people they pretended to be?

Was anyone? Was there even such a thing as "just a cheerleader"?

"Damn," I said under my breath. "I seriously need to chill." It must have been the mint smell that was still assaulting my senses. The conditioner was obviously playing funky beauty-product mind games with me and making me all weepy and philosophical.

I was officially never letting the twins give me an unmarked bottle again.

I looked down at my watch and decided that I really didn't care how long *Laguna Beach* was supposed to be. I was done.

I closed the book, slid it back under my bed, and stood up. I must have stood up too fast, because the blood rushed from my head, and everything went dark around the edges for a moment. Then again, maybe it had nothing to do with how fast I'd stood up and everything to do with the concussion the doctor had seemed confident I didn't have. Or it could have been that the conditioning treatment was actually mildly hallucinogenic.

Not liking any of the choices, I stumbled into the bathroom, closed the door behind me, stripped off my clothes, and hopped into the shower. I turned the water on and let it beat against my hair. Possible concussions aside, I wanted the trippy conditioner out.

Standing there in the shower, the smell of mint slowly subsiding, it occurred to me for the first time to wonder which one of the perky girls I'd seen in the book was Brooke's mother.

Probably whichever one was captain, I thought wryly. Like mother, like daughter.

CHAPTER 13
Code Word: Practice

When I woke up the next morning, I still hadn't come to any brilliant conclusions about the Jacob Kann situation. Instead, I'd spent most of the night having naked dreams, half of which featured homecoming, and half of which involved exploding cars—which, FYI, were at least three times more traumatizing if your clothes disappeared mid-BOOM.

By the time five in the morning rolled around, I was thankful to be getting out of bed, which just goes to show that there really is a first time for everything. Little-known fact about cheerleaders: They keep schedules that would make grown marines cry. Between before-school practices and after-school meetings/practices, some days I felt like I spent my entire life cheering. At least this morning, I had more to look forward to than a rousing rendition of "Clap Your Hands."

I might not have accomplished anything the night before, but when Brooke had ordered me home, she'd already been forming a course of action that involved analyzing the TCI audio and tracking data and scanning Kann's hard drive for clues about what had brought these particular members of the watch list to Bayport to begin with. Based on previous experience, I was willing to bet that the other girls had already managed to zero in on some key piece of information. In fact, I would have wagered my combat boots on it.

There were few things besides coffee that could actually get me going before noon, but mystery and intrigue numbered among them. It took me all of two minutes to get dressed. The twins had idiot-proofed (or as they liked to call it, "Toby-proofed") my wardrobe, so all I had to do was grab a preselected outfit off the hanger, stuff it in my duffel bag, and throw on a pair of cotton shorts and a sports bra, and then I was ready to go.

After getting dressed at warp speed, I actually managed to drive all the way to high school before I realized that I'd forgotten my morning coffee. Mystery, intrigue, and naked dreams aside, that didn't bode well for my chances at making it through the morning without killing myself. Or someone else.

The first person I saw when I walked into the gym was Brooke, who looked distinctly miffed in her own super polished way.

"You're late."

I ignored Brooke's greeting and proceeded to the locker room. She followed, and as I threw my bag into a locker, she repeated herself, and I repeated my nonresponse. I was two minutes late. For me, that pretty much meant I was early, and the only thing that kept me from snipping right back at Brooke was the conversation I'd had with Zee the day before. Of everyone in this room, our captain was probably the only one who'd actually had a more stressful night than me.

Plus, she was the one who got to decide whether or not I was going to be a part of the next stage of our mission—whatever that might be—which meant that aggravating her more than necessary probably wasn't wise.

"Holos are on, Brooke!" Lucy was the only person I knew who spoke with an exclamation mark in her voice at the crack of dawn.

Brooke arched one eyebrow at me. "Holograms are on," she said dryly. And then, without another word, she stalked past me to the showers, which held one of the many secret entrances to the Quad.

Five minutes later, the ten of us were seated at our conference table, and I was taking in just how much I'd missed the night before.

"In the twelve hours since we placed bugs and trackers on the TCIs, none of them have shown obviously erratic patterns of movement. Amelia Juarez spent the night at her hotel, and our bugs didn't register any incoming or outgoing calls from either her cell or the hotel phone."

Chloe smirked in my general direction when Brooke said the word *cell*, and it only took me a few seconds to figure out why. Tara and I hadn't gotten a bug on Kann's cell, just his hotel phone, which—had he actually lived—probably wouldn't have proved that useful. Somehow, April and Chloe had one-upped us.

"Anthony Connors-Wright appears to have eaten dinner in Walford Park, but beyond the fact that he voluntarily chose to pick up food from the KFC drive-through on the way there, his pattern of movement wasn't sketchy in the least. Ditto for his phones.

"Because he's our prime suspect in the surveillance we found on the other TCIs, the Big Guys instructed us to pay special attention to Hector Hassan, and we kept a live trace on him last night." She smiled. "Good thing, too, because Hector Hassan drove to three different pay phones between two and four in the morning." The second the words were out of her mouth, I knew we'd hit pay dirt. Young, suave businessmen didn't use pay phones unless they were up to something.

"We contacted the Big Guys, and they tracked down outgoing and incoming calls from each of the pay phones and compared the phone log with the times Hassan was there." Brooke paused, letting the tension build in the air. "Two of the three calls were received from untraceable phones, but the third . . ."

Okay, enough with the dramatic pauses.

"The third was an outgoing call to an individual who's much, much higher than Hassan on the Watch List."

In other words, Hassan wasn't just a Terrorist-Connected Individual. He was an individual who'd spoken with his terrorist connection the night before.

"Have you passed this information on to the Big Guys?" I asked.

Brooke flipped her hair over her shoulders and rolled her eyes, a gesture I took to mean "why, yes, Toby, yes I did."

"Any word back yet?" This time, the question came from Chloe, and Brooke offered a real answer.

"I'm expecting the call any minute."

"What about the data I got from Kann's laptop?" I asked,

risking Brooke's wrath for messing with her dramatic timing again.

To my surprise, Brooke smiled, and I realized that even though two of the other teams had managed to bug their marks' cell phones, the information Tara and I had retrieved might just prove itself to be even more useful.

Take that, Chloe!

"Chloe, you want to debrief everyone?" Brooke spoiled my moment of victory by turning the floor over to Chloe, thus reminding me that while I'd been "resting," Chloe had been enjoying the spoils of my hacking prowess.

"Most of the data on Kann's hard drive was useless," Chloe said, sitting up straighter in her chair, her eyes lingering on me as she delivered the last word. "But I did manage to analyze his inbox and sent mail for patterns consistent with the timing of the TCI influx, and it looks like our boy was definitely here to purchase something. We've got the alias of the seller, but haven't managed to ID him yet."

"What kind of purchase are we talking about here?" Tiffany asked. Of all of us, the twins probably spent the most time making purchases themselves, so the question seemed oddly natural coming from Tiff.

Chloe had an answer ready, and it was clear that she was thrilled to have been asked. "That's the other thing we managed to pull off the disk. We don't have specifics, but we do have reason to believe that Kann was here to purchase . . ."

Chloe mimicked one of Brooke's dramatic pauses, and I couldn't help but add theme music to the situation. "Dum dum DUM!"

Everyone at the table glared at me in one synchronized motion. Like I was the only one thinking it.

When Chloe spoke again, her voice was soft. And deadly. "Kann was here to purchase some kind of biological weapon," she said. "And then he was going to turn right around and sell it."

Based on the meaning of the TCI acronym, I was going to go out on a limb and guess that Kann probably wasn't planning on selling it to the good guys. For the millionth time since the day before, the explosion replayed itself in my mind's eye, but this time, part of me couldn't help but see it differently. Murder was bad, but so was equipping terrorists to commit more of the same, and that was what Kann was planning to do before he died in that blast. I couldn't decide what to think about that, or if I even wanted to think about it at all, and a moment later, the air of solemnity around us was suddenly and completely shattered by the sound of pop music blaring from Brooke's cell phone.

"Please tell me that wasn't who I think it was singing," I said as Brooke excused herself from the table and went to answer the phone. "Celebutantes should not be allowed to pretend they're pop stars."

"What?" Lucy said. "It's catchy."

Oh, dear God.

"I'll pass on any information that you . . . you'd like to what? Oh. Okay. Sure. No problem." Brooke's voice started out sharp, crisp, and professional, and morphed into forced and perky. She shut her phone and then turned back to the rest of us.

"There have been some developments," she said.

"And they are . . . ," Chloe prompted, a twinge of attitude in her voice.

"They want to talk to all of us," Brooke said. "You can hear about the developments for yourself."

At those words, I actually stopped breathing. During my first mission, we'd gotten our instructions straight from our superiors. Since then, everything they'd communicated to us had been communicated through Brooke. Normally, I might have played at being Zee and attempted to analyze Brooke's reaction to the fact that the Big Guys wanted to talk to all of us, but even once I started breathing again, analyzing was out of the picture.

I didn't know much about the Big Guys. I knew there were several of them. I knew they were somehow part of the CIA. And I knew that one of them was Jack's uncle.

"Good morning, girls." The screen flipped on, and a neutral, male voice greeted us.

John. It's Alan. I need to talk to you. It's about Jack.

I never had figured out what Uncle Alan had wanted with Jack. For all I knew, he'd been calling about wanting to take his nephew to a baseball game or something. Still, the sound of the Voice, which I hadn't heard in weeks, but hadn't been able to forget, either, had me wondering all over again. How was it that Jack's father was the head of what basically amounted to a terrorist cell, but Jack's uncle was part of the CIA?

And, perhaps more importantly, what did this say about Jack?

The Voice continued laying down the facts in a cool, calm manner, oblivious to my line of thought, and I forced myself to pay attention to the case at hand, tucking all questions and objections concerning good old Uncle Alan neatly away for the time being.

"The data you sent us yesterday has proved invaluable,

Brooke. Hector Hassan has been taken into custody, officially as a suspect in Jacob Kann's death."

And unofficially, I filled in, because of the calls he'd exchanged with terrorists the night before.

"What about the email address we sent you?" Brooke asked, slightly appeased by the fact that despite demanding to talk to all of us, the Voice had still made a deliberate effort at recognizing her as our leader.

"We're still tracking down the alias," the voice answered. "Whoever this guy is, he knows how to cover his tracks."

Somehow, it escaped everyone's attention but mine that uncovering tracks like those was more or less my forte.

"In the meantime, you girls don't need to worry about uncovering the identity of the seller, or the details of the biological weaponry for sale. We've got people on that here."

I could actually see the effort Brooke was putting in to not frowning at that little announcement.

"What we need you girls to do is stay on the remaining TCIs. With Kann dead and Hassan in custody, Amelia and Anthony are our only remaining links to this case. We've got agents in the area, but starting at 1500 hours today, I want two of your teams on each of them. You girls can get closer than we can, and we can't take any risks. These people could be dangerous, and until we can identify the threat and neutralize it, tracking the buyers is our only option.

"I want a fifth team staking out the firm and keeping a complete log of who's coming and who's going. If someone's selling a biological weapon in Bayport and Peyton, Kaufman, and Gray doesn't have a hand in it yet, I think it's safe to assume that they will soon."

And here I'd been hoping that my homecoming date's father *wasn't* involved in the national security risk du jour.

"Understood, sir." Brooke's tone bordered on sounding military. "We'll handle it. Have the results come back yet on yesterday's explosion?"

"We're expecting the labs back this afternoon, and that leads me to the point of this conference call." The voice paused. I was starting to see where Brooke and Co. got it from. "This case is sensitive, girls. It's dangerous. And we've officially designated it a Do Not Engage. Under no circumstances are *any* of you to engage your marks. If you see something suspicious, call it in, and one of our teams will take care of it. Your mission is strictly observational. Have I made myself clear?"

For a moment, there was silence, and then at Brooke's nod, the rest of the Squad, minus me, chimed in. "Yes, sir."

I said nothing. For one thing, I wasn't exactly keen on speaking in unison, and for another, I wasn't about to make any promises I couldn't keep.

"Toby."

I jumped in my seat. The Voice actually knew my name. And somehow, he had the freaky ability to ascertain that of all of us, I was the one who hadn't responded.

"Do you understand?"

I contemplated telling him that what I didn't understand was his familial relationships, but stayed momentarily silent, causing everyone within a three-foot radius to kick me under the table at once.

"Ow!" I cleared my throat. "I mean, yes." I didn't throw the *sir* on the end, but apparently, that was good enough for the Voice.

"Excellent. Report in tonight, and we'll have more information for you all tomorrow. And girls?"

"Yes?"

"Congratulations on the homecoming nominations. We're all very proud."

And with that, the line went dead, and I was left trying to figure out what part of this exchange (aside from the obvious Jack's uncle factor) had been the most surreal: the official commendation from the government on being nominated for homecoming court, or the fact that Brooke had chosen the poppiest of pop ringtones to signify a call from the CIA.

"Okay, guys. You heard the man. We'll meet back here for seventh period and head out from there." Brooke looked down at her watch. "We still have an hour before class starts. Who's up for tumbling?"

At that point, I realized something. The most surreal part of this entire morning had nothing to do with ringtones or homecoming and everything to do with the fact that I had enough energy and potential frustration built up inside of me that the physical release of tumbling actually sounded good.

CHAPTER 14
Code Word: Luscious

Word to the wise. Never let a high school junior try to teach you how to do something called a layout, because either you won't be able to do it, in which case you'll feel like the cheertard everyone else thinks you are, or you will be able to do it, in which case, the aforementioned junior might take it upon herself to teach you something harder.

On a related note, I really, really do not recommend trying to do anything with your body that includes the phrase "full twist."

After forty-five minutes of tumbling, every muscle in my body was rebelling, and I'd added several bruises to the arsenal I'd started the day before. Unfortunately, the twins didn't see any of this as a reason to go easy on me on the personal appearance front. The second we got back to the locker room, they insisted on signing off on my outfit and did so only after supplying me with yet another pair of boots to supplement my growing collection.

I got all of ten minutes of peace while everyone was getting dressed and primped for the day before the twins returned to gaily consider my newly conditioned hair, anxious to see the results up close and personal.

And I mean personal. Tiffany actually stuck her nose into my hair and took a big whiff. After some whispering behind their hands, the twins informed me that my Bounce Index had improved considerably, and I was clear to go for a day at Bayport High.

Call me crazy, but I found it difficult to care about whether or not I qualified as "sufficiently luscious" when we were mere hours away from a mission so large that all five Squad teams would be deployed: two to each of the TCIs, and one to Peyton, Kaufman, and Gray.

I mean, yes, this was just an observational mission, and yes, we had been explicitly forbidden from making contact of any kind, but the thought of getting out there again and doing what the ten of us were born to do was enough to make me submit to the twins' high-speed primping and fluffing without issuing so much as a single death threat.

I was still smiling with anticipation a few minutes later when I left the Quad and headed up to my first hour. My mind on reconnaissance missions and tailing hostile individuals who may have posed a threat to our national security, I wasn't watching where I was going, and as I rounded a corner on the way to my geometry class, I ran smack into a large, smirking Jack-shaped object.

I bounced off of him and stumbled backward, falling to the ground. I jumped immediately back to my feet, the way I would have in the middle of a fight. Jack caught me in his arms and grinned.

"Happy to see me?" he asked, taking in the goofy smile that was still plastered to my face and ignoring the reflexive narrowing of my eyes that hit me the moment his hands touched my arms.

"I have to say, Ev, the whole smiling thing really works for you. Not that your little scowl isn't cute, too, but . . ."

I tried to glare at him, but he just touched the side of my face.

"See?" he said. "Cute scowl."

Just then, I didn't care who his father was, or his uncle. All I could think was that I'd show him cute.

"Vote for Toby!"

Any violent and/or furious kiss-related thoughts rising in my mind were immediately quelled when I heard a familiar voice that sounded way too self-satisfied for its owner's good.

"Vote for Toby. Vote for Toby. Hey, baby. How you doin'?" Slight pause. "Vote for Toby."

Jack glanced over his shoulder at the source of the voice and then turned back to me, incredulous. "Does your brother have a death wish?" he asked.

"Toby Klein—the people's candidate. Voting for Toby is like voting for yourself, except it's not at all narcissistic. Vote for Toby. She'll— Well, hello there, gorgeous. Call me. We'll do lunch."

I opened my mouth and then closed it again.

"Vote for Toby!" Whatever he was doing, Noah was getting progressively louder.

"Yes," I said, answering Jack's question. "He has an obvious death wish. He must also be a masochist, because this is going to hurt."

My moment with Jack temporarily forgotten, I stalked off, rounded another corner, and came face to face with my brother.

He was wearing a sandwich board with my photo plastered to the front.

He was handing out buttons and flyers with my name on them.

And, unless I was mistaken, he'd gotten his friends to do the same.

"Vote for Toby."

"Vote for Toby."

"Vote for Toby."

All up and down the hallway, the biggest goofballs in the class below me were actually encouraging their peers to throw their homecoming votes my way. From this distance, it looked like Chuck might have even been handing out candy.

I may be short, but it only took me three hugely angry steps to be standing directly behind my brother. I tapped him on the shoulder—harder than required to get his attention—and he turned around.

"Vote for To—" he started to say, but the moment he saw the look on my face, he changed his mind. "Hey there, big sis," he said in a little-boy voice especially designed to remind me that I was his older sister, he was the baby, and my family had a strict no-maiming policy.

He needn't have worried. I wasn't going to maim him. I was going to *end* him.

"Noah," I said through gritted teeth. He waited, and I couldn't even go on. Instead, I gestured at his sandwich board, the buttons, and the various other freshmen watching our interaction, their hands full of VOTE TOBY posters.

"Explanation," I barked, knowing that nothing he said would make this any better, but feeling as if I should allow him to have some final words other than "hey there, big sis."

Noah said nothing.

"Now." My voice started off low and dangerous, but it rose to a yell.

"I told you," Noah said, his grin never faltering, even as he showed the beginning signs of preparing to run. "I'm your campaign manager."

"I don't want a campaign manager," I said, stepping even further into his personal space. "I don't want to win."

"I know," Noah said. "That's why you'd be perfect!"

I grabbed the lapels of his shirt, even though the fact that he had three or four inches on me meant that I had to reach up a little to do it. "If you don't make all of this disappear in the next five minutes," I said, "you'll be perfectly dead, and Mom and Dad will never miss you. Clear?"

"Crystal," Noah replied. Then he raised his voice. "Okay, guys. We have a no-go. That's a no-go on the posters, buttons, and boards."

I released him, and as he scurried down the hallway, I heard him yell one last thing.

"Proceed to Plan B."

"Death wish," Jack said, coming up beside me. "Clearly."

About that time, I realized that due to the volume of the threats I'd issued to my brother, everyone had heard me sounding about as dangerous as I get. This type of behavior didn't exactly qualify as flying under the radar and taking advantage of the cheerleader stereotype to convince people that I couldn't possibly be anything more than I seemed.

The Squad would not approve.

"Uhhh . . . Go Lions," I added. My audience let out a collective shrug and dissolved.

"How long until that hits the rumor mill?" I asked Jack below my breath.

"Seven-point-eight seconds," Jack answered solemnly. "But don't worry, Zee'll come up with something more interesting for people to talk about. She always does."

He was right. That was part of Zee's job, orchestrating gossip that served our purposes and stomping out rumors that hurt them. Sometimes, Jack was so perceptive that it truly freaked me out. The only thing I was sure about when it came to Jack's family was that Jack didn't know what his uncle did, or, for that matter, what I did. Whether or not he knew the full extent of what his father's firm did was up in the air. Of all the people who could potentially discover our secret, Jack was the candidate whose discovery would devastate our operation the most, and he was the one person most likely to actually sort things out.

And he was my homecoming date.

"I don't know if Zee will be able to do anything about it," I said, trying not to let him see that his comment had really rocked me. "It doesn't get much juicier than a cheer-leader-issued death threat."

"Oh, come on, CDTs happen all the time," Jack said solemnly. "Usually it's over stuff like two girls wearing the same outfit, or someone telling someone else that a third person said they were a slut, but still, cheerleader death threats are old news."

He was trying to make me feel better, and there was a chance he was right, but those stupid VOTE TOBY posters were still plastered all over the walls, and it was hard for me to be optimistic about anything with my own face staring back at me, reminding me that the world hated me and wanted me to suffer.

"But you know, Ev, if you really want them talking about something else, I could probably help you out."

"Yeah," I said. "Right."

He took my words as a challenge, pressed me to a wall, and kissed me so long and hard that even once I knew we had an audience, I couldn't pull away.

This was wrong. There was a conflict of interest here, and besides which, he was at the top of a hierarchy I hated. Forget that I was on top, too. I wasn't the kind of girl to go weak at the knees just because someone was . . .

The most incredible kisser. Ever.

His hands moved from the side of my face down my neck and to my waist.

I hated him. I hated being a cheerleader.

I hated that I didn't actually hate him or being a cheerleader. But most of all, I hated it when we stopped kissing.

"Miss Klein! Mr. Peyton! Perhaps the two of you should invest in a room?" Mr. Corkin pushed to the front of the crowd that had gathered around the two of us while I'd been lost in my own thoughts and Jack's lips.

"I don't suppose you'd know where we might get one?" Jack inquired, his face a mask of civility, his tone overly polite.

Mr. Corkin sputtered.

"No?" Jack said. "In that case," he flicked his eyes over to mine, "maybe the two of us should go to class?"

"Jack Peyton is HOT!" someone from the audience yelled.

"Toby Klein is HOTTER," a male voice argued, and I almost went into an epileptic fit of disgust at both the words and the tone.

"Now, now," Jack said, raising his hands. "Don't be ridiculous. Mr. Corkin is clearly the hottest."

Corkin turned bright, bright red, and I couldn't help it. I laughed.

Jack Peyton was everything I shouldn't want in a guy—including, given his background, potentially evil—but I had to admire someone who could make Mr. Corkin turn a nice shade of fuchsia without ever even suggesting that a posterior-kissing might be in order.

Jack wrapped his arm around me. I forced myself to shrug it off, but as the two of us walked through the crowd, he put it back and bent down so that his mouth was right next to my ear.

"See, Ev?" he said. "By lunchtime, no one will be talking about any death threats you may have allegedly issued toward your younger brother. Everyone will be talking about what just happened between the two of us."

He sounded vaguely like a lawyer, and I remembered all of the reasons that I didn't want the rest of the school talking about him and me any more than I wanted them talking about the fact that my little brother could provoke even the sanest of cheerleaders to homicide.

"Let me guess," Jack said, taking in my silence. "You don't want them talking about us, either."

"Give the man a prize."

He fixed his eyes on mine, and for a moment, he looked almost sad. "They'll always talk, Toby."

My real name, for a rare moment of real seriousness between the two of us.

"That's the life. People watch you, and they talk about you, and they expect you to act a certain way until no matter what you do, they see it as part of whatever it is that you're supposed to be."

Now he wasn't talking like a lawyer. He was talking like someone who knew way too much about my life, way too much about the Squad and the reason it worked. Or maybe he was just talking like someone who'd lived the high life for way too long.

"It sucks," I said.

Jack shrugged. "You get used to it," he said. "And it's not all bad." His eyes lingered on mine.

At that exact moment, four scrawny guys ran by wearing nothing but ski masks, boxers, and paint on their chests. As they passed us, I tried to make out the writing on their chests and realized that each guy bore one letter.

T. O. B.

"Y." Jack completed the sequence for me. "I have to hand it to your brother. He's inventive. And brave."

And, I thought, so incredibly dead.

Obviously, no combination of mystery and intrigue was going to be enough to gear me up for this day. I even had doubts that coffee would do the trick. My first class hadn't even started yet, and I'd already publicly threatened to exact physical revenge upon the creature formerly known as my little brother, engaged in some serious PDA with someone I wasn't supposed to have actual feelings for, and watched the aforementioned brother-creature and his friends streak by wearing nothing but boxers and my name painted on their chests. Not to mention the part of the equation where I'd gotten an operative assignment so dangerous it had been designated "Do Not Engage."

Tomorrow, I was going for at least three cups of coffee, just to be on the safe side.

The bell rang, and without a word, Jack and I went our separate ways, and I found myself thinking disturbingly girly thoughts along the vein of "how can he like me if he doesn't really know me?" and "does he really like me, or is it just that I'm the only girl who's ever turned him down?"

Forget the coffee, I thought, wanting to ram my head into something quite hard to discourage my subconscious from any more probing thoughts. Tomorrow morning, I'm going with cyanide.

CHAPTER 15
Code Word: Boyfriend

"It was like the hottest thing I've ever seen."

"And then this teacher was all 'get a room,' and I was all 'yeah, please do.' "

"I hear they're going to be on *Survivor: Couples' Edition*."

"Really? I heard they'd already accepted an offer from *Real World: Bayport*."

"I soooooo wish I was Toby Klein."

By lunchtime, Jack and I were the primary topic of conversation in the cafeteria, and bits and pieces of conversations assaulted my ears as I made my way toward the central table. I was beginning to feel like I couldn't sneeze without making front-page news: *God Squad Member Toby Klein Sneezes; Allergies Are IN!*

Of course, some of the whispers were less than flattering. Jack was the number-one hottie at our school, and Chloe (Jack ex number two) wasn't the only one whose hackles were up at the thought of a Toby/Jack pairing.

"She is such a slut."

Yup. Jack was the only guy I'd ever kissed, and we hadn't done anything but, so clearly, I was Slut Girl. Of course, given the fact that the person who was slinging the s-word around was in fact much "friendlier" toward the opposite sex than I was, the insult didn't carry much of a punch.

"And her technique is total crap."

At first, I thought they were talking about my kissing technique—WHAT WAS WRONG WITH MY KISSING TECHNIQUE?—but then I realized that when junior varsity cheerleaders say "technique," they mean one and only one thing.

"I mean, did you see that back handspring?"

Insults were one thing coming from Chloe; whether or not we were friends, we were teammates, and that meant something, but these JV girls didn't know me, and I was getting damn tired of people picking on my handsprings.

"You know," I said, sauntering up to their group and inserting myself into their conversation. "Maybe you're right. The other girls on varsity think my standing back tuck is much cleaner than my back handspring, and even my back handspring back tuck has a little more oomph, so maybe I just shouldn't bother with the easier stuff at all." I paused and looked at each of the JV cheerleaders in turn. "This morning, Bubbles was teaching me how to do a layout. Maybe next year, we'll start requiring more advanced tumbling skills for new recruits."

The girls shut their mouths one by one. As jealous as they were, and as much as they hated me, I'd just reminded them that I held their futures in my hands. There were four seniors on varsity this year, which meant that we'd have four open slots on the Squad next year, and as far as these girls knew, the remaining members simply voted in new ones on whims. None of these girls had made varsity as sophomores, but they were still pretending that they stood a chance junior year, and some of them might have.

If they managed to go that long without really pissing me off.

"Go ahead and up the tumbling requirements," Hayley Hoffman sniffed. "My back handspring back tuck is flawless."

"But your personality," I said, "well, let's just say that they invented the term *fatal flaw* for a reason, Hayley, and as far as the varsity squad is concerned, you're dead to us."

Okay, so it was cheesy, but I wasn't used to issuing popularity threats. It must have been potent enough, though, because all of the other girls gasped a little and took a step back. It was so over the top and ridiculous that I couldn't believe it was really happening, let alone that I was an integral part of it, but these days, suspension of disbelief was my forte.

"If you're still on the God Squad next year," Hayley said, "I wouldn't want to be. Being varsity used to mean something, but apparently, they've lowered their standards."

She looked to the others for support, but they remained quiet.

"Kiki," Hayley hissed, and one of the girls cleared her throat.

"Ummm . . . yeah," she told me. "Unless . . . do you think if I could stick a back tuck that maybe . . ."

"Kiki!"

"Never mind," the girl mumbled. Since April had joined the Squad, Hayley had surrounded herself with new minions, and it looked like at least one of them was taking orders, albeit clumsily.

"Well," I said, "I should go eat lunch. With my boyfriend. And the rest of the God Squad. Feel free to talk amongst yourselves. It's not like anyone who matters is listening."

I turned on my heels and walked toward the central table. And that's when it hit me . . .

I was turning into one of *those girls*.

It wasn't pretend. It wasn't just a cover. I'd just threatened a bunch of girls with cheerleading annihilation. I'd referred to Jack as my boyfriend and thrown it in their faces. I'd told Hayley she was "dead to us."

What in the name of all that was good and holy was the matter with me?

This wasn't me. I didn't take crap, but I didn't play games, either. I didn't care what other people said about me, and I certainly didn't think the fact that I was going to homecoming with Jack gave me the right to use him as a weapon against lesser females.

Oh, no.

I'd just mentally referred to someone as a lesser female.

It was too much. This wasn't what I signed up for. I wasn't supposed to actually change. That was never part of the deal. I'd agreed to pretend to be a cheerleader, pretend to play the popularity game, but it was just supposed to be that: pretend. Make-believe. I was still supposed to be me. I wasn't supposed to become the kind of girl I'd always hated.

That was the thing, though. Being around the other girls had made me realize that I didn't hate them, not even Chloe, and I'd done a complete one-eighty on my views of cheerleading in general, so maybe that was why I'd changed. I'd learned to respect them. I even liked them for the most part, and now . . .

Was I doomed to become another Chloe? Two years

from now, would I look at some new girl on the squad and snip at her the way Gadget Girl did at me?

No, I thought. No way. The next time someone called me a slut, I was going to do one of two things. If it was a girl, I was going to ignore her—who cared what people said or thought? The old me certainly hadn't. Gossip was nothing more than a minor annoyance, and *that* I could deal with, especially if it kept me from having these identity crises on a regular basis.

And if a guy called me a slut? Well, then I'd be forced to take him down. I couldn't in good conscience beat the crap out of someone smaller than or as small as me, but football players were fair game, especially if they didn't respect women. And, to be quite honest, I kind of missed bringing the odd football player down every once in a while. Call it a hobby.

"Hey, Toby. If you're done with your inner rant/identity crisis, you might want to join us. Everyone's talking about you and Jack, and I want the inside scoop." Zee put her arm around my shoulder and guided me to our table. Somehow, I wasn't surprised that she knew exactly what was running through my mind. Same old, same old.

"There is no inside scoop," I told Zee as we took our seats. "We're going to homecoming together. He kissed me in the hallway. End of story."

Luckily, before the others could pump me for more information, Jack sat down at our table, and the topic of conversation turned away from our social lives and toward our chances of beating Hillside on Friday. The amount of enmity the people at our table showed for the Hillside Bobcats made the cool, detached way we dealt with terrorist threats look like rhythmic gymnastics.

"We're going to massacre them! Those SOBs won't know what hit 'em." Chip waxed poetic about Hillside's impending doom. "We're going to demolish them. They won't even see it coming, those ‾ . ."

"They're totally going down," Lucy chimed in.

"They'll forego the rest of their season out of sheer embarrassment." That one was from Tara.

"We'll crush 'em." Chip again.

"Kill them?" Bubbles asked, not quite sure if that was the appropriate response.

"Yeah," Chip agreed. "And you girls will put their cheerleaders to shame. Next to you, they'll look like dogs." Chip was losing a little of his steam now that he wasn't speaking in terms of violent metaphors.

"Really ugly dogs," one of the Chiplings assured us.

"So their cheerleaders are ugly, their football players are wimps, and they're our archrivals because why?" It was either ask the question, or try to join in with the rabble-rousing by making some kind of comment about crushing our enemies' bones to powder, and I opted away from the melodrama.

Everyone at the entire table paused at my question, and I realized this was one of those times when I just should have kept my mouth shut. Forget orders not to engage the TCIs. I should have adopted a strict No Engagement policy with the football team.

"She's right," Jack said, and I got the distinct feeling that I was the only one who could hear the sarcastic undertone to his voice. "We're going to beat them so badly that next year, they won't have the cajones to call us their rivals."

The Chipling sitting nearest Zee, who I inferred was probably her homecoming date, spoke up then. "That's right, son," he said, pounding his fist into the table. "Bayport High doesn't have a rival. Nobody can touch us."

Eventually, the conversation tapered off, and once I'd actually managed to ingest my food, I decided to make a quick exit before somebody brought up me and Jack again, or before I became possessed by enough school spirit that I felt compelled to actually insult the collective manhood of the Hillside football team.

"I'll be back." I lied through my teeth, knowing as I did it that there wasn't a girl on the Squad who I would fool. "Just going to run to the bathroom real quick."

Immediately, Lucy and Bubbles stood to follow. Over the past few weeks, I'd come to accept the fact that it was a law of girl nature that for reasons I couldn't quite grasp, going to the bathroom required as much backup as even the most dangerous reconnaissance maneuvers. The three of us passed Noah's table on the way to the bathroom, and I knew better than to hope that he wouldn't notice. Noah's cheerleader radar was more advanced than anything the government could possibly develop. Zeroing in on the incoming hotties, he stood up. For one horrifying instant, I thought that he might have more Toby for Homecoming Queen shenanigans up his sleeve, but ultimately, his flirting impulse won out, and I was left trying to decide which of the two was a lesser evil.

"Hello, ladies." Noah grinned in a way that he probably thought was suave, but that actually made him look like a kid with his hand in the cookie jar.

"Goodbye, Noah," I said, trying to put an end to this interaction before he could proposition one of my Squadmates.

Bubbles and Lucy, however, either didn't catch or chose

to blatantly ignore my not-so-subtle hint that we were leaving. The two of them looked at each other and then at me, and before I could stop her, Bubbles offered Noah the same greeting she'd given me the first time we'd met.

"I can put my feet behind my head."

Noah's mouth dropped open, and for a moment, he was speechless.

Quick, I thought, while he's still recovering! "Come on, guys," I said, grabbing their arms and pulling them forward. "Let's go."

"You can put both feet behind your head," Noah repeated, his voice full of reverent awe. "There is a God." And with that pronouncement, he fell to his knees and raised his arms heavenward. "Hallelujah!"

Beside me, Lucy giggled, and even though I half expected her to match Bubbles's overture, just to tease me, she didn't. Instead, she did something much, much worse. She smiled shyly at Noah, and he grinned goofily back, both of them eerily subdued compared to their normal selves.

"Hi." Noah climbed to his feet, and instead of dishing out one of his many standard pickup lines (none of which were effective; most of which were severely idiotic), he just offered Lucy an earnest smile.

"Hi," Lucy returned, ducking her head a little and matching Noah's grin with another of her own.

My brother and our resident weapons expert were officially having a moment. No good could come of this.

"We have to go," I said again. I tightened my hold on Lucy's arm and pulled her forcibly toward the bathroom. Bubbles trailed after us, leaving Noah in our wake. When we made it to the sanctuary of the girls' room, I turned my full-force glare on Lucy.

"What?" she said innocently.

"You know what."

"Yeah," Bubbles said, and then she frowned, utterly lost. "What?"

I took a deep and cleansing breath and prepared myself to patiently explain to them that phrases like *do not engage* were specifically invented with little brothers in mind.

CHAPTER 16
Code Word: Flirt

My reward for making it through the rest of lunch and Mr. Corkin's class without making any kind of scene (or being sent to the office) was my sixth period: computer science, also known as free time on the net. The administration at Bayport High was somehow completely unaware of the fact that all of the students were members of the computer generation. I'd hacked into the Pentagon at the age of thirteen, and though my classmates were significantly less skilled in that department, they were connoisseurs of MySpace and Facebook, so a lot of what this class professed to teach us, all of us already knew. Our first few weeks had been devoted to Microsoft Office. Now, we'd moved on to the ins and outs of designing websites.

Really, they shouldn't have even called the class "computer science," because "how to use a computer" would have been a much more appropriate title. Not that I was complaining. I'd finished my website the first day and had been able to spend the past week surfing the net and accessing the high school's most guarded databases.

Leaning back in my chair, I swiveled side to side, debating how best to spend my free time today. What I really wanted to do was dig up more information on the TCIs, or hack into the Big Guys' mainframe to see if there was anything they weren't telling us about yesterday's explosion, but I knew better than to give in to temptation on that front. I was good, but I was also smart enough to know that using a public computer to do that kind of thing wasn't the best idea. High school computer labs aren't exactly the most secure places for any kind of data transfer. This is especially the case when the heir apparent of the Law Firm of Doom is sitting at the computer next to you.

I glanced at Jack's monitor, wondering what he was working on, and his website assignment stared back at me. Between the moving graphics and the handmade font, it was definitely a step up from what most of our class was making. In fact, given that he'd actually put some effort into it, there was a distinct chance that it was better than mine.

And—be still, my heart—the site appeared to be dedicated to classic rock, proving once and for all that Jack was not afflicted by musical tastes capable of causing me massive amounts of psychic pain.

JackOfDiamonds: Like what you see?

The message popped up on my computer screen. I looked from the screen to Jack. He kept his eyes locked on his own monitor, but even from a limited side view, I could tell that he was biting back one of those smirky smiles.

How in the world had Jack Peyton gotten my IM name? Besides the rest of the Squad (all of whom had obtained it from the file the Big Guys had developed on me before I'd joined up), no one at school knew my IM name. I could count on one hand the number of people I'd given it to *ever*, and none of them were Jack.

JackOfDiamonds: Speechless, Ev?

I snorted and let that serve as my answer, since he could hear me perfectly well. Meanwhile, I angled my computer screen away from him so that he couldn't see what I was doing, and then I set to work. Somehow, he'd figured out my instant messenger name. I planned to do him one better. I had his screen name. Now, I was going to figure out his password.

JackOfDiamonds: You liked what you saw so much that you need some privacy? A little alone time? I'm flattered.

I leaned around my computer screen and glared at him again. He pretended not to see me.

JackOfDiamonds: Come on, Ev. Talk to me. You know you want to.

I was too busy trying to hack into his account to put much thought into it, but lest he get suspicious, I shot off a quick reply.

TaeKleinDo: Do I?

It was short, it was cryptic, and it poked holes in that annoying "I'm so charismatic" confidence of his.

JackOfDiamonds: You probably shouldn't, but you do.

I hadn't had any luck guessing his password yet, which meant that Jack was significantly savvier than certain TCIs I could think of.

TaeKleinDo: Why shouldn't I want to talk to you?

I was still going on autopilot for my side of the conversation, so I didn't even realize I'd asked him a question until he answered it.

JackOfDiamonds: Because you're you and I'm me.

That sounded vaguely like an insult.

JackOfDiamonds: And you deserve better.

Now this was a side of Jack I'd never seen before. Smirky confidence? Sure. Subtle self-loathing? That was new.

TaeKleinDo: Most people would say you're the one who deserves better.

Including, I thought, about a dozen JV cheerleaders I can think of.

JackOfDiamonds: Most people are idiots.

I totally couldn't argue with that sentiment. And he knew it.

"Mrs. Hanson?" A high-pitched voice next to me broke me from my thoughts. "Can you come help me with the thingamajig?"

I quickly straightened my screen and minimized the chat window. By the time our computer science teacher was standing behind us, I appeared for all intents and purposes to be diligently working on my web page, which, unlike Jack's, wasn't so much a tribute to classic rock as it was a page dedicated to encouraging Bayport High spirit.

Can I tell you how much that wasn't my idea?

"Kiki, what seems to be the problem?"

The girl next to me frowned, and I recognized her as Hayley's poor excuse for a minion from lunch.

"I can't get this centered," she said, pointing to a piece of text on her screen. "And it's not big enough."

Considering the fact that we had a handout with the HTML codes for font size and centering on it, Kiki's statement went a long way to explaining how it was that she'd come to be following Hayley Hoffman's lead. Obviously, she wasn't the sharpest tool in the shed. Or, to put it in cheer terms, the puffiest pom in the JV set.

I waited for Mrs. Hanson to answer the question and marveled at her patience. Five minutes later, she was gone, and I went back to my attempts to hack Jack's IM.

JackOfDiamonds: Miss me?

I looked at him out of the side of my eyes, but if Jack noticed, he didn't give any visible reaction.

JackOfDiamonds: Check your email.

I'd just about concluded that Jack was the one person in this entire school who used a random assortment of numbers and letters for his password when I registered the content of his last IM. My email? Why did he want me to check my email?

Somewhat warily, I entered the URL of my Bayport High email account, half expecting some kind of elaborate, sardonic Jack Peyton gesture, but instead, I discovered that I had five new emails, all of which were from Noah.

Beside me, Jack snickered.

I opened up the first email and found a picture of the world's most adorable puppy wearing a sign around his neck that said VOTE FOR TOBY. SHE LOVES PUPPIES. As best I could tell from the "to" section of the email, Noah had sent this delightful piece of Toby promotion to the entire student body.

Dreading what would pop up next, I hit the next button and waited to see just how badly my brother wanted to die.

Email number two had a kitten. I didn't get past email number three, which was a public service announcement from the Toby Saved Our Lives Club. If my brother was looking for a way to make me regret ever having defended him and his equally goofy buddies from jock-wielded violence, he'd found it.

I trashed emails four and five before reading them. I could only hope that Noah's efforts would annoy the rest of the student body as much as they annoyed me. The way I figured it, the Irony Gods owed me that much.

"Mrs. Hanson? I need help with the—"

I cut Kiki off before she could get the rest of the request out of her mouth. "I'll help her." The last thing I needed was our teacher standing two feet away while I figured out a way to disable Noah's Bayport High email account—an action which was now a much higher priority than hacking into Jack's IM. In any case, whatever I was going to be doing on this computer, chances were it was the kind of thing the administration tended to frown upon, and I didn't need a member of the faculty staring over my shoulder.

I turned my chair to the side and leaned over to Kiki. "What do you need?" I asked, my voice completely flat.

She gave me a tentative smile. "I like think this would look better in purple, but when I tried the thingy . . ."

"HTML code," I corrected.

"Yeah, that. Anyway . . ."

"You want it to be purple?" I asked, commandeering her keyboard and fixing the code. "What else?"

"Can you show me how to put in a picture?"

It was on the tip of my tongue to tell her that pictures were just too hard for me to manage, but the desire to wreak internet havoc on Noah (and an equal desire to get back to my not-quite-a-conversation with Jack) kept me in check. "Sure," I said. "Where's the picture?"

She held up her phone.

Fifteen minutes later, I'd transferred the pictures from Kiki's phone to her computer, and showed her how to upload them to a photo-hosting site. She blinked several times, as if she couldn't quite believe the miracle before her.

"Which one do you want on the site?" I asked.

"That one." She pointed, rather than identifying the picture by its number. "See, the site is for this mother-daughter book club, and that's me and my—"

"Whatever." I cut her off, but as I captured the URL for the picture in question, I realized that Kiki's mother looked very, very familiar in a president of the PTA kind of way.

"There," I said. "Done."

"Wow," Kiki said. "You're really good at that." She paused, and I flinched, preparing myself for some gratuitous hugging. Instead, Kiki looked down at her hands. "You . . . ummm . . . you won't tell Hayley you helped me, will you?"

Some thanks. I practically built her entire web page for her, and she was afraid that her new BFF would find out that she'd talked to me. Then again, I vastly preferred her course of action to her mother's reaction to everything, which was to go all touchy-feely and start talking about what a precious time this was in my life. I was, to say the least, grateful that such actions weren't hereditary.

"Ummm . . . Toby?"

I narrowed my eyes at her. "Hayley and I aren't really on speaking terms. Your secret is safe with me."

"Cool." She paused another beat. "So you know what you were saying at lunch about the tumbling requirements for varsity?"

I was officially never helping anyone ever again. I kept my brother from being beaten up, and he dedicated his life to torturing me. I helped a JV cheerleader build a mother-daughter book club website, and she took that as an invitation to grill me about her chances of making varsity. I kissed Jack, and he had the gall to come up with a password I couldn't figure out on my own.

Okay, maybe that last one was stretching it just a bit.

"Toby?" Kiki prodded. "About the—"

"Hey Keeks," Jack cut her off, leaning back in his chair to get a better view of the girl in question.

Kiki got really obviously flustered at the attention. Unlike most cheerleaders I'd met, concealing her emotions really wasn't her strong suit.

"Yes?" she squeaked. Despite her squeaking, she made a masterful attempt at batting her eyelashes at *my* homecoming date.

"I like your sweater."

Jack's compliment left Kiki speechless. Five seconds later, a new message popped up on my IM.

JackOfDiamonds: You're welcome.

Apparently, I was supposed to thank him for flirting with another girl. Then again, I thought as I logged into my brother's email account and began messing around with his settings, aforementioned flirtation had distracted Kiki from talking to me, which just confirmed my suspicion that Jack Peyton was the kind of guy who always knew exactly what to give a girl. Some girls liked diamonds. Some girls liked pearls. I liked having someone running interference between the rest of the student body and me.

And, as much as I really, truly, deeply hated to admit it, I liked Jack.

TaeKleinDo: Shut up.
JackOfDiamonds: Yeah, Ev. Love you, too.

When the bell rang a moment later, I wasn't sure whether I was thankful or disappointed. In fact, the only thing I knew for certain was that I'd wreaked enough havoc on Noah's email account that he wouldn't be sending out messages of any kind for a very, very long time.

CHAPTER 17
Code Word: Blend

By the time I got to the Quad, everyone else was already there.

"Hello, Toby."

One look at the half smile on Tara's face had me preparing myself for her trademarked understated form of teasing, but Tara didn't get the chance to say whatever she'd planned to, because the others beat her to it.

"I hear that you love puppies." Brittany stole Tara's thunder.

"Yup, Toby just wuvs cute wittle bitty—"

"Shut up, Tiffany. Don't you guys have something to glitter?" It occurred to me a second after I spoke that encouraging the twins to apply any sort of cosmetic product to anything was seldom a good idea—especially since there was at least a ninety percent chance they'd choose to apply it to me.

"What's wrong with puppies?" Bubbles asked, mystified. Of all of the girls, Bubbles was the only one whose inner depths I'd never discovered. I was pretty sure that she didn't actually have depths. She'd joined the Squad because of a freakish ability to contort herself into odd, but useful positions. It was an incredibly handy skill, and Bubbles was probably the single stealthiest person I'd ever met in my life, but she wasn't exactly a rocket scientist.

"There's nothing wrong with puppies," I told Bubbles, shooting daggers at the twins with my eyes and daring them to say something else. "I'd just prefer it if the puppies of the world weren't endorsing my candidacy for homecoming queen."

Bubbles frowned. "The puppies are voting for *you*?"

She sounded equal parts confused and offended. Oh, Bubbles.

"Noah just sent this email thing around," Lucy explained. "It had the cutest picture of a puppy in it. I think it's sweet that he's trying to help you, Toby."

"He's trying to drive me nuts," I corrected her. "And it's not sweet. It's pathological. And in the future, please do not use the words *Noah* and *sweet* in the same sentence."

Lucy chose to pretend I hadn't spoken at all, forcing me to wonder what was going on in that cheerful little mind of hers. Was she actually into Noah?

Like I was actually into Jack. . . .

"Are we going to get ready for our missions or what?" I cut off my own train of thought with a question. If I could just flip into spy mode, then I wouldn't have to worry about anything that existed within the walls of this high school. I could concentrate on terrorists, biological weapons, and reconnaissance, which was a definite step up from boys, brothers, and homecoming.

"I agree with Toby." At Brooke's words, the world stopped spinning on its axis. "We may just be tailing the TCIs, but this mission is important. If we want Washington to deal us in on the action when things go down, we need to nail this." She paused. "That means following orders. Don't let the TCIs out of your sight, but don't engage them. Get as much video and audio feed on them as you can, but don't let them see you. The night shift will take over at 2100 hours, but until then, the TCIs are ours."

The "don't screw it up" on the end of Brooke's sentence went just barely unstated.

"We'll be working in three groups. Group one will be following Anthony Connors-Wright. Chloe and April, you'll be working with Bubbles and Lucy on this one. Strategy is up to you, but we want as many angles of surveillance as possible. Same goes for team number two. Britt, Tiff, Tara, and Zee, you'll be tailing Amelia Juarez."

"What about me?" I narrowed my eyes at the captain. Tara was my partner. We worked as a team. So why had Brooke assigned Tara and Zee to work together? Shouldn't Zee have been working with her partner?

"You'll be with me." Brooke's words reminded me just who Zee's partner normally was. "I want Zee in the field. The closer we can get her to the TCIs, the better she'll be able to read their body language. You and I will be stationed near Peyton, Kaufman, and Gray, so that we can keep an eye out for anything there. As bad as having a biological weapon in Bayport is, it would be much worse if the firm got a hold of it. If we see something suspicious, the Big Guys will be sending a team in, but if they can't get there fast enough, it may be up to us to make sure nothing goes down."

Brooke dangled the chance of action in front of me like a carrot.

"Besides, I don't trust you to stick to orders. If I sent you to tail one of the TCIs, you'd probably manage to get yourself killed."

"I would not!"

"Get yourself killed or go against orders and engage your mark?"

She had me there. "The first one."

"Says the girl who almost got blown up yesterday." Brooke waved away any further objections on my part with a flick of her wrist. "Brittany, Tiffany, go prep the salon. Given the nature of our mission, all teams will be going with a B3 cover."

Brittany nodded, and Tiffany—for reasons that eluded me—sighed. "We'll be ready in five." With that, the twins headed off to their torture chamber (or, as they preferred to think of it, their "beauty lab").

"Chloe—"

"Cameras, video cameras, binoculars, communicators, and standard bug sets are ready to go." Chloe didn't give Brooke a chance to finish her order. "They're already camouflaged to go with a B3."

Brooke smiled in a way specifically designed to convey the fact that she was annoyed, but wasn't going to say anything about it. "Great. Luce?"

"Yeah huh?" Lucy didn't have quite the siblingesque rivalry with Brooke that Chloe did, and she docilely awaited her orders accordingly.

"I want Tasers and knockout patches, plus bulletproof push-up bras all around. We're not engaging the enemy, but we're not going to take any chances, either."

"Awesome," Lucy said. "I redid some of the knockout patches to look like stickers." She turned her toothy grin on me. "You can have the puppy, Toby."

Sometimes, it was really hard to tell when Lucy was being serious and when she was teasing, because she used the same earnest tone and expression for both.

Paying no heed to the puppy comment, Brooke continued dishing out orders. "Lucy, Chloe, get things set up in the guidepost, and then report to the salon. Everybody else, let's get a move on. The TCIs aren't going to tail themselves."

There's not much you can do to mentally prepare yourself for a makeover, especially a makeover of the scale and caliber the twins routinely pulled off. They'd pretty much single-handedly turned me from the slacker no one noticed to the reluctant teen goddess I was today. Since my initial transformation, I'd avoided their lab at all costs, but today, there was no way to avoid a B3. Whatever a B3 was.

"Care to explain?" I asked Tara. "About the B3 thing?"

"You'll see." Tara was less than forthcoming.

I knew that the twins' job description included designing costuming for each mission that would play up whatever attributes would offer us the most advantages, but this was the first time I'd gone on a mission as anything other than my cheerleader self. The Squad worked because we hid in plain sight. Nine times out of ten, the stereotype was the only cover we needed.

Apparently, today's mission was the tenth. I knew that it was ridiculous that car bombs didn't scare me, and teenage fashion dictators did, but no amount of mental pep talking could convince me that giving the twins carte blanche to alter our appearances was anything less than bone-chilling.

"I'm not sure I'm ready for another makeover," I muttered

as we entered the twins' lab. "I almost didn't survive the first one."

"Makeover?" Brittany said, wrinkling her nose. "Who said anything about a makeover?"

"Brooke did," I replied. "You know, a B3."

Tiffany joined her twin in giving me a blank look.

"You guys live for makeovers." I stated the obvious. "It's practically your middle name!"

"Silly Toby." This was from Bubbles. As in, the girl who thought that puppies got to vote for homecoming queen. "A B3 isn't a makeover. It's a make*under*."

"A makeunder?" April repeated the term. It was times like these that I was grateful that I wasn't the only new member of the Squad.

"We need to blend." Brooke elucidated the situation. "If we go out in groups of four looking like this, we're going to attract a lot of attention, and since the TCIs aren't supposed to even know we're there, that's not exactly a good thing the way it would be if we were planning to interact with them, but didn't want to be seen as a threat."

"A B3 makeunder is constructed with that goal in mind," Tiffany said, her tone absolutely, deathly serious. "Although we can't disguise our more striking features, we will be downplaying them. Some people call it 'the natural look.' We've spent a lot of time designing outfits and makeup/hair schema that will serve a dual purpose. To the casual observer, we'll look average."

Brittany took over where Tiffany left off. "But if we happen to run into anyone from school, we need to look nice enough that they won't get suspicious. These outfits aren't about being unfashionable; they're about being subtle. The perfect B3 will allow its wearer to blend in, but on closer focus, she'll stand out because of the ensemble's simplicity."

"A B3 says, 'I'm pretty without trying to be,'" Tiffany continued. "It says, 'I'm not wearing makeup,' even though you will be. It says, 'Don't look at me, don't remember me, but if you know me, be impressed with my effortlessness.'"

I think the twins might have gone on indefinitely if Brooke hadn't sped them along. Instead, they multitasked, punctuating my makeunder with theoretical explanations I paid no attention to whatsoever. By the time they finished with me and moved on to the next person, I wasn't sure what to expect. What was the logical result of spending a great deal of time and effort attempting to look natural?

A quick examination in the mirror revealed my answer. I didn't look like the old me, but I wasn't exactly Cheer Toby, either. I was a Neutrogena commercial, clean and cute. I didn't look average, but I did look generic. Because of my height and the way the twins had styled my hair, I also looked about thirteen.

Makeunder complete.

CHAPTER 18
Code Word: Girl Talk

Brooke and I got ice cream at a shop down the street from the firm and then set up camp on a bench outside the shopping center. Along the way, we also stopped at a few stores, just for good measure, and our packages were spread out on the ground near our feet.

"So what now?" I asked Brooke.

She pulled her feet up and folded them gracefully under her body. "Now we talk." She took in my skeptical look. "Trust me. It's something girls do."

So that was our cover. We weren't cheerleaders. We were just *girls*. I maneuvered to get myself comfortable, until I was sitting cross-legged on the bench, my ice cream balanced precariously on one knee. "And what do girls talk about?" I asked.

"Boys. Other girls. World domination."

I was about eighty percent sure she was kidding on that last one, but this was Brooke, who dominated our high school world with seemingly little effort, so I wasn't willing to completely discount the possibility that she might be serious.

"Which other girls?" That one seemed the safest.

"Whichever ones are pissing us off." Brooke didn't sugar-coat it.

"And if no one is?"

Brooke rolled her eyes. "Then you're lying."

"Are you trying to say I'm an angry person?"

"Well, yes. But it wouldn't matter if you weren't. This is high school. Everybody's mad at somebody."

"So who are you mad at?" I asked.

Brooke shrugged. "Chloe for being a brat. Zee for analyzing what's none of her business. You for almost getting blown up."

"So, as girls, we're supposed to sit here talking about how you don't like me?"

Brooke rolled her eyes. "Technically, we're supposed to talk about the people who aren't here."

Brooke's phone beeped, and she flipped it open to read a text message. Then she dug into her purse and pulled out an iPod. I stared at it warily, unsure whether this was the communicator iPod that Chloe had given us, or the one that doubled as a high-voltage Taser.

Brooke put one of the earpieces in her ear, and I came to the conclusion that as painful as sitting here with me obviously was for her, she probably wasn't frustrated enough to resort to Tasering herself. Yet.

"What's up?" I asked her.

"Just a song I like," she said lightly, and I got the message. She was coordinating the tails on the TCIs, but she wasn't going to give any verbal indication of what she was doing—not even to me. Considering we were only twenty yards away from the institution our Squad was designed to combat, I couldn't chalk that one up to anything but common sense, as much as I would have liked to blame it on Brooke's more PMSy tendencies.

Her fingers flew across the keypad of her cell phone at high speed, and I wondered what kind of orders she was dishing out. Given an infinite amount of time and all of the technology in Chloe's lab, I might have been able to figure it out, the same way that a hundred monkeys could eventually produce the works of Shakespeare, but I didn't have that kind of time, or the technology, or the monkeys, so I settled for taking another bite of ice cream and watching the parking garage across the street. Trying to appear as though I were gazing vacuously off into space, I zeroed in on a car that was preparing to turn into the Peyton parking garage.

I brought my free hand up to the simple chain at my neck and fiddled with the charm. An almost inaudible click told me that my necklace, which was actually a high-definition digital camera, had taken a picture that might have been of my collarbone, but that I hoped was of the car across the street. I glanced over at Brooke and saw that her dark hair was tucked behind her left ear, clearing the way for a clean shot by the video camera installed in her earrings.

Between the two of us, we were wearing more or less an entire Radio Shack, and thanks to Lucy, I had a puppy sticker in my pocket that, if applied to a person's bare skin, would render them unconscious in less than a second.

"Come on, Toby. There must be someone you don't like." Brooke was back to making conversation. It seemed like the most natural thing in the world coming from her, like she didn't normally roll her eyes at me eight million times a day. And that was when I realized something.

Brooke and I weren't hanging out. Brooke's cover was hanging out with my cover. We were supposed to be friends, just two girls chilling on a bench, eating ice cream and talking about boys and shopping and the girls on our metaphorical hit lists. So that's what Brooke was doing, and she was doing it well.

Two could play that game.

"Hayley Hoffman," I said. "Her JV mafia. Chip. Mr. Corkin." I decided to stop listing people, lest I appear to be the angry girl she already viewed me as.

"Hayley's not that bad," Brooke said.

"If by 'not that bad,' you mean 'unholy spawn of evil,' then, yeah."

"I mean, yes, she's kind of a bitch, but there are worse things to be. She wants things, and she goes after them. People follow her."

"So tell me. Are we talking about you or Hayley?"

Brooke snorted. "You've been spending way too much time with Zee. And we're talking about Hayley. If we were talking about me, we'd be using words like *fabulous*."

Even as we talked, Brooke's fingers raced across her keypad. She had an uncanny ability to text without looking, and to carry on a conversation with me, whilst listening to reports from the other four teams, issuing orders, and keeping an eye on Peyton, all at once.

Personally, I was struggling with eating ice cream and watching the building across the street.

"Get your phone."

It took me a second to realize that Brooke was talking to me, even though there wasn't anyone else around. I dug my phone out of my purse.

"You know that guy you like?" she prodded.

Jack? My mind went there before I could stop it.

"That guy," Brooke said again, and I followed her gaze to a guy across the street. She glanced just briefly down at my necklace, and I got the picture. With another absent-minded fiddle, I'd captured his image, and a few keystrokes to my cell phone allowed me to download the pictures without ever connecting the two. Chloe may have been a brat, but she was darn good at her job.

Once the picture had loaded on my phone, Brooke grabbed it out of my hand and passed me hers. While she keyed in the access code for comparing the picture to the Big Guys' watch list database, I scrolled through the last few messages she'd sent to the teams.

Team A was at Walford Park with Anthony Connors-Wright. They'd followed orders and kept from engaging, and were currently monitoring him from four different viewpoints. Chloe wanted permission to go in closer, but Brooke had denied the request. No engagement meant no engagement, not even minor physical contact. Nobody on the Squad was so much as going to brush up against a TCI on Brooke's watch, and her text messages made that abundantly clear in a manner suited to an alpha female.

Team B was following Amelia Juarez in two different cars, careful to keep the tails as subtle as they could. On Brooke's orders, the girls fell back a mile and followed the tracker we'd planted on the car rather than the car itself. Brooke had notified the Big Guys' of her decision, and they'd approved.

From the way Brooke was playing things, you would have thought No Engagement meant No Risks. For someone who *made* the rules at our high school, she was awfully hesitant about breaking them elsewhere.

"I don't think you guys are a very good match," Brooke said, handing my phone back. It took me a second to read the meaning in her words: the guy I'd photographed didn't match anyone in the Big Guys' database.

Soon thereafter, I confirmed something they don't tell you in spy movies. Recon is boring. So boring, in fact, that I might have actually preferred to be doing toe touches. Brooke and I sat there for hours, repeating the same motions over and over again, thinking of new ways to make them look natural. We rotated locations, going from the bench, inside a lingerie store (near the window, of course), then down the street on the other side, and finally, we ended up back on the bench, eating Chinese food for dinner.

From what I'd been able to glean from Brooke, none of the other teams had noticed anything sketchy, either. Anthony Connors-Wright was still wandering around the park, which might have been a sign of mental instability, since the park wasn't exactly a hot spot of activity, but probably wasn't a sign of nefarious activity. He hadn't actually talked to anyone, other than a hot-dog vendor whose background check had turned out clean when the girls ran his picture through the database.

Amelia Juarez had spent most of the night shopping, which meant that our second team had been able to camouflage themselves without much effort at all. Given the fact that the girls knew the closest mall inside and out (including all of the potential hand-off locations), they felt that they could say with high levels of certainty that Amelia wasn't up to much other than biding her time.

My mind began to construct scenarios, as Brooke and I sat there, talking about nothing over chow mein, just to keep up the appearance of talking. We'd downgraded to talking about celebrities (most of whom I knew absolutely nothing about), their hairstyles, and their misguided relationships.

Of the scenarios I'd managed to construct, Scenario one went a little something like this: Peyton, Kaufman, and Gray wasn't at all involved in this biological-weapons scare. Since Jacob Kann was dead and Hector Hassan was in custody, that just left Amelia and Anthony, both of whom were waiting on a call from the biological-arms dealer before moving forward with their plans, whatever those might be.

Scenario one was my favorite, mostly because it meant that my relationship, or non-relationship, or whatever-it-was with Jack wouldn't come into spy play. If Peyton, Kaufman, and Gray wasn't involved, I was in the clear. Scenario one also had the advantage that it would be pretty simple for us to save the day. We'd keep track of the TCIs until the Big Guys identified the seller, and then we'd take him—and the weapon—out of the picture.

Scenario two was the pessimistic one. In that one, Peyton, Kaufman, and Gray was either responsible for brokering the deal that had brought the TCIs to Bayport in the first place, or they'd noticed the influx the same as we had. Either way, they were now in the center of everything, and at any given moment, one of the most insidious, impenetrable rogue operations in the country would have access to a weapon we still knew nothing about.

Scenario two had the plus side that it might mean that Brooke and I would eventually see some action, but the Jack factor was enough to make me resign myself to discussing celebrities' bangs and hoping that the rest of the night would be equally tame. By the time we finished dinner, I didn't even have to think about working my camera anymore, or checking pictures or license plate numbers against our database, and I'd developed an eerie sense for reading Brooke's reactions to the news she was getting through her communicator.

I was also bored enough that I considered using the puppy in my pocket to knock myself out.

And then, just as I was cursing my own boredom, Brooke abruptly switched topics. "So," she said. "You and Jack."

There was something underneath her tone that I couldn't quite read. Jealousy? Intensity? Heartbreak? Or maybe it was just that her tone was so painfully neutral that I couldn't help but read into it all of the above.

"There is no me and Jack," I said.

"You're supposed to be able to lie better than that," she informed me blithely.

"It's . . ." I was going to say that my involvement with Jack was just part of the job, but I didn't. "It's complicated."

That was, quite possibly, the biggest understatement that had ever been uttered.

"Things with Jack Peyton are always complicated."

This was my opportunity to ask her about Alan Peyton and his involvement with our organization. Unfortunately, I couldn't risk it. Not in public. Not so close to the firm. Instead, looking at the expression on her face, I found myself wondering for the first time if Brooke or Chloe had ever really liked Jack. Chloe's jealousy wasn't enough to convince me that she had, and most days, Brooke didn't even show any emotion—including jealousy—unless she wanted other people to see it. I'd always just sort of assumed that the other girls had used Jack to get to his father and the firm. Brooke was all Squad, all the time, half cheerleader/half agent, and nothing left for anything else, and Chloe was basically the wannabe Brooke. They'd dated Jack because he was popular, and because he was the easiest way to the firm.

But technically, those were the reasons I was dating Jack, too. Only I *wasn't* dating Jack. I'd decided not to date him. Homecoming was simply an unavoidable fluke.

"You like him." Brooke spoke the words carefully, enunciating each one.

"No, I don't." My first reaction was always to argue, especially when I didn't want to consider the fact that Brooke was absolutely right.

"Yes," Brooke gritted out. "You do. And you're not supposed to, and it's going to come back to bite you in the ass."

So much for the two of us pretending to be friends. We couldn't even keep up appearances for a few hours before things went to heck in a pom bag.

Then, without warning, Brooke began cursing, quietly and possibly in more than one language.

I guess she felt more strongly about this Jack thing than I'd realized.

"You know that thing Tara and Zee were doing?" Brooke said.

I nodded.

"Well, they kinda lost it."

Lost it? As in lost their mark? As in a TCI was out there, completely unsupervised, quite possibly acquiring a weapon we really didn't want her to have?

"Yeah," Brooke said, her voice conveying so much pissed-offedness that I got the feeling that the safest thing to do would be to back away slowly. "They lost it."

I didn't have to ask if the twins had lost Amelia as well.

Despite Brooke's calm outward appearance, she was freaking out, and that meant that things were bad.

Brooke's fingers flew across the keys of her cell, and I wondered if she was giving instructions to the others, or if she was reporting the situation to the Big Guys. I wondered that right up until I saw a green sedan pulling into the parking garage across the street.

"Brooke," I said, throwing caution to the wind. "What color is You Know Who's car?"

Hopefully, if anyone was listening to me, they'd be up on their *Harry Potter* slang and think I was talking about Voldemort.

"Green," Brooke said, and then she followed my gaze.

I recognized the license plate. My memory for numbers never failed me, and I knew even before Brooke confirmed it that something completely unexpected had happened. The other teams had lost their TCI, and we'd found her.

At Peyton, Kaufman, and Gray.

CHAPTER 19
Code Word: Fun, Fun, Fun

My first instinct was to bolt across the street and fling myself at Amelia Juarez the second she stepped out of her car, hence preventing her from entering the Peyton building and bringing this entire mission to a crashing halt. Brooke's first instinct was to make sure that I didn't engage in mine. She grabbed onto my ponytail in the stealthiest of all possible ways and literally held me back. She didn't say a word, she just stood there, holding my hair like a leash and silently compelling me to heel, while she listened to the audio feed coming in through the earpiece in her right ear. Then her cell phone rang, and she quickly traded the communicator for another type of secure line—one that would allow her to talk back.

"Hello?" She said, tightening her grip on my ponytail with one hand as she flipped her ringing phone open with the other. "Hey! OMG, I haven't talked to you in so long. What's up?"

If I hadn't been almost positive that she was talking to our bosses, I would have been completely fooled by the tone and content of her words. "Really? That's like so awesome. You must be so psyched!"

I tried to imagine what listening to both sides of this conversation would have been like, Uncle Alan or one of his colleagues imparting crucial information in an overly serious tone, and Brooke responding like a Valley girl, heavy on the Valley.

"Do you want me to call him for you? Ask him if he's interested? Because I can totally do that for you. It's not a proble—" Brooke stopped talking abruptly. "Oh. Okay. Yeah, I get it. You don't need my help on this one. That's cool."

Brooke loosened her hold on my hair, but I curtailed my ongoing impulse to dive into the action headfirst for two reasons. First, Amelia Juarez was no longer in my sight and was, in all likelihood, already inside. And second, unless I was reading too much into Brooke's side of this conversation, there was a distinct chance that we'd been called off this case.

Brooke flipped her cell shut and confirmed what I'd suspected. "Come on," she said. "I'll give you a ride back to the school."

Just like that? We'd been staked out here all day, and now that something had finally happened, we were leaving?

Recon sucked.

Brooke picked up what was left of her Chinese carryout and threw it in the closest garbage can. I followed suit. If this had been the movies, we would have been passing on some secret information in the remains of our chow mein, but this was life, and trash was just trash. If anyone happened to suspect that we were more than what we seemed and came to check up on it, all they would have found was a bunch of half-eaten noodles and a fortune cookie that promised me an exciting future.

Apparently, the fortune cookie lied.

Brooke and I gathered our bags, and I couldn't help but cast a longing glance over my shoulder. I'd nearly made my way onto the casualty list working this case. Didn't that buy me anything with the Big Guys? Brooke and I could have stopped Amelia from going to that meeting. We could have prevented it.

"Toby, just let it go. We're cheerleaders. That's all."

That was probably the biggest lie any member of the Squad had ever told, but I tried to dig through the crap to get to Brooke's meaning. The best I could come up with was the fact that the firm couldn't ever know we were more than cheerleaders. If we blew our cover to the one enemy our operation was maintained to watch, the Squad would be demoted to mere cheerleaderdom in a heartbeat.

In retrospect, it was probably a good thing Brooke had held onto my hair.

Given the amount of mental processing I was doing, there is a slight chance that I wasn't paying enough attention to where I was going, and as Brooke and I crossed the street, I found myself stepping out onto the road, in front of oncoming traffic. I jumped back, startled into paying attention, but almost instantly, a minivan barreling down the road swerved toward me. I stood there on the sidewalk, in complete denial that the van was no longer on the road, and the nanosecond before I would have jumped out of the way myself, Brooke flying tackled me, pushing me out of the car's path. The two of us fell, a tangled mess of limbs on the ground, but at least this time, I didn't hit my head.

"You okay?" Brooke asked me.

I nodded, and as we stood up, I glanced down the street. The van was gone.

"Let's go." Brooke didn't seem to be quite as affected by my second brush with death in as many days as I was.

"That person almost hit me. I was on the sidewalk, and they almost hit me."

"Probably a drunk driver," Brooke said, "though don't ask me who hits the bottle on a Wednesday at nine."

As we walked to Brooke's car, I kept seeing the van speeding at me, kept feeling myself freezing, and for some reason, the part of the experience that my brain insisted on dwelling on the most was the fact that I'd now been flying tackled by other members of the Squad twice. I was well on my way to getting sacked more often than any of our Neanderthal football players.

The second Brooke and I were in the car, and she'd turned it on and set the radio to the faux station that was programmed to run an automatic check for listening devices, Brooke leaned her head back against the headrest, closed her eyes, and sat that way for several seconds.

"Brooke?"

Her eyes snapped open, and it was suddenly like nothing had ever happened. Team B hadn't lost the tail on Amelia Juarez. The Big Guys hadn't told the two of us to leave. A crazy driver hadn't almost turned me into a Toby pancake.

"What?" Brooke's tone was high and clear and absolutely brittle.

"What just happened back there?" I'd gotten the general gist of the Big Guys' orders, but I wanted specifics.

"We went shopping," Brooke said, playing dumb. "We ate ice cream and Chinese food and talked about boys. It was fun."

"That's one word for it."

"Just drop it, Toby."

I snorted. If she thought that was going to work, she wasn't nearly as smart as I'd given her credit for being.

"Are the Big Guys sending a team in?" I decided to try my luck with a very specific question.

"No." Brooke's answer surprised me. She didn't elaborate.

"What do you mean, 'no'? An individual who we think is in Bayport to purchase a biological weapon just went into the evil law firm of destruction and doom, and the Big Guys don't think this merits a team?"

For a split second, I found myself doubting the conclusion I'd reached about the CIA knowing about Alan Peyton's connection to the firm. What if they didn't? What if he was a double agent and nobody realized it but me? What if the people calling the shots on our mission were working for the enemy? What if . . .

"Amelia doesn't have the weapon." Brooke finally imparted some useful information in my general direction, and it stopped my what if–ing in its tracks. "Our superiors have ID'd the seller, and whatever the bioweapon is, he still has it. The deal isn't going down until later this week."

Well, that was the first piece of good news we'd had all day. Incidentally, it also made me feel like an idiot for every ridiculous question I'd let enter my mind. Lest Brooke sense that I was silently berating myself for that, I pressed on.

"And?" I prompted her for more information.

"And what?"

"That's not all they told you." Somehow, I was sure of this fact.

Brooke blew a wisp of hair out of her face and took the car around a corner a little faster than was strictly necessary. "Do the math, Toby. If Amelia doesn't have the weapon, why would we stop her from meeting with Peyton? We still have an audio feed in one of their offices. The signal's scrambled, but some intel is better than none."

I felt every bit as stupid as Brooke's tone said I was for not making the connection earlier. I was the one who'd planted the bug at Peyton. This was our chance to use it.

"What about the weapon?" I asked. This was about as far into "sharing" mode as Brooke got, and since the two of us were stuck in a car together anyway, I was going to press her for as much information as I could, even if her glare suggested that this course of action might not be in my best interest healthwise.

"After they ID'd the seller, the nature of the weapon became apparent."

"And?"

Brooke slammed on the brakes as we came to a stoplight. "And apparently," she said, her voice full of false cheer, "we'll be debriefed in the morning."

The Big Guys knew what the weapon was and who had it, and they expected us to wait until morning? No wonder Brooke was in such fine form.

"So what now?" I asked as Brooke pulled into her parking spot at the school.

"Now?" Brooke said. "Now I try to figure out how Amelia Juarez, whose only claim to fame is her family's crime empire, managed to lose not one, but two of our tails, and dismantle our tracking chip, and you go home."

"Go home?" I was getting the strangest sense of déjà vu.

"Be back for practice tomorrow morning." Brooke eyeballed me. "And this time, don't be late."

And with that, she slid out of the car, shut the door without slamming it, and walked into the gym like she wasn't a moving ball of stress and fury. I considered following her, but ultimately decided that I liked my head right where it was—on my shoulders, with my ponytail intact. So for the second night in a row, I followed Brooke's orders and drove home.

I didn't realize how tired I was until I walked through my front door, and then something in my mind clicked, and staying vertical suddenly became very difficult. Who would have thought sitting around all day, doing nothing, was so exhausting?

"How was your day?" My mom accosted me in the front hallway. If she noticed the zombielike glaze that had settled over my eyes, she said nothing.

How was my day? I considered my response. I'd spent the morning getting debriefed by our contact at the CIA, followed immediately by flaming the gossip fires by kissing Jack in the hallway, had watched my brother have a "moment" with a cheerleader, had discovered that Jack actually knew how to create a password I couldn't crack, had girl-talked with Brooke while staking out Jack's father's law firm, had discovered that the Big Guys knew more than they were telling, and to top it all off, I'd nearly been hit by a car.

"Fine," I grumbled.

"That's nice, dear," my mother said. "Now, you wouldn't happen to know why your brother's email stopped working, would you?"

Noah was such a tattletale.

"Not a clue," I deadpanned, and then, before my mother could say another word, I climbed the steps and headed for my room, stopping only long enough to hear Noah on the phone.

"We've got to go *bigger*. We've got to be inventive. My friends, it's time to think outside the box. It's time for . . ." Noah pitched his voice lower, like a TV announcer. "Homecoming: the next generation. This is an all-new frontier of advertising, gentlemen. So ask yourselves this question: are you ready?"

As soon as I developed the strength, I was going to short-circuit my brother's telephone line. For now, however, all I wanted was to fall asleep, because the sooner I slept, the sooner morning would come.

CHAPTER 20
Code Word: Flat

"Vote for Toby! She loves puppies."

Puppies? Again? I glance around the room, looking for Noah. Instead, I see a room full of puppies, all of whom are staring straight at me. Something about their beady little puppy eyes has me looking down at my body, but thankfully, I'm fully clothed.

Unfortunately, I'm wearing a puffy pink monstrosity. It's so big and fluffy and pink that I can't even move. I hate dresses, and this one is trying to kill me.

"Nice dress." And then Jack's there, only instead of wearing a tuxedo, he's wearing boxer shorts. Well. This is certainly an interesting (and not entirely unwelcome) turn of events.

"Toby?" Jack says.

I look down at my dress, hating it, and then a moment later, it disappears, and I would give anything to have it back again. I cover myself with the poms I'm suddenly holding in each hand, but Jack doesn't seem to notice at all.

"Toby?"

"Go away!"

"Toby?"

The puppies are closing in, and when they open their mouths, I see razor-sharp teeth. This is so not good. Rabid puppies, disappearing fluffy dresses, and Jack just keeps saying my name over and over again.

"Toby? Toby? Toby?"

And then we're at the dance, and he's holding my arm, escorting me up to the stage, and I'm wearing the pink dress again, but I know with every fiber of my being that the second I step onto that stage and accept that crown, it's going to disappear.

"Clap your hands, everybody!"

Where is that cheering coming from?

"Toby?"

"Everybody, clap your hands!"

"Toby?"

I'm cheering along with them. I can't help it. I'm walking toward the stage and cheering, and Jack is calling my name, and the puppies are gnashing their puppy teeth, and I know this just isn't going to end well.

"Toby?"

"What?" I spit out.

Jack reaches out to touch my face. "Run."

The second the word exits his mouth, there's an explosion, and as I fly backward, the world around me engulfed in flames, my last conscious thought is that my fluffy pink dress has disappeared again.

For the second morning in a row, I woke up before my alarm. This was getting seriously ridiculous. A girl can only take so many naked dreams before she commits herself to a life of insomnia.

Looking at my watch, I ascertained that if I got dressed as quickly as I had yesterday, I'd have time for at least two cups of coffee. When I staggered into the kitchen wearing my standard cheer practice uniform—tiny cheer shorts and a sports bra—I wasn't expecting to be greeted by a large percentage of the freshman class, but there were at least a dozen freshman boys in my kitchen, eating donuts and engaging in some kind of robust debate.

Given the fact that Noah was even less of a morning person than I was, I took this as a very bad sign of things to come.

"Toby!" Noah was either happy to see me, or very, very nervous. "Going to practice?"

I didn't reply. Instead, I glowered at each and every person in the room, stole one of their donuts, and grabbed a thermos of coffee to go. This morning, dealing with my brother was going to have to wait. At some point, you have to prioritize, and right now, the morning's debriefing won out. Maiming Noah was but a distant second.

Lucky for him.

As I walked out of the back door, the boys went back to their plotting, and I tried very hard not to wonder what the much-contested "phase three" entailed.

On the drive to the school, my mind checked out, and I went into the zone, completely absorbed in my own thoughts, but somehow able to navigate the early-morning traffic. There were so many questions swimming around in my head. The Big Guys owed us so many answers, and my gut instinct told me that we weren't going to get all of them.

If I were the CIA, I probably wouldn't tell my teenage

operatives everything, either. That didn't make this particular pill any easier to swallow, and I wondered what they would hold back. Not information about the bomb in Jacob Kann's car—they owed me that much. Not information about the seller's ID and the nature of the weapon for sale—without the information I'd torn from Kann's laptop, they might never have made the connection. And they could hardly hold back on what had transpired between Amelia and the higher-ups at Peyton the day before. I'd been the one to plant the bug at Peyton in the first place.

On second thought, if I were the CIA, I'd tell us everything.

Someone tapped on my car window, and it took me a second to realize that I'd parked it. Grabbing my coffee and my bag, I turned the car off and slipped out.

"Good morning." Tara's voice was just slightly hoarse.

"Long night?" I asked her.

She inclined her head slightly. "I couldn't sleep."

I thought back on my naked dreams. "That makes two of us."

"You didn't lose a tail yesterday." Tara's words surprised me. She almost never talked about spy stuff so plainly, especially outside of the Quad.

"Yeah, well, I've been naked in every dream I've had for the past forty-eight hours."

That got the slightest hint of a smile out of Tara. "You win."

I waited until we reached the safety of the locker room before I voiced a more sensitive question. "What do you think they'll tell us?"

"Whatever they want us to know."

Those weren't exactly the kind of words that inspired confidence.

It's amazing how quickly even the most extraordinary things can become routine. I barely even registered our journey from the locker room to the conference table, but soon, I was drinking my coffee, and Brooke was giving us the rundown on Amelia Juarez in anticipation of the Big Guys' call.

"She shouldn't have been able to lose any of you."

Brooke's words didn't have a visible effect on anyone in the room, but I somehow doubted that Zee had gotten any more sleep last night than Tara had. As for the twins, they weren't polishing each other's nails, which put them toward the more solemn end of the Britt-Tiff spectrum.

"But she did lose you, and that tells us something. It tells us that there's a lot we don't know about Amelia Juarez, because the four of you are good. And if she lost you, then she's much, much better than we gave her credit for. Zee?"

Zee nibbled on her bottom lip, and for a split second, I could see the awkward little kid she must have been her first time through high school. "I did some more digging. The profiles the Big Guys gave us were explicit, but far from complete. We knew that Amelia had a need to prove herself to her family. She's the youngest of five and the only girl. Her family is known for being brutal, merciless. They control everything from prostitution to the drug trade in at least three states. From what I've been able to tell, Amelia hasn't been allowed to take much of a leadership role in the business."

"What does that tell us?" Beside me, Tara cut quickly, but smoothly to the point.

"Her family is smart, but they rely more on strength, intimidation, and power to get things done." Zee paused. "I dug up some old aptitude tests from Amelia's elementary school. They're outdated, but they tell us one thing for sure. Her family is smart. Amelia is smarter."

If Zee was impressed with Amelia's scores, that meant the TCI gave new meaning to the word *genius*.

"This wasn't entirely our fault." Brooke was sure of that. "We weren't given any reason to believe that Amelia had ties to Peyton. If our superiors had suspicions, they didn't share them, and they underestimated Amelia, too."

"She found the tracker on her car," Chloe offered suddenly. "But she didn't get rid of it. She reprogrammed it. That's how we lost her. We followed the signal, and the signal lied."

A supersmart TCI who was deeply involved in the world of organized crime, working for Peyton, Kaufman, and Gray. This could not possibly be a good thing.

At that exact moment, an all-too-familiar pop song started blaring from Brooke's cell phone, and in response, she tapped the access code into the keypad on her chair's arm, and the flat-screen television clicked on.

"Good morning, girls."

Good morning, Uncle Alan.

"As you know, yesterday, Amelia Juarez met with associates at Peyton, Kaufman, and Gray. Unfortunately, they did not conduct this meeting within the typical range of our audio surveillance. We were, however, able to go back over the audio feed and match a recorded sample of Amelia's voice to trace sounds recorded in the background. As a result, we managed to reconstruct a very small portion of the conversation. While this provided very little new pertinent information, it did allow us to confirm our previous assessment of the situation.

"Amelia has been in contact with an individual who has dangerous technology that the firm considers rightfully theirs. While this individual believes Amelia came to Bayport representing her own interests, she was in fact recruited by the associates at Peyton, Kaufman, and Gray to do two things: acquire the technology and take out the seller."

Take out? The way Jacob Kann had been "taken out"? We'd suspected Hector Hassan was behind the bombing, because all signs indicated that he'd been the one to plant the bugs we'd discovered on each of the other TCIs. But if Amelia was brought here to take out the seller, what would stop her from taking out other potential buyers?

While I was pondering this question, a picture appeared on the screen: a middle-aged man who practically had the word *nerd* emblazoned on his forehead.

"Phillip Ross," the voice informed us. "Ross holds a triple PhD, one each from Harvard, Oxford, and Bayport University."

Let's see, I thought, which one of these things does not belong?

"What are his degrees in?" As the resident PhD herself, Zee quickly zeroed in on this question.

"Biomedical engineering, nanotechnology, and genetics."

I took this entire conversation to mean that Phillip Ross was smart. Smart enough to develop a new kind of biological weapon. The image on the screen changed, and this time, words appeared.

Nanotechnological Advances in the Field of Gene Targeting: A Study of Technobiological Viruses in the Common Mouse (Mus musculus).

"This is the title of Ross's most recent dissertation, from the University of Bayport—where, incidentally enough, his research and schooling were supported by the prestigious Kaufman Grant for Advances in Science."

Kaufman. As in Peyton, *Kaufman*, and Gray.

"So the firm was bankrolling his research," Brooke concluded.

"Correct," our contact confirmed.

"And then his research started going really well, and Ross realized that he might get a better offer elsewhere." That was from Chloe.

"So he starts making subtle inquiries." Tara.

"Invites the interested parties, or their emissaries, to Bayport." Brooke again.

"And he figures that if he keeps a low enough profile by only negotiating with people who aren't normally considered true players in their own right, Peyton won't find out about it." Zee provided that bit.

"Except they did find out about it." Now it was my turn, teamwork at its best. "So they made Amelia an offer, and now they're counting on her to get the weapon for them."

There was a brief pause, and then April added in the last piece of the puzzle. "And to make sure that Ross never backstabs them again."

Even given the seriousness of the situation, some petty part of my mind couldn't help but think that growing up with Hayley Hoffman as a best friend, April probably knew a lot about backstabbing and retaliation.

"So what do we know about this weapon?" Chloe asked. Our contact wasn't immediately forthcoming with information, so Chloe started musing on her own. "Whatever he was testing on mice for his dissertation, he must have found a way to apply it to humans. Nanotechnology means we're dealing with something so small it can't be seen by the naked eye, but so technologically advanced that it has some sort of computational ability. Gene targeting means we're talking about DNA. And the fact that the words *virus* and *weapon* are used suggests that whatever the nanotechnology does to genes, it ain't pretty."

"Very good, Chloe. In generic terms, you've hit the nail on the head. I'm afraid we can't share specifics at this time, but rest assured that the resulting technology is incredibly dangerous. We cannot allow it to fall into enemy hands."

I stared at Ross's dissertation title on the screen and memorized it. My dad was a career scientist with a PhD of his own, and I'd absorbed enough physics babble over my lifetime to know that dissertations were usually published—if not in a scientific journal, at least in some kind of university collection or database. Good old Uncle Alan might not be gung ho on giving us specifics, because he was so very good at leaving out important details, but with a little more information on Ross's dissertation research, we could probably figure it out for ourselves.

While I was staring at it, the image on the screen changed, this time to reveal a picture of a building.

"Ross's lab is located here," the voice said. "On the fifth floor. Security is tight, and while we could break in, we need to do so in a way that won't advertise our presence to Peyton, Kaufman, and Gray. We need to acquire this technology, but if Peyton doesn't realize we've done so, they may proceed with their plans."

And if they proceeded with their plans, the Big Guys might actually be able to pin something on them. Maybe not the whole firm, but at least some of the associates.

"We need to get in and get out, and the configuration of the building eliminates the possibility of going in unseen. That means we have to go in unnoticed, and that means we need you girls."

The next picture on the screen made me wonder if there was a slight chance I was still dreaming.

"Cheer Scout cookies?" I asked.

"Cheer Scout cookies," the voice said. "This is your cover. As of 1500 hours this afternoon, all five teams will commence fund-raising at strategic locations spread throughout Bayport, specifically, large, commercial buildings."

It took me a second to realize that one of the locations in question was the building that housed Ross's lab. I must have been playing this game for too long now, because in a twisted way, this whole cookie thing made sense. If we were all doing "fund-raising," then the fact that a subset of us chose to do it at Ross's lab wouldn't raise suspicions. Clever.

"Girls, I must stress the incredibly sensitive nature of this case. We must acquire the weapon prototype that Ross has constructed, replace it with a decoy, and get out without raising suspicions. Due to the danger involved in penetrating Ross's lab, we've designated the active part of this mission as eighteen and over. We'll be sending two operatives in; the rest of you will be acting as decoys across town."

Eighteen and over meant that the CIA wasn't comfortable handing this part of the case over to minors, which meant that dangerous was an understatement. The last time a case had been given this designation, Zee and Brooke had been caught in a crossfire in Libya.

"Unfortunately, however," the voice continued, "after a deeper analysis of Ross's technological capabilities, psychological profile, and security detail, the task force assigned to this case has recommended that at least one of the operatives sent on the primary mission have a strong technological background, superior fighting skills, and . . . errrrr . . ."

Chloe preened, sure the voice was describing her.

"The psychological profile revealed that our best chance at countering Ross's paranoia is to go in with someone young, female, and unintimidating."

As far as I could tell, that description fit each and every one of us.

"Specifically, it has come to light that Ross is more likely to implicitly trust a young female with a particularly small chest."

I didn't even want to know how they'd come to that psychological conclusion. Nor did I want to know why everyone in the room was suddenly looking at my breasts.

Or lack thereof.

"I'm in," I said, ignoring the fact that I'd gotten the coveted assignment based on the flatness of my chest.

"So am I," Brooke said. "Assuming we only need one operative with that last . . . special attribute."

Brooke was admirably trying to be diplomatic about the boob issue.

"I'm sending through all of the information you girls need," the voice said. "Remember, get in, acquire the weapon, replace it with the decoy, get out. Stealth is the name of the game, girls."

And with that, the screen went dark, and the phone line went dead.

"You heard the man," Brooke said, visibly relieved that we'd managed to keep this mission a Squad operation. "We meet back here for seventh period, and at fifteen hundred hours, Operation Cheer Scout begins."

CHAPTER 21
Code Word: Envy

When you spend your morning on speakerphone with the CIA, the normal ups and downs of high school just don't quite carry the same punch. During first period, three people asked me where I'd bought my shoes. Halfway through my English class, we had a pop quiz, because the teacher, in all of her wisdom and glory, had noticed the fact that no one was paying attention to a word that she said. When I went to the bathroom in between English and chemistry, I noticed a somewhat unflattering message about me scrawled across the bathroom wall.

Then, just as I was heading back from the bathroom, I ran into Jack, and the two of us may or may not have staged a reenactment of our kiss from the day before. As a result, I discovered that the only thing that stacked up to the kind of morning I'd had was the feeling of Jack's lips on mine. The warmness that spread up my spine and over my entire body was enough to make me consider the possibility that I'd been missing out by beating guys up instead of making out with them all these years.

Because I clearly have mental problems (or as Zee would

say, "intimacy issues"), the fact that anyone could have this kind of effect on me was enough to make me lash out and slug Jack in the stomach, but this time, he was ready for me, and without a word, he sidestepped the punch. "Nice try," he murmured, nuzzling me as he took my hands in his. "Didn't anyone ever tell you that violence isn't the answer?"

"No." I glowered at him, trying to resist the power of his nuzzles. There were a million reasons I shouldn't have been kissing him, and only one that made me want to do it again.

He turned his head so that his lips were near my neck. I could feel his breath on my skin as he spoke. "Me neither." He kissed me again, softly, his lips just barely grazing mine. "But sometimes, Ev, it pays to play nice."

I'm sure something must have happened in my fourth period, but I couldn't for the life of me tell you what. By the time lunch rolled around, the entire school knew about The Kiss, Part Deux, and I was starting to think that if I was going to be helplessly girly and turn to Toby mush whenever Jack "played nice," it might be to my benefit to find a less public venue for our next rendezvous.

Brooke and Chloe apparently concurred, and they demonstrated this agreement by spending the first half of our lunch hour glaring at me in their own, individual it-doesn't-look-like-we're-glaring-but-we-really-are ways. Given the fact that Brooke and I were going on an over-eighteen mission in less than three hours, I had to infer that this probably wasn't a good thing.

"Jack, you dawg!" Chip greeted Jack in a way that reminded me why I'd spent most of my life beating guys up instead of making out with them. "Is she a wildcat, or what?"

Jack let his popularity shield drop just long enough for a single-sentence response. "Chip, you're an idiot."

"Whatever, man," Chip said, perfectly affable. "You dawg!"

Tara leaned over to whisper in my ear. "You might want to switch to SDA mode," she advised. "Brooke probably won't kill you for the PDA, but Chloe might."

I didn't have to ask what PDA was, but I tried to sort out the other acronym.

The barest hint of a grin flicked across Tara's face at my puzzlement. "Stealth Displays of Affection."

Based on the looks the twins—our resident flirting experts—were giving me, I could only conclude that as soon as we wrapped up with Operation Cheer Scouts, there might be an SDA tutorial in my future.

Not nearly soon enough, the topic of conversation changed to a teen slasher movie coming out the next weekend, and I felt a piece of paper being shoved unceremoniously into my lap under the table. In an attempt to prove that I could be stealthy, I unwrapped it and read without anyone else at the table noticing.

I need to talk to you.

For a note from one of my Squadmates, it wasn't very high-tech. No codes. No invisible ink. But then again, the message wasn't exactly the stuff that national security was made of. Girls across the country probably passed notes like this every day. I scanned the table, trying to figure out who'd sent it to me, and when my eyes landed on Chloe, I groaned internally.

She was staring straight at me, and her not-a-glare glare changed into something else. She held my eyes for a moment, and then spoke. "OMG. I totally forgot to pick up the banner paint, and we were going to make banners for Friday's game at practice today. I'm going to go see if Mr. J will let us sneak out to pick some up. You want to come with, Toby?"

I really didn't, but since Chloe had never voluntarily spent time in my presence, I got the distinct feeling that whatever she wanted to talk to me about, it was big.

"Sure!" I tried to match her peppy tone. "I've always wanted to pick out banner paint."

I could see Brooke repressing an eye roll at my response, and even I had to admit that it wasn't exactly one hundred percent believable, but if any of the guys at the table thought it was strange, they didn't comment on it. Even Jack just looked at me, a half smile on his face, like he knew that banner paint was seriously up there on the list of things I couldn't have cared less about, but wasn't going to blow my cover, because he was the master of pretending to care about things that didn't matter himself.

As Chloe and I walked away from the table, part of me had to wonder whether I fell into that category, or if I was the only thing in Jack's charmed life that didn't.

"Arrrrr, mateys! It be homecoming season, and we be the homecoming pirates."

Dear God, I thought in silent prayer, when I turn around, please don't let that be Noah.

"Arrr!" a dozen more voices chorused.

I turned around, and there was Noah, along with Chuck and the slew of freshman boys who'd been at my house that morning. All of them were dressed up like pirates, and three of them were actually standing on a table in the middle of the cafeteria. Noah brandished a makeshift sword.

"Who you be voting for, mateys?" he asked his pirate followers.

In what I can only conclude was the product of a great deal of rehearsal, the other boys chorused in unison, "The homecoming pirates be voting for Toby Klein. She be worth her weight in pirate's gold. Arrrrrr!"

What was my brother thinking? Did he honestly think making a complete fool out of himself would encourage anyone to vote for me? That was insane. Or, at least, I hoped it was insane, because if by some miracle Noah's pirate act actually convinced so much as a single person to write my name down on that ballot, I was going to stuff not one, but both of my poms into a part of his anatomy where the sun doesn't shine.

"Arrrr!"

To her credit, Chloe didn't so much as glance over her shoulder at the boys, and a large portion of the student body followed her lead. Still, I couldn't help but notice as we left the cafeteria that a disturbing amount of freshmen and sophomores were cheering Noah on.

As Chloe and I walked toward the vice-principal's office, the silence between us was nearly tangible, but I finally broke it.

"If there was a way to deport my brother to Antarctica, you'd tell me, right?" That was about as much of a peace offering as I could give her. If we were going to be stuck in the same room for any amount of time, I preferred to get rid of any latent hostilities first.

"If you win homecoming queen," Chloe snipped, "I'll deport him myself."

Something about the expression on her face convinced me that she wasn't joking, and I spent several seconds hoping that senior members of the Squad didn't actually have a way of deporting people, because I couldn't actually let someone ship my brother off the continent.

Chloe rolled her eyes and snorted simultaneously. "Gullible much?"

Chloe's tone reconfirmed two things for me. First, that when it came to me, hostility was Chloe's middle name, and second, that my first impression of this whole homecoming situation had been entirely accurate.

Things were definitely going to get ugly.

On the plus side, though, talking Mr. J into excusing us from our last two classes turned out to be a piece of cake. After all, heaven forbid we run out of banner paint!

"You do realize how twisted this is, right?" I didn't particularly want to talk to Chloe, but once we were safely away from the office, I couldn't keep the opinion to myself.

"Don't look a gift vice-principal in the mouth," Chloe said glibly. Almost belatedly, she rolled her eyes, as if she'd remembered at the last second who she was talking to and that an eye roll was the mandated response. "But, yes, for the record, I do get that this is ridiculous. We all do. We're not stupid." Chloe paused as the two of us entered the Quad, and when she continued, her voice was slightly less blatantly nasty and marginally more condescending. "Look at it this way—if Jacobson didn't have a job at Bayport, he'd have a job somewhere else, and the cheerleaders at that school probably wouldn't be skipping class to deal with terrorist threats."

That was, in all likelihood, an understatement.

All things considered, though, it was a miracle that

none of the other parents had ever complained. Then again, if any of the parents did complain—about their kids not making the varsity squad, about the blatant favoritism in the school, about the fact that there wasn't a single noncheerleader nominated for homecoming court—the Big Guys Upstairs would probably just pull some strings and have that parent transferred out of the Bayport school district, the same way they'd somehow managed to have me transferred in.

The longer I spent on the Squad, the more I started thinking that maybe the paranoid people in the world had it right. Big Brother was totally watching.

"So what's the deal?" I asked. "Why did you need to talk to me?"

Chloe didn't say anything. She just kept right on walking through the Quad, up a flight of stairs, through a labyrinth of hallways, and into her lab. "Don't touch anything."

Like I was going to mess up her precious inventor's lair. Then my eyes lit upon something that looked vaguely like some kind of microscanner, and Chloe's voice broke into my techno-daydreams.

"Let me rephrase that. *Don't touch anything.*"

Now it was my turn to roll my eyes. "What do you want?"

Chloe reached over to her desk and picked up a thick stack of papers. "It's Ross's dissertation," she said. "Brooke doesn't know I have it, and neither do our superiors, but I'm not letting the two of you go into this mission blind because they don't feel like telling you what you're up against."

I wasn't sure what surprised me more: the fact that

Chloe was so adamant about protecting us, or that she'd had the exact same idea I had about finding a copy of Ross's dissertation.

"It wasn't easy," she told me. "He originally submitted it for publication, but retracted it only a few weeks later. It was like he suddenly realized he could make a lot more money off of this thing underground than above. He wiped every trace of it off of the web, but the university still had a copy of it in their database."

"You hacked it?" Compared to most of my jobs, this was kiddie play, but still, I was the hacker, and this was Chloe treading on my turf. And she knew it.

"Is that a problem, Toby?" she asked sweetly. "From the look on your face, you'd think somebody stole your boyfriend or something."

Subtle she was not. Forget the fact that I'd been *ordered* to date Jack in the first place, and the fact that the two of them had been over long before I'd come into the picture. Clearly, I'd stolen her boyfriend, and therefore, her stealing hacking jobs was my just reward.

"So do you want the Cliff's Notes, or do you want to read it yourself?" Now that she'd gotten in her jab, Chloe was all business.

"I'll read it myself."

An hour and a half later, Chloe grinned at me. "So do you want the Cliff's Notes version, or do you want to read it yourself?"

On the one hand, I wanted to tell her to shut up. On the other hand, I still hadn't managed to make sense of the dissertation, and we were running out of time before seventh period.

"Fine," I said. "Cliff's Notes."

To Chloe's credit, she didn't make me say "please."

"Basically, Ross managed to combine his degrees in biomedical engineering, nanotechnology, and genetics to design a nanotechnological device . . ." Chloe paused and then made a show of dumbing down her words for me, her smile broadening. "He built a teeny, tiny computer type thingy that is capable of targeting and altering DNA in a prespecified manner. These nanobots . . . I mean, these *thingies* he designed basically go in and rewrite a person's genetic code."

"Are we talking about the dissertation or a really bad science fiction movie?" I may have been stronger in math than in science, but even I knew enough to be skeptical. I was pretty sure the type of thing Chloe was describing shouldn't have been possible.

"In terms of gene therapy, this is definitely a breakthrough," Chloe said. "The really amazing thing is that these bots, as small as they are, can actually carry programs."

I knew enough about technology to know that should have provoked skepticism on my part.

"This is real, Toby," Chloe said. "I don't know how, but it's real. And it's bad news."

Nothing Chloe had said so far sounded particularly like bad news to me.

"At the point in time that Ross wrote his thesis, there were still some glitches in the programming. He managed to rewrite the DNA, but in a way that makes the information genes contain utterly useless." Chloe's eyes glazed over as she searched for the appropriate metaphor. "Think of a computer. What happens if you swipe your hard drive with a very large, very powerful magnet?"

"It wipes all of the data, the programs, everything. And then . . ."

"And then your computer is pretty much dead," Chloe finished. "At the end of his thesis, Ross presented two alternatives for future research. One involved working out the kinks in programming so that the bots could be used for gene therapy, but that could take decades, maybe longer."

"And the other alternative?"

"The other alternative involved two steps: adapt the prototype for use on humans, and make it airborne."

"Airborne as in—"

"As in you release these nanobots, they spread out, permeate the skin, and start destroying every inch of code it can find."

Now the phrase *technobiological weapon* was starting to make sense.

"This is what you and Brooke are retrieving," Chloe said. "They must be containing them somehow, but if those bots get out . . . It's bad, Toby. It's very, very bad, and the two of you deserved to know."

Translation: The Big Guys should have told us.

"We've got to tell Brooke," I said.

Chloe grabbed my arm and held it. "We can't tell Brooke. If we could, trust me when I say that I would have been talking to her and not you."

I jerked my arm out of Chloe's grasp.

"When it comes to this school, Brooke does what she wants, when she wants to do it. She's in charge. She makes the rules. But when it comes to the Squad, she's a different person. She doesn't break the rules, Toby. She doesn't ask questions, and she doesn't apologize." Chloe paused and looked away. "This is highly classified information, and

Brooke can't know that we know. She's their good little soldier, their *captain* . . ." Chloe's voice got very quiet. "But she's my best friend, and there's no way I'd let her go in there unprepared."

So. There it was. Chloe couldn't tell Brooke, so she told me. Standing there, looking at Chloe very carefully not looking at me, I wondered if this was the first time Chloe had kept a secret from Brooke, and just like that, I knew that it wasn't.

"Brooke doesn't know, does she?" I asked the question in a voice every bit as quiet as the one Chloe had used a moment before.

"I just told you that she can't know about this," Chloe snapped.

"Not about this," I said. "About Jack's uncle. She doesn't know."

I'd assumed that when it came to the Squad what Chloe knew Brooke knew, but the way Chloe's lips tightened at my question was enough of an answer to tell me that I'd assumed wrong.

Brooke didn't have a clue that one of the Big Guys was a Peyton. Apparently, Uncle Alan's identity was an even bigger secret than I'd thought.

"There you guys are!" Bubbles popped out of the woodwork. I hadn't even heard her come into the lab. "Brooke's looking for you guys. You missed the debriefy thingy! We're ready to go on Operation Cheer Scout, and you guys still need to hit the salon."

If Bubbles had heard Chloe's monologue, she didn't give any indication of it. She tilted her head to the side and wrinkled her nose, looking almost comically quizzical. "What are you guys doing up here anyway?"

The intensity that had been clear on Chloe's face seconds before melted away, and she smirked at me and then provided Bubbles with a cover story that wasn't amusing in the least.

"Toby begged me to give her some tips on SDA."

CHAPTER 22
Code Word: Crazy!

After leaving the twins' beauty lab, I had confirmed my lurking suspicions that I preferred the makeunder to its high-ponytailed, perky, extra-highlights-in-my-hair, paw-print-drawn-on-my-cheek counterpart. I also discovered that this uniform, which showed a substantial portion of my midriff, was even more uncomfortable than the one I'd worn for the pep rally.

My mind, however, didn't have time to dwell on either of those decisions. When you're getting ready to break into a high-security lab to steal a technobiological weapon that could mangle your DNA and kill you where you stood, polyester, paw prints, and ponytails just can't compare.

"You missed the debriefing." Brooke was markedly displeased with me, but she never stopped smiling. "This is the most dangerous, most important mission you've ever gone on and will ever go on until you're actually old enough to be doing over-eighteens in the first place, and you missed the debriefing."

I mimicked Brooke's forced smile. "My bad."

She handed me a small, pearly pink Game Boy that

someone had meticulously covered in rhinestones. "This contains a copy of the floor plan to the building as a whole, and to Ross's lab. It's set up like a conventional office space, with the actual laboratory in the back, and offices, a copy room, and reception in the front. The biggest area of interest, however, is the small kitchen, situated just off the lab."

"The kitchen?" Somehow, I doubted Ross was keeping his potentially lethal technology in the refrigerator.

"An infrared scan of the building revealed increased concentration of heat and light in that area."

I fiddled with the buttons on the Game Boy, and it zeroed in on the kitchen for me.

"Lasers," Brooke said. "They're located in the oven, which we believe is nonfunctional and concealing some kind of safe. You're going to need to dismantle the security, which will mean finding the control panel. We believe it's in the kitchen, but if it's not, you may have to improvise."

First killer nanobots, and now lasers. My life had definitely become a James Bond movie.

As if sensing my thoughts, Brooke leaned over, took control of the Game Boy, and suddenly, I was looking at a diagram of the air ducts in the office.

"Lucky for us," she said. "You're small."

Yet another reason cheerleaders made for good secret agents: most of us were tiny, though some of us had smaller chests than others.

"Let's go. We've got a tight time frame to work with here. I've got your goody bag from Lucy, and we'll go over the exact plan on the way. If you've memorized the floor plans, you can leave the Game Boy here."

I did as instructed. My memory was close to photographic, and floor plans were close enough to geometry that my mind immediately absorbed the numbers and angles in question.

Still, as Brooke and I made our way out to her convertible, I had to wonder how exactly it had escaped her notice that this whole plan was insane. The Big Guys were insane. Our cover story was insane. And the fact that I was supposed to crawl through air ducts in a uniform this tight?

Stretchy fabric aside, still insane.

Fortunately, sanity has never exactly been my strong point, and even now, the adrenaline was pumping through my veins, telling me that we could do this, that I had to do this.

Besides, even if things got dicey, Ross wouldn't murder two cheerleaders in broad daylight, and even if he tried, I was pretty sure I could take him. The nerds of the world don't exactly strike fear into the hearts of black belts armed to the hilt.

Speaking of which . . .

I waited until Brooke started her car and raised the convertible's top before I asked the question on the tip of my tongue. "What's in Lucy's goody bag?"

"Weapons are a last resort," Brooke told me. "Ideally, we won't have to use them at all. We get in, we get the bots, we get out. Remember, we were assigned this case because Peyton won't suspect us of anything. If we break out the weapons, our superiors will have to send in backup."

I was somewhat comforted to know that if things got truly dicey, the Big Guys would have our backs. Then again, these were the guys who'd kept us in the dark about the fact that the weapon we'd been instructed to retrieve could kill us, so it wasn't like I had a great deal of trust that they had our best interests at heart.

"If they have to send in a cleanup team, we won't worry about replacing the target with a decoy. Our main agenda then is to get the target, and preserve our covers. If the Big Guys send a team in, Peyton will know that something is up, and we'll need to ensure that they don't realize that that something involves us."

She was throwing so much information in my direction that I almost forgot what I was waiting for. "Weapons."

"Last resort," Brooke said again.

"Gimme."

With a roll of her eyes, Brooke handed me a small gift sack. Lucy considered "weapons" and "prezzies" to be synonymous.

I reached into the sack and withdrew a small baggie filled with pins that had words embossed across them. GO! one declared. FIGHT! WIN!

"The spirit buttons double as throwing stars," Brooke said. "Twist the pin on the back, and they'll morph."

I did as she instructed and immediately decided that despite all evidence to the contrary, Lucy was a genius.

"What about this?" I asked, picking up a small, half baton.

"Spirit stick," Brooke said. "It also shoots blow darts. One will stun, two will paralyze." She paused slightly. "Don't shoot the same person three times."

I didn't have to ask what a third dart would do. I looked at the potentially deadly spirit stick with new respect, but at the same time, my stomach flipped at the idea that with these weapons in my hands, I could be lethal.

Even as a last resort, I wasn't ready for that. Putting the spirit stick gingerly aside, I took out two pairs of bobby socks.

"Grenades?" I guessed. Lucy had this thing for bobby-sock grenades.

"Yup. Put them on over your socks. If you need to launch them, they'll tear off, but once you tear them, you only have ten seconds until detonation."

The only thing left in the bag was a clipboard with a single piece of paper attached. Written on it were several names and addresses and what appeared to be orders for Cheer Scout cookies.

"What does this do?" I asked curiously.

"It makes us look legit," Brooke said.

"Oh." I was somewhat disappointed. I mean, after exploding bobby socks and throwing-star cheer pins, who wouldn't be?

"We'll hit up some of the other offices in Ross's building before making our way to his. If he knows some of the other people who've ordered Cheer Scout cookies, any suspicions he might have about us should go way down."

I couldn't hear the term again without asking. "Cheer Scout cookies? Is there really such a thing as Cheer Scout cookies?"

Brooke executed an eloquent shrug and merged onto the highway. "There is now."

As we drove closer and closer to Ross's building and to our target, the deadly nanobots contained within, Brooke went through each step of our plan with me again and again, and I sorted through them on my own, forming a mental checklist.

Weapons? Check.

Memorized floor plan? Check.

Cover story? Check.

Plan for getting to the kitchen? Check.

Method for deactivating the security system? Hmmm.

"What kind of technology are we talking?" I was good enough to hack into almost any system on my own given enough time, but considering we'd only have a few minutes, a few technical boosters couldn't hurt. Brooke nodded toward a central compartment and I opened it. My eyes fell on a small black box, and I smiled.

Eureka.

If I could find the security panel and it was computer-based, with any luck, I'd be able to rig the black box (also known as one of the seven wonders of the modern technological world) to scramble its signal.

"Where's the decoy?" I asked. Brooke handed me a small, silver box. I frowned. "If we don't know what the target looks like, how exactly were the Big Guys able to make a decoy?"

I mentally encouraged Brooke to come to the conclusion that our bosses were holding out on us more than she realized.

"We've got an approximation." Brooke had an answer ready, and I wondered who had fed it to her and if she'd been in contact with our superiors since the phone call that morning. "Beyond that, it doesn't matter. Ross may be able to tell the difference between the target and our decoy, but nobody else will, and if he's willing to double-cross Peyton to sell his technology to the highest bidder, I seriously doubt he'll balk at swapping a decoy in for the real thing."

"Speaking of the evil nerdling, what's his deal? Why

aren't we just knocking him out the second we get there and giving him something to alter his memory?"

Memory-altering drugs weren't nearly as worthy of science fiction as nanobots that could rearrange DNA, so it seemed like a reasonable question.

"Funny you should ask," Brooke hedged. "Phillip Ross may be a nerd, but he's an extremely paranoid nerd with heavy security detail."

And she was just telling me this now?

Keeping one hand on the wheel, Brooke tapped a command into the radio panel of her car, and a flat-screen popped out of the dashboard.

"Show bodyguards."

The car responded to Brooke's verbal order, and three pictures popped up on the screen, each depicting a man uglier and more massively enormous than the one before him.

"Larry, Moe, and Curly?" I guessed.

Brooke shrugged. "I was going to go with Flopsy, Mopsy, and Cottontail, but whatever."

Okay, I thought. Three gargantuan security guys, a paranoid (and perhaps rightly so) scientist, and in all likelihood, less than three or four minutes until they realized I was up to something.

"If you were eighteen, you would have two and a half years of training before you got a mission like this," Brooke said, "but you're not, so you haven't. If you can't cut it, tell me now, and I'll put in a request for a non-Squad hacker with no breasts and an adrenaline addiction. Believe me when I say you're replaceable."

Believe me when I say that I didn't believe her. She

followed orders, and she'd been told to take me with her on this mission. If they'd given her a choice, Chloe would probably be sitting in this seat with some kind of breast-reduction bra on.

"I'll be fine." In that moment, I actually believed it. Insanity definitely has its perks.

CHAPTER 23

Code Word: Cookies

"Hi, I'm Misty," Brooke said brightly.

"And I'm Fawn," I added.

"And we're selling Cheer Scout cookies," we chorused together.

By the time we made our way into the foyer of Ross's office, Brooke and I had the Cheer Scout routine down pat. The security guard who'd answered the door eyed us distrustfully.

"And spirit pins," I said earnestly.

"And spirit sticks."

"And we're having a car wash next Saturday."

"And we're trying to get Krispy Kreme to sponsor us, so maybe if you buy something now, we can get you free donuts later."

The security guard seemed taken aback, but he didn't move at all.

"I can do the splits," Brooke volunteered, sounding as air-headed as Bubbles at her worst.

"Ronald, what's going on out there?" a voice called from further back, inside the office.

Ronald—who I'd decided looked like a Mopsy—turned around. "Some girls selling cookies," he called. "They can do the splits."

Moments later, Phillip Ross exited his lab and made his way to the reception area, where Ronald/Mopsy, who was eyeing us slightly more speculatively, had nevertheless kept us in the hall, instead of inviting us in. Looking past Mopsy's shoulder, I could see Ross, who looked every bit as nerdy in person, flanked by another security guard—Flopsy. I could only infer that Cottontail was in the lab or the kitchen, safeguarding the loot.

"What school do you guys go to?" Ross asked, peering around Mopsy's massively broad shoulder.

"Bayport," Brooke said. Fake names, real school. It was a combination specifically designed to discredit Ross's story if he happened to try to pass it on. After all, if we were parading around in our own school's uniforms, oozing Bayport High spirit from our very pores, why would we bother with fake names? It made no sense, and that was exactly why we did it.

Ross appraised us through his thick, wire-rimmed glasses. "Maybe you're from Bayport and maybe you're not. Won't you come in?"

The invitation sounded ominous. Apparently, inventing an incredibly dangerous little doodad had convinced Phillip Ross that he was a badass. I could only imagine that he was inviting us in to determine if we were who we said we were, and if he didn't buy it . . .

Well, then I'd get to really use this so-called spirit stick.

"Awesome," Brooke said, and the two of us stepped into the office. The doors closed behind us.

I held out the clipboard. "You can sign up for cookies

here," I said. "The Sis-Boom-Baked Chocolate Chip are my favorite."

"But the Go, Fight, Cinnamon are also really good," Brooke put in.

The fact that we were even managing to do this with a straight face was remarkable.

"Or you could buy a pin," I said, holding one up for his inspection. He took it, turned it over, and then handed it back to me.

"So you girls are cheerleaders," he said.

We nodded.

"You cheer?"

We nodded again.

"Prove it."

Man, this guy really was paranoid. Then again, he was also right, but that was completely beside the point.

"Prove it?" I repeated dubiously.

Brooke wasn't nearly as thrown as I was. "Clap your hands," she said, and then she went into major cheer mode. "Ready? Okay!"

My response to those two words was purely instinctual. It had been drilled into me over and over again, and I knew exactly what to do.

"Clap your hands, everybody! Everybody, clap your hands!"

We threw ourselves into the cheer, and I managed to keep up with Brooke, move for move, head bob for head bob.

"Goooooooooo Lions!"

Cheering without the entire Squad felt slightly sacrilegious, but it was far preferable to being shot by Flopsy or Mopsy, and Brooke and I finished with bright smiles on our faces.

"They're cheerleaders," Flopsy grunted. "Can't fake that."

"So, do you guys like want some cookies, or what?" I threw an extra *like* in there, just for good measure. "The guys downstairs bought like a ton."

"Let me see that," Ross said, taking the order form. "You guys want anything?" he asked the bodyguards. "I think I'm going to get a couple boxes of Rah-Rah Rum Raisin."

Do not laugh, I ordered myself silently. Do not laugh.

"That last jump made my tummy all rumbly," I said instead, sticking out my lower lip and feeling like the idiot I was pretending to be. "Is there a bathroom in here?"

Ross amiably pointed me toward the bathroom, all suspicion he might have once harbored toward me flying out the door. I was young, I was a cheerleader, and—as every single member of the Squad had pointed out—I had the world's flattest chest, which, for some reason, meant that I was the exact type of person that Ross instinctually saw as unthreatening and trustworthy.

He must have had some bad experiences with big boobs in the past.

I made my way to the bathroom, aware as I walked that Flopsy had slipped away from the group to follow me. I opened the bathroom door, stepped inside, and locked it. I crouched and listened, until I could see Flopsy's feet right outside the door.

Now I just had to undo the vent and climb into the air-conditioning ducts without making any noise that might tip my good friend off to the fact that I was dealing with more than a rumbly tummy.

Luckily, I was good at improvising.

I put the toilet seat down and stood on top of it to reach the vent. I took a bobby pin out of my hair and began to unscrew the screws holding the vent in place, and to cover the noise, I did something that no other member of the Squad would have thought to do.

I pressed my lips against my arm and blew, making an incredibly loud and disturbingly realistic fart sound. There were some pluses to having grown up with a little brother, and this talent, nay, this *gift* was one of them.

I took another screw out and let out another juicy noise. Outside the door, I could see the bottom of Flopsy's feet as he took a cautionary step away from the bathroom.

Chalk one up for fart noises.

The vent finally came off, and I let out one more massive faux fart, and just for good measure, I groaned a little.

Outside the door, Flopsy backed further away.

"I . . . uhhhh . . . I think I might be a minute," I called.

Flopsy was too traumatized to reply. Excellent.

I set the vent cover down and boosted myself into the air duct. All things considered, it was a minor miracle that this building had air ducts big enough for me to fit into. Most modern buildings didn't, and honestly, you would think that if a person was planning on being an evil mastermind, he would invest in an office that didn't provide his enemies with a convenient route of passage through his wannabe lair.

Once I was inside the duct, I started crawling. It was dark, but my eyes adjusted quickly, and I made my way as fast as I could toward the kitchen. My brilliant performance in the bathroom had probably bought me a couple of minutes (Flopsy wasn't exactly going to be anxious to break down the bathroom door), but I couldn't count on more than that.

I counted inside my head, imagining how fast I was going and calculating the distance between the kitchen and the bathroom, and finally, I stopped over another vent. There, right below me, was Cottontail.

He was bigger than either of the guards I'd already seen, and he looked significantly more deadly. Someone who's had as much martial arts training as I have can spot another master a long way off, and the guy below me was good, no question. Very quietly, I reached for my spirit stick blow gun. I'd been instructed to use it as a last resort, but time was passing, and the only way to ensure that I didn't engage the enemy was to take him out now. Besides, if Ross wasn't going to advertise the fact that he'd lost his prototype and acquired a decoy, I doubt he'd take out billboards announcing that one of his guards had fallen asleep on the job.

As for Cottontail, from what I understood of the darts, he wouldn't remember a thing.

Positioned directly above someone this dangerous, I was struck by a momentary fear that he would look up, but just as he began to gaze unwittingly toward me, I heard a voice from the other room.

"Hey, Merv? You want any cookies?"

If he said yes, I wouldn't have to go against orders and dart him. And even if he said no, at least the question distracted him long enough to allow me just enough time to double-check my aim.

"No," Merv barked. "No cookies."

All right, I thought. One . . . two . . . three!

Pffft. Pffft.

I shot two darts in close succession, and both of them hit Merv in the side of the neck. He dropped to the floor. I winced at the sound and hoped that they hadn't heard it in the other room.

"The lion sensation is taking the nation—blue and gold . . . let's go!"

Brooke's voice carried and I breathed a sigh of relief. Her cheerleading antics would hopefully keep Mopsy and Ross occupied long enough to let me disarm the security and swap in the decoy.

I pushed the vent aside and dropped down from the ceiling, landing in a crouch on the floor. First things first, I retrieved the darts from Merv's neck and checked to make sure there was no visible sign that they'd ever been there.

Excellent.

I began sweeping the room. Of all of the aspects of the mission, this one—locating the security panel—was probably the one I was least qualified to do. My basic training had included several sessions on sweeping a room, but I hadn't done it enough for it to be automatic, and right now, I didn't have time to think.

I just had to act.

If I was a hidden security panel, where would I be? I walked along the length of the walls, looking for a loose panel, uneven paint, or anything that might give me the answer I desperately needed.

Think of it as a code, I told myself. A giant, living code. Where's the aberration? Look for natural repetitions in the room and find something that breaks the pattern.

Think of everything you know about Ross, about this room.

I continued searching the room manually and visually with no luck, until I opened the refrigerator. No way should a mad scientist's fridge have been this neat and tidy. And what was with having multiple kinds of milk in one refrigerator? I reached up to examine the milk, and when I tried to pick one of the containers up, I encountered some resistance. I pulled harder, and with a pop, the back of the refrigerator opened to reveal a security panel.

In a twisted way, it made sense. If the guy had laser-sensors to protect a safe in his oven, of course the security system would be based in his refrigerator.

Now that I had access to the security panel, I concentrated on disarming the system. I pulled my black box out of the bag of tricks I'd brought with me. With a little technological ingenuity, I hooked it up to the hardware inside the panel and keyed in what I could ascertain about the make of the system.

Luckily, the black box came equipped with pictures, and once I narrowed the choices down, it quickly recognized what kind of system we were dealing with, which meant that it knew how many digits the password was. The box heated beneath my hand, and I waited as it accessed a satellite that would hopefully allow it to hack directly into the security provider's system.

I looked down at my watch.

Hurry, I thought. Hurry, hurry, hurry. If Ross had actually invested in a system that was more secure than the black box could hack, I might have to get creative, and for once in my life, I really, really didn't want to get creative.

Beep.

I took in a sharp breath at the sound, but the lights on the system went off, and I breathed out a sigh of relief.

Black box, I thought, how I love thee, let me count the ways.

As I moved toward the oven, I spent one second devoutly hoping that the box would pull its last trick—scrambling any remote signals that the system might be sending to the security provider.

I opened the oven door and stared at it for a second. To say that I'm not familiar with cooking or any of the tools used to do so would be an enormous understatement, so I wasn't exactly sure if there was anything unusual about this oven, but time was running out, so I strong-armed it, and a back panel popped inward.

There, just within my grasp, was a small silver box. I grabbed the decoy, which was more of a gray, out of my bag of tricks and moved to swap the two. With any luck, I could make my way back to the bathroom, and Brooke and I could walk out of there with the weapon before anyone realized that Merv was in dreamland.

Unfortunately, the second before I made the swap, things began falling apart at warp speed.

I felt Merv behind me before I saw him, and I turned. He was easily three times my size, but he was groggy from the sedatives, and I was quick. I sank a punch to his stomach and kicked the gun out of his hand. He lunged at me, but I dodged and planted a hard kick to his groin, pushing him back. Once I had enough space to move, I steadied myself and then prepared my go-to move.

I was halfway through the roundhouse when I saw a flash of black and realized that Merv and I weren't alone. But before I could figure out who our new black-clad friend was, we were interrupted by Flopsy realizing at high volume that I was no longer in the bathroom.

Seconds later, I registered a male scream, as Brooke attacked either Ross or Mopsy in the foyer.

Midturn, I appraised the situation without ever slowing down. I had to take Merv out quickly. Brooke was in the other room with Ross and two security goons. That meant at least three guns, and as good as she was, she couldn't stop a bullet, even though Lucy's bulletproof push-up bra had been known to stop one or two in the past.

Ignoring the sounds and sights assaulting my senses, I threw my momentum into finishing my roundhouse, and microseconds after my foot connected with his neck, Merv went down for the count.

My movement propelled by adrenaline, I zeroed in on the next threat and whipped out my pin/throwing stars, activated them, and starting launching them at the mysterious person in black, but even when I heard them hit, the person—whoever it was—didn't stop.

And then the mystery intruder grabbed the silver container—the one I'd so kindly left sitting clearly visible on the stovetop—and it was up to me to get it back.

"You wanna dance?" I asked, advancing, ready for a fight. "Then let's dance."

Gunfire sounded from the direction of the reception area where I'd left Brooke. I wavered for a split second and then did the only thing I could do.

I ripped the bobby sock off my left foot and launched it toward the person in front of me, hoping that it would be enough to slow him or her down (but not enough to release the nanobots themselves) and then I ran toward the sound of the gunshots. Toward Brooke.

As I ran down the hallway and into the reception area, an explosion sounded behind me, but I barely heard it, because the situation in front of me demanded every ounce of attention I could muster. Brooke had managed to take Ross out, and he was lying in an unconscious heap on the floor, but the guards were a different story. One of them had a gun pressed to her temple. As my breath caught in my throat, the hired goons took their eyes off Brooke just long enough to look at me, and Brooke jabbed a spirit stick into Mopsy's leg. She must have somehow triggered the release of the darts, because the oversized guard crumpled to the floor, and then it was just me, Brooke, and one guy with a gun.

I leapt toward him, not heeding the obvious danger, and as he swung his gun to aim it at me, Brooke went for his legs. The gun went off, but missed us both, and within seconds, Brooke had managed to grab his head between her feet, and with some pretty fancy footwork, she executed a perfectly flawless standing back tuck and came damn near close to breaking his neck.

As his eyes rolled back in his head, Brooke knelt down next to him to check for a pulse.

"Alive," she said. "Did you acquire the target?"

And then I remembered the person in the kitchen and took off running without offering Brooke any kind of verbal answer to her question.

The kitchen was in shambles when I got there, scorched and burning as a result of my bobby sock grenade, but the black-clad figure, the silver box and the dangers contained within were nowhere to be found.

I swore. And swore. And swore.

"The hostiles are secured," Brooke told me, coming

into the room on my heels. "The backup team will have registered the gunfire and should be here any moment." She broke off, processing for the first time the obscenities currently pouring from my mouth. Then she noticed the decoy, which had fallen to the floor.

"There was someone else," the explanation flew from my mouth like projectile word-vomit. "They made it through a half dozen throwing stars and a grenade, and they moved . . ." I thought back over the other person's motions. "They moved like one of us."

Brooke and I came immediately to the same conclusion. "Amelia."

We'd underestimated her once, and she'd reconfigured our tracking chip. Then a figure in black showed up here and stole the biotechnology Peyton had hired her to acquire. The aforementioned figure wasn't nearly big enough to be Anthony, the only other TCI at large, and I had serious doubts that Anthony could have pulled something like this off in the first place.

The math was simple. Amelia Juarez had DNA-wiping technology, and for all we knew, she was on her way to Peyton, Kaufman, and Gray as we spoke.

This time, Brooke was the one who swore—long, hard, and in ways that struck even me as disturbingly creative.

When the backup team arrived to clean up the mess and take Ross and his guards into custody, Brooke and I disappeared back into the building, which, because of the layout and thickness of the walls of these offices, remained blissfully unaware of the chaos in Ross's lab.

As hard as it was for either of us to act even the least

bit normal, Brooke and I did the only thing we could to maintain our cover and exculpate ourselves from any and all suspicion in the Ross affair.

"Hi! We're members of the Bayport Varsity Spirit Squad, and we're selling Cheer Scout cookies!"

"The Go, Fight, Cinnamon are to die for."

CHAPTER 24

Code Word: Mommy Dearest

"That's it," Brooke said finally. It was the first thing one of us had said that wasn't (*a*) something that would have had to be bleeped out on most major broadcasting networks, or (*b*) a pitch for our cookies.

Shortly after we'd returned to "selling" our cookies, the police had arrived and ushered out all of the occupants of the building. We told them we didn't know anything, and either because they took one look at our faces and were apt to believe that we indeed knew nothing at all or because the Feds were secretly pulling their strings, we were quickly and quietly allowed to leave. Now the two of us were in Brooke's car, presumably driving back to the school to lick our wounds and further obsess over our failure.

"That's it." I repeated Brooke's words.

"We lost the one object we couldn't afford to lose. We caused a huge disturbance. If you'd detonated your right sock instead of your left one, we might have taken down part of the building."

So now she tells me that one grenade had more firepower than the other.

Brooke, oblivious to my train of thought, continued emotionlessly recapping our experience. "Shots were fired, and we both could have been killed."

I considered her words. "Yup. That about sums it up."

"You don't get it," Brooke said, heat entering her tone for the first time. "We were supposed to try to avoid actual danger. The weapons were for the worst-case scenario, and that scenario happened. They sent us in to get a weapon without being noticed, and we almost blew up the building *and lost the weapon to the one person we were trying to keep it away from.*"

"That's bad."

"There are no words for how bad this is."

"Okay, so we do damage control," I said. "We find Amelia and take her down before she can give the weapon to the firm."

Brooke actually laughed then, and it was a brittle, brutal sound. "You think they're going to let us do that?" she snorted.

I'm not sure what gave her the impression that I intended on asking.

"This isn't just an over-eighteen case now, Toby. This isn't just a Do Not Engage. I can guarantee you that this is no longer a Squad operation. Now it's up to the professionals, and we'll be lucky to see action again before I graduate."

"We could—" I started to say, but Brooke cut me off.

"We can't do anything. They won't let us. God, talk about disasters. I'm never going to hear the end of this." Sensing that I was going to interrupt her the way she'd interrupted me, Brooke plowed on, not giving me the chance. "They didn't even want us on this case after the explosion. They had to be talked into it, but I told them I could handle it. I promised them I could handle it. I even told them *you* could handle it."

"And you were going to share this with me when?"

"Puh-lease, Toby, no whining right now. I can't deal with it. I really can't. We have much bigger problems than this right now."

Hey! I was not whining.

"What problems might these be?" I asked. "And where are you going?" I hadn't noticed, because I'd been too busy trying to process Brooke's rant, but she'd pulled off the highway, and now we were driving through a residential area.

"Home," Brooke said tersely.

"Home as in your home?" I asked.

Brooke nodded.

"And why are we going there?"

Brooke took a deep breath. "Because that's where the Big Guys live."

"Excuse me?" I felt an undying need to start swearing again.

"If you want to get technical," Brooke said, "that's where one of the Big Guys lives. She's one of the smaller Big Guys actually, not based in Washington, not on active duty, but she still calls her share of shots, and right now, all of those are aimed at me."

Brooke pulled into a driveway and ran a hand angrily through her hair. "Not good," she muttered. "So not good."

A second later, someone tapped gently on the driver's side window, and Brooke, pushing all signs of aggravation off her face, rolled it down.

A woman stood there. She was probably about my mom's age, maybe a few years younger, but she'd aged well.

She was trim and fit, her hair was dark and every bit as thick as Brooke's, and her eyes were wide set, her lashes long, and her face almost wrinkle-free.

In fact, the only reason that I guessed she was near my mom's age was the fact that I had a deep and abiding suspicion that this was, in fact, Brooke's mother.

"Hello, Brookie," the woman said, a tight nonsmile on her face. "I see you brought a friend."

"Mom, Toby. Toby, Mom." Brooke made the introductions, her smiling matching her mother's exactly.

"Hello, Toby," Mrs. Camden said. "Won't you two join me inside?"

She sounded like your average PTA mom—chipper and faux sweet and like she'd have cookies waiting for us in a jar on the counter, but I knew better. Brooke's mom was one of the Big Guys, and, quite frankly, she scared the hell out of me.

Where were Flopsy, Mopsy, and Cottontail when you needed them?

Brooke rolled her eyes. "Come on," she told me under her breath. "She's not going to kill *you*." The emphasis on the last word did not escape me, and as I slipped out of the car, I couldn't help but think of everything Zee had told me about Brooke's relationship with her mom. I'd known Mrs. Camden was a former Squad member herself, known that she'd groomed Brooke for this and that (according to Zee's latest spiel), she put a lot of pressure on her, but I'd never realized that Brooke's mother was actually in on our operation.

First Jack's uncle and now this. Who was going to be next? The twins' little sister?

With happy-homemaker efficiency, Mrs. Camden got us settled on the couch in her living room, and she actually did bring us cookies. Neither of us ate them.

"Tell me what happened," she said simply.

I couldn't read anything in her tone, but Brooke looked like she'd been slapped.

"We entered the premises on the mark's invitation and immediately identified the locations of all three nonmark hostiles. We convinced all of them of our cover, and I played decoy while Toby exited the room under the guise of going to the bathroom. The first hostile followed her, but she managed to escape the bathroom through the air duct as planned. The mission progressed accordingly for approximately four and a half minutes . . ."

"That long?" Brooke's mother mused. She arched an eyebrow at me. "He didn't break down the door for four and a half minutes? Impressive."

I made the executive decision not to illuminate Mrs. Camden on the method I'd used to procure as much time as possible. Somehow, I didn't think this particular desperate housewife would appreciate it.

"I continued distracting the second hostile and the mark while Toby disabled the third hostile and began searching for the security panel. She located the panel, deactivated the security, and found the target, but unfortunately, the third hostile woke up just as the other two realized that she was not, in fact, in the bathroom. I disabled the mark first as instructed, and engaged in hand-to-hand with the other two until one of them managed to pull a gun. He fired a single shot. I succeeded in diving out of the way, but the second hostile caught me and held me at gunpoint. At that point in time, Toby came into the room, providing enough of a distraction that I was able to disarm the hostiles and render them unconscious. Toby returned to the kitchen while I secured the hostiles and the mark, but the target we were sent to retrieve was gone, presumably taken by an unidentified intruder whose arrival had coincided with the third hostile's awakening and the others' discovery that we were not who and what we claimed to be."

If by *unidentified*, she meant "almost certainly Amelia Juarez."

"An unidentified entity, an 'intruder' as you so blithely put it, has the weapon you were sent to retrieve?" Mrs. Camden asked, her voice still sickly sweet.

"Yes." Brooke's answer was short, and her voice was neutral, but I could feel the tension beneath the surface of her tone.

I expected Mrs. Camden to yell, or to lash out physically, or to do something drastic, but instead, she just sighed.

"Oh, Brookie. What are we going to do with you?"

"It wasn't her fault," I surprised myself by saying. "It's mine. If I'd taken Amel—errr—the intruder out the first time I'd seen her, this wouldn't have happened."

That was true enough.

Mrs. Camden considered me, her face the epitome of polish and homemakerly grace. "You're green," she said. "And you'll learn."

I got the feeling that from her, this was high praise. Beside me, Brooke stiffened.

"Don't wrinkle your forehead, dear," Mrs. Camden chided. She must have had incredible eyesight, because as hard as I looked, I couldn't make out a single wrinkle.

"You'll have worry lines before you're thirty." Then, without sparing Brooke so much as another look, she turned her attention back to me. "Why didn't you disable the intruder?"

I hedged around the question. "When I first noticed her, I mean, when I first noticed another person in the room, I was engaged in combat with the . . . uhhhh . . . third hostile."

"And then?" Mrs. Camden prodded. She was sharp. Nothing got past this woman, and there was no way around telling her the truth.

"I went to help Brooke."

"And why did you need help?" Mrs. Camden asked her daughter, like someone talking to a very young child who's been quite naughty.

"I didn't disarm them fast enough."

"Which," Mrs. Camden said, "wouldn't have been a problem if you'd been properly armed."

Brooke looked away.

"Tell me, Brooke, if they'd had knives instead of guns, do you think you would have been able to disarm them quicker? Or what if you'd had a gun as well?"

I didn't see where this line of questioning was going, but Brooke apparently did.

"I'm not sure."

"Yes," her mother said, "you are. One of these days, Brookie, you're going to have to get over this thing you have with guns. You'll have to use one eventually, and you can't freeze up every time you see one, not even for a second."

"It wasn't like that," Brooke said, her calm exterior cracking just a bit.

"Don't get worked up, dear," her mom said. "And don't

talk back. Right now, I don't want you to even worry about the operations end of things. I'll smooth things over, and you'll have a new case before you know it. I'll make everything all right. You just worry about homecoming."

I read the look in Mrs. Camden's eyes and the expression on Brooke's face and translated them into words, even though neither Brooke nor her mother actually said a thing.

Mrs. Camden: Try not to screw that one up, too, Brooke.

Brooke: I won't. I'm not a screwup. Screw you. Don't be mad.

And before I knew it, Brooke was walking me to the door.

"Do drop by again, Toby," Mrs. Camden called. "We expect great things from you."

Sure, I'd drop by again. WHEN HELL FROZE OVER.

On the way out, we passed a bookshelf full of pictures. All of them were of Brooke, and in each and every one of them, she was cheering. In the earliest picture, she was probably about five or six. Trophies sat on the top shelf, and I squinted, making out the names of several individual cheerleading competitions.

1ST PLACE.

1ST PLACE.

1ST PLACE.

Why did I get the feeling that first place was the only place that Brooke or her mother understood?

"I'll see you tomorrow," Brooke said evenly. "We should practice before school. Big game on Friday."

Her voice sounded the same as it always did, but I felt like there was something missing, something dead.

"Okay," I said, trying to keep my own voice sufficiently subdued.

I didn't realize until I stepped out of her house and onto the front porch that I didn't have a way home. I pulled out my Squad-issued phone and dialed the other girls one by one.

Tara didn't answer.

Neither did Zee.

I got Bubbles on voice mail, which was somewhat amusing, because she'd had technical difficulties programming her phone, and the whole prerecorded message was just her going, "Is this thing on? Is it working? If I like say something, will . . . oooh, what's that beep?"

I had no desire to call Chloe, and I wasn't exactly looking my best postmission, so I decided to avoid calling the twins as well. I tried Lucy—who, after all, deserved some major kudos for the bobby-sock bomb, even if it hadn't saved our mission. When Lucy didn't answer, either, I dialed the last number on my list.

April.

She answered on the third ring.

"Toby?"

"Yeah," I said, feeling more than a little awkward. Of all the girls, April was the only one my age, and the one I'd interacted with the least. We didn't really know each other, and once upon a time, she'd been Hayley Hoffman's second-in-command, which meant that the few times I'd registered on her social radar pre-Squad, she hadn't exactly been friendly. "Listen, I'm at Brooke's house, and I kind of need a ride. Do you have your license yet?"

"No, but I have a car," April replied. "Actually, I have two, so it's no big if I wreck one. I'll be there in a few minutes—it's on Calloway Street, right?"

I wasn't sure, but that sounded good to me. "I think so."

"Okay. Just hang tight and give me five. Later!"

I hung up my phone, and as I stepped off Brooke's front porch and walked down her driveway, I hoped that April would hurry.

The sooner I could get away from this place, the better.

CHAPTER 25
Code Word: Kisses

While I was waiting for April, my phone rang. It was Zee.

"Sorry I missed your call," she said. "I was doing yo-galates."

I wasn't exactly sure how to respond to that.

"Don't roll your eyes at me," Zee said, and I realized that was exactly what I had been doing. "There's nothing wrong with yogalates. You can't honestly expect me to spend all of my spare time working on my latest criminology dissertation."

"I didn't even know you were writing one," I said. "And honestly, I thought you didn't answer because you were either still selling Cheer Scout cookies, or because you were on the line."

Gossip queens and phones sort of went hand in hand.

"What do you need?" Zee asked. She seemed to know that I wouldn't have called unless I really needed something, and that even though I'd accepted my position on the Squad, I was loath to ask for help.

"I just needed a ride," I said. "April's coming to pick me up."

"Good," Zee replied. "You two haven't spent much time together."

She sounded like some kind of twisted matchmaker. I was about to hang up, but just as April's car pulled into view, I remembered that there was one thing about the conversation with Brooke's mom that was still bothering me.

"Zee? What's Brooke's deal with guns?"

Zee didn't answer, which caught me off guard. Zee always had an answer.

"Zee?"

"You don't want to know," she said, "and if you do, look it up yourself. There's an information superhighway out there, and you're the web equivalent of a biker babe."

I just loved crappy metaphors.

"Tell April hi for me," Zee chirped, and then she hung up.

I climbed into April's car, and at that moment, all I wanted was to be at home.

"Where to?" April asked.

"The school. I need to pick up my car."

April nodded and flipped on her stereo. I listened to the music for a few minutes and nodded my approval.

"Not bad," I said. It wasn't exactly good music, but compared to the crap the rest of the girls listened to, it wasn't horrible.

God, how could I even think about music right now? What was wrong with me that I could do what I'd just done and know what I knew and just sit here, in April's car, like this was normal? Maybe, after a while, you get so used to living a double life (or in my case, given the whole popularity thing, maybe a triple one) that it just comes naturally to shut off one part of the brain and boot up another.

"That's the thing about me," April said lightly, unaware of the serious turn my thoughts had taken. "I'm really not that bad. I'm not a bad person. I'm a good cheerleader, and even if I'm not as good at the secret-agent thing yet, I'm picking it up."

Apparently, the story about my bombed mission hadn't circulated yet, because April thought I was good at this.

"I know you think it's kind of weird that I just ditched Hayley once I made varsity," April said. "And I know that you and I were never friends before all of this."

Understatement.

"But the thing is, Hayley and I weren't really friends, either. I didn't ditch her. I transcended her, and the only thing she misses is having someone to boss around."

"She has someone to boss around," I said. "Kiki . . ." I searched for Kiki's last name, reminding myself that she was the PTA president's daughter.

"McCall," April provided. The light turned green, and April accelerated.

After that, I expected the conversation to go somewhere. April certainly seemed on the verge of spilling her Poor Little Rich Girl heart, but she didn't. Instead, she just said, "I don't mind not having friends, but I like having you guys. Does that make sense?"

Oddly enough, it did. Especially now.

Ten minutes later, when April pulled up to the school, I realized that I didn't find her company totally abhorrent, which was probably a good thing. Barring any deadly explosions, the two of us were going to be around each other pretty much constantly for the next three years. Eventually, I was going to have to see her as someone other than Hayley's former sidekick.

"Thanks for the ride." Things weren't exactly getting less awkward as time went on, but at least they weren't getting any worse.

"Anytime," April replied. "Have to get in plenty of practice before I turn sixteen."

Her sense of logic was a beautiful thing.

"Hey, April," I called as I got out of the car. "Do me a favor?"

"Depends on the favor."

At least she was honest.

"You know that whole homecoming princess thing?" I asked.

She nodded.

"Please win it."

She grinned. "Done."

I walked toward my car and was surprised to see Noah sitting on the hood.

"Wasn't someone supposed to give you a ride home?" I asked. Noah ignored the question.

"Which one was that?"

"Which one was what?"

"Toby, a cheerleader just came within a hundred yards of my person, and I didn't notice until it was too late. This is a very serious matter." It was hard to take Noah seriously when he had that goofy, puppy dog smile on his face.

"It was April," I said, "and she's not interested."

Noah rolled his eyes. "That's what you always say."

I thumped him in the shoulder. "It's always true." I walked past him and opened the driver's side door. "Get in the car."

By the time we got home, Noah had actually managed to distract me from thoughts of our failed mission, the weapon that Peyton would probably sell to the highest bidder if the Big Guys didn't stop them first, and the conversation I'd just had with April in the car.

The only thing I couldn't stop thinking about was Brooke's mother, and as soon as we got home, I went to join my own in the kitchen.

"Want to help make the salad?" my mom asked, not commenting on the fact that I was home early for the second time this week.

I shrugged. "Sure."

She handed me a knife, and I began chopping up lettuce.

"You're thinking about something," my mom said. It was a simple comment, and she left it up to me if I wanted to share what I was thinking. No pressure, no wheedling. That was my mother.

"I went over to our captain's house today after school," I said. "Her mom was a little . . ." I decided to go with Zee's word of choice. "Intense."

"An intense cheerleading mom?" my mom feigned shock. "Never."

"You're not surprised," I concluded.

"When you were little," my mom said, handing me some carrots and peppers to go in with the lettuce, "there was a big scandal about this mother in Texas whose daughter hadn't made the cheerleading squad. She was so upset about it that she took matters into her own hands."

"Complained to the school board?" I guessed.

"No," my mom said, sliding the salad dressing down the counter. "She hired a hit man to take out one of the other girls."

"Seriously?"

My mom nodded. "Seriously. It made national news. So if your friend's mom is a little intense, well . . . it's an intense sport, Toby."

The fact that she'd called it a sport didn't go unnoticed. I thought about the fact that we were going to be actually practicing tomorrow morning, and that instead of finishing up a case and safeguarding the world, we'd be flipping and flying and doing all kinds of motions that would inevitably make my armpits hurt.

That was the thing about cheerleading. The jumps were torture on your leg muscles, and the conditioning could be hell, but at the end of the day, your armpits were always sore. Or maybe that was just me.

"Mom?"

"Yes?"

"Thanks for not being a crazy cheer mom."

"No problem." My mother paused. "Though in fairness to all of those mothers out there who are only partially crazy, I did enroll you in martial arts classes when you were really young, and that world can be just as competitive."

My mom was a karate instructor, and she was right—I'd been kicking butt for as long as I'd been walking.

"But you weren't . . . intense about it," I said, choosing my words carefully again. She'd never forced me into competitions. She'd never looked at me and said "Oh, Toby" in that put-upon way.

More importantly, she didn't give a rat's bum about homecoming. Thinking of homecoming reminded me of something.

"By the way," I said conversationally, "I should probably

tell you that if Noah stages one more publicity stunt on my behalf, I am going to hurt him."

"What did he do?" my mother asked.

I gave her the grand total for the past couple of days. "Ran through the school in his boxers, walked around wearing a sandwich board with my face on it, sent out mass emails to the whole student body, and pretended to be a pirate in the middle of the cafeteria."

My mom showed no signs of surprise, but she did let out a single giggle.

"Mom!"

"Toby, you have to admit, the pirate thing is just a little bit funny."

I most certainly did not have to admit that, and I didn't have to stand there and take the abuse, either.

"Just consider yourself lucky that he didn't open a kissing booth to raise money for your campaign fund," my mom said. "I'd be surprised if the idea hasn't crossed his mind."

As we have already established, my mother is never surprised, which led me to conclude that Noah had, in all likelihood, considered the idea. And if Noah had considered the idea, he probably wouldn't have had the foresight to decide against it.

"I'll be right back," I said. I stuck my head into the living room. "Noah?"

"Yes?"

"How much money did the kissing booth make?"

"It's not really the amount of money per se that determines the success of a booth," Noah opined. "It's the number of girls I managed to kiss before some . . . errrr . . . *angry* young men shut down my operation."

"And what is that number?" I asked.

Noah grinned. "Two."

That was it. Absolutely it. The twins had to be stopped, whatever the cost. I'd beg if I had to, and if that didn't work, well, I still had my second bobby-sock grenade, and it had even more firepower than the first.

CHAPTER 26

Code Word: Rebel

That night, I sat in front of my computer for a long time thinking about exactly two things. The first involved Brooke, her aversion to guns, and Zee's insistence that I could find out on my own, and the second was peripherally related to the fact that when I was little, and report cards were made up totally of S (for satisfactory) and N (for not satisfactory), I'd always gotten an N in two areas—plays well with others, and, more importantly, follows directions when they are given.

I had a healthy disrespect for authority, and for as long as I can remember, when someone said "don't do that," what I heard was something more along the lines of "doing that would probably be fun."

Based on our interaction with Brooke's mom, and the way she'd told Brooke to concentrate on homecoming and not worry at all about the biotechnological weapon now in the hands of some anonymous independent operative, I could only conclude that we'd been given the official (if subtle) cease and desist that Brooke had seen coming.

I didn't feel much like ceasing or desisting. If I'd managed to take the operative down and still saved Brooke, we wouldn't have been taken off the case. If I hadn't almost gotten blown up the first day, the Big Guys wouldn't have been watching this particular mission so closely to begin with. We'd been pulled off this case because of me, and I felt vaguely like Brooke's mom and her superiors were dangling all of the answers just out of reach, doing the covert version of "nanny nanny boo boo!"

The fact that the phrase *nanny nanny boo boo* had just crossed my mind made me briefly question my own sanity, but that didn't change the feeling in my gut. I'd been told to stay away from this case, and what I heard was "diving into this case headfirst would rock your world."

I didn't really care if the Big Guys Upstairs gave me an N on my espionage report card. I didn't even care if I was, as Brooke had so sweetly put it earlier that day, "replaceable." I wanted answers. I wanted to know if anyone else had even come to the same conclusion Brooke and I had about the identity of our faceless intruder. I wanted to know where Amelia Juarez was. I wanted to know if the Big Guys had a tail on her. I wanted to know when she was going to give the weapon to the firm, and what could be done to stop her. And while I was at it, I wanted to know what the CIA knew about Alan Peyton.

After I figured all that out, I wanted to stop the bad guys, save the day, and flip Brooke's mom the metaphorical bird.

What can I say? I'd tried being a good little girl who didn't hack into government databases, but that just wasn't me. This was. I organized my plan into steps. Step One: Access Squad database. Step Two: Hack the Big Guys' database to see what they were holding out on us. Step Three: Victorious evil laughter.

Okay, so Step Three wasn't exactly a step, but I figured that planning too far ahead was a waste of time. The name of the game was improvisation, and sometimes, plans just got in the way.

"Okay," I said. "How to access the Squad's database . . ." I pondered out loud. If I'd wanted to, I could have gone up to the school. I could get into the Quad—I had the entry codes and my own key to the school, courtesy of Mr. J's lack of foresight and natural trust of girls in uniform. But I didn't want to go back up to the school. I was tired, and on the off chance that I had been the target of the original bomb, I didn't think traipsing around Bayport by myself at night was the world's best idea.

And they say I have no impulse control, I thought wryly.

That left me with exactly two options. I could try to hack into the system blind, which would be time-consuming and possibly futile, or I could call Chloe to see if she'd built a remote-access mechanism into my Squad-issued cell phone.

Let's see, I thought. Hundreds of hours worth of work, or thirty seconds on the phone with Chloe? It was a tough call and would have been even tougher if I'd thought for even a second that Chloe might turn me in. Given that she'd done some illicit hacking of her own that afternoon, I wasn't too worried, but that didn't mean that I was looking forward to this particular phone call.

While I mulled over my choices, I pulled up a search engine and typed in Brooke's name. And then I typed in the word *gun*. And then I almost hit enter, but couldn't quite bring myself to do it. I wasn't really sure why. Maybe it was something about the way Zee had sounded on the phone, or maybe it was the depths of the undercurrents I'd sensed between Brooke and her mom on that particular topic. Maybe it was the fact that I couldn't imagine Brooke Bow-Down-and-Worship-Me Camden being afraid of anything, let alone a weapon she'd probably been exposed to from a very young age.

Or maybe I was just crazy. That could have been it. After all, here I was planning to hack into one of the U.S. government's most secure databases on a whim. Again. The first time had gotten me recruited to the Squad. The second time could get me kicked off.

Nanny nanny boo boo, I thought. And then I picked up the phone and called Chloe.

"If you're not calling to tell me that you've been horribly disfigured or had a sex-change operation, I don't want to hear it."

"You know, Chloe," I said. "Most people just opt for 'hello.' "

She didn't dignify that comment with a response.

"Have you heard from Brooke?" I asked her.

Silence. I took that as a no. I knew something that she didn't, which just added to the resentment I could practically hear from her side of the telephone.

"The mission didn't go well," I said. "We lost the weapon to an intruder—probably Amelia Juarez—and the Big Guys took us off the case."

I actually heard Chloe take in a sharp breath.

"Brooke's mom is unhappy," I said simply.

"I'll call her," Chloe said quietly. "Not her mom. Brooke."

Some days, it was easy to forget that the two of them were best friends, as well as rivals. Between the tone in Chloe's voice now, and the way she'd leveled with me before our mission, today wasn't one of those days. The two of them had been through a lot together, and if anyone understood the relationship between Brooke and her mom better than Zee, it was probably Chloe, who'd been along for the ride since she and Brooke were eleven years old.

"You should," I agreed. "Now, I'm going to ask you a hypothetical question." I paused. "Hypothetically speaking, if I wanted to access Squad files remotely from my room, would my cell have some kind of technology that helped me to do that?"

"Hypothetically speaking," Chloe said, "you're crazy, but if you hypothetically wanted to do that, you'd set your phone to D mode, type in your passcode, and flip the switch on the very top of the phone to the far right."

"What's my passcode?"

"If I told you that," Chloe replied, "you might actually start to think I like you. Hypothetically speaking, of course."

"Of course."

"You're the hacker. Figure it out your hypothetical self."

She was a hypothetical bee-yotch, but she'd answered my first question, and she was going to call Brooke, and that was going to have to be enough for me.

"Goodbye, Chloe." I didn't wait for a response before I hung up the phone. I followed Chloe's instructions and immediately set about figuring out the passcode. It took me two and a half hours, and by the time I hit on the correct one, I was ready to upgrade Chloe's status from hypothetical bee-yotch to actual to enormously huge.

I funneled my energy into the work, selecting the files I wanted the phone to download. A warning popped up on my phone's screen, letting me know that these files would self-destruct within two hours of download, and that I wouldn't be able to access them from this phone again. As far as security measures went, it was a must, but in terms of my difficulties with speed-reading late at night, it was unfortunate.

I finished selecting the pertinent files, hit the send button, and entered my passcode again. The phone started downloading, and as it did, I turned my attention back to the open window on my computer.

Brooke Camden. Gun.

I hit enter. The search returned too many hits, and I narrowed it down by adding one last parameter.

Bayport.

And there it was. A small news blurb, and below that, an obituary. I opened the blurb first, and somehow, I knew exactly what to expect.

Christopher Camden, age thirty-two, died on Friday at Bayport General after suffering three gunshot wounds to the chest. The circumstances surrounding his death are somewhat unclear, and the BPD has no leads at this time. Camden is survived by his wife, Karen Madden Camden, and a daughter, Brooke, age four.

The obituary was simple and sweet and said only that Brooke's father would be missed. A second news article mentioned, albeit briefly, that there had been one witness to the shooting. One guess who.

It was no wonder that Brooke had an "aversion" to guns. I probably would have found them pretty averse if I'd seen my father killed with one, too. And her mother! How could she just sit there and act like it was something Brooke should just magically be over by now?

If I hadn't already decided to stick it to Brooke's mom

and the whole damn system by solving this thing myself, reading these articles would have been enough to push me in that direction. As it was, it made me view Brooke, her relationship with her mom, and her domination of our school in a whole different way.

Mainly, though, it made me realize that if Brooke didn't win homecoming queen because of Noah's rare and annoyingly undiagnosable personality disorder, I'd deport him myself.

CHAPTER 27
Code Word: Girly

Remotely accessing the Squad's database didn't tell me much that I didn't already know. We still had data coming in on Anthony Connors-Wright's location. He'd apparently been at the park again that afternoon, while the figure in black (*cough* Amelia *cough cough*) had been stealing our target. Since this officially eliminated him as a suspect, I wasn't any more interested in what he'd done with the rest of his day than I was, for example, in Chip's philosophical ponderings on the topic of love. Ross had been taken into custody for his mad scientist hijinks, and with no one around to sell him weapons, Anthony posed no threat as a buyer. Whoever had Ross's nanobots now (and I could only hope that the answer to that question wasn't Peyton, Kaufman, and Gray) would be looking to deal with much bigger fish than an intelligence brat with a chip on his shoulder. Anthony could go to the park to his heart's content, and neither I nor the government particularly cared.

Beyond that, the only information I immediately gleaned from our database was the fact that the Big Guys had actually sent us an official electronic cease and desist order. If they thought that would in any way deter me, they clearly weren't paying their profilers enough.

I scanned through the rest of our files, looking for anything that might tip me off to what Amelia Juarez planned to do next. I read Amelia's profile again and again, looking for a clue about who exactly Amelia was and wishing that I had Zee's uncanny ability to make outlandish, but accurate, predictions based only on personality indices, body language, facial expressions, and what she referred to as an individual's background/environmental matrix.

As I read over Amelia's files, I kept coming to the same conclusions over and over again. She was smart. She came from a dangerous family. She wanted to prove that she was more than just the baby and the only girl. And somehow, that had led her to Bayport, to working for Peyton, Kaufman, and Gray, and—if she really was the one who'd crashed our last mission—to stealing a top-secret, high-tech biological weapon. I tried my best to convert the facts into numbers, to solve the equation that would tell me where to find her and how to stop her, but again and again, I came up with a whole lot of nothing.

Oh well, I thought with a wicked grin. On to Step Two.

Hacking the United States government was *so* much fun.

A mere forty-five minutes later, I was in. I'd like to claim that I'm a genius—and I am—but if I'm being perfectly honest, it didn't hurt that I still had access to the Squad's mainframe and that the mainframe and the Big Guys' systems were configured to file-share, even if there were some major firewalls in place on their side of things. With a flick of my wrist, the sweat of my brow, and what I can only describe as the hacking hokeypokey, I managed to locate the exact system portal that I needed to hack. After that, it was just a matter of using a few of my pet programs—all of which I'd designed myself—to force my way into a system that should have been impenetrable.

It was almost as if the Big Guys *wanted* me to hack them.

Since I had the distinct feeling that my presence wouldn't go undetected for long, I set several of my decrypt-and-search programs to looking at once, and before I got booted out of the system, I managed to access their file on the current case (shockingly easy—perhaps because they'd originally planned on sharing it with us to begin with?). I wasn't entirely sure that the files weren't encrypted with something that would crash my computer, but luckily, Bessie (my laptop) was a tough old girl.

She and I had a lot in common.

As I read through the files I'd managed to borrow (*steal* is such an ugly word), I came to a disturbing conclusion. High school cheerleaders are much better at writing intelligible reports than government operatives are. Reading the government files was like trying to read a book with the plot of Edith Wharton's *Ethan Frome* (worst book ever, and one of the English department's faves) that just happened to be written by a dyslexic Viking writing in iambic pentameter.

In other words, it was worse than trying to read Ross's dissertation, and this time, I didn't have Chloe to translate. Piece by piece, bit by bit, I managed to parse what I was reading into something more manageable, and slowly, what the Big Guys had been up to since we'd been pulled off the case became clear.

They'd apprehended Ross, as well as the three security

goons, run interference with the local cops to prevent a formal investigation, and confirmed through interviews and a variety of anonymous sources that no one had made a connection between the chaos and any cookie-peddling cheerleaders in the near vicinity. Ross and his cohorts were being interrogated, and they were slated to later have their memories chemically altered. By the time the Big Guys were finished, nobody would remember that Brooke and I had been in Ross's office, except for the mysterious figure in black who'd caught me red-handed.

The Big Guys hadn't yet positively ID'd the intruder, but the dominant theory did seem to be that it was Amelia Juarez, working on behalf of Peyton, Kaufman, and Gray. The firm was under constant surveillance, with upward of eight teams ready to swarm in the second Amelia appeared within a five-mile radius of the "hot zone."

Additionally, the Big Guys were working on "minimizing the threat" posed by the "loss" of the biotechnology. Their motto was more or less "Contain! Contain! Contain!" They wanted this threat contained to Bayport, and they wanted it done yesterday. As such, they were keeping a close watch on all of the airports and bus stations, and they'd set up roadblocks on the way out of town.

"Okay," I said out loud, "you're making sure Amelia can't get through to Peyton and that she doesn't get out of town, but where is she *now?*"

The most disturbing thing about reading the Big Guys' files wasn't the complete lack of writing skills; it was the fact that they didn't have an answer to my question. They knew Amelia wasn't at Peyton, and they knew she hadn't skipped town, but beyond that, they weren't even looking.

In my twisted mind, all of this information led clearly to

a single conclusion, a solution as clear as 4 to 2 + 2. The Big Guys could watch Peyton. They could contain! contain! contain! to their hearts' content. That wasn't enough for me. The costs of this mission had been huge. Too much had happened for me to just shrug it off. Somebody had killed Jacob Kann. Somebody had stolen a weapon I'd been sent to retrieve. Between the explosion, the car last night, and the security gorilla with a gun this afternoon, I'd had not one, not two, but three near-death experiences while on this case.

I didn't want to contain the threat. I wanted to eliminate it, and that meant finding Amelia Juarez, even if I had to do it myself.

"Somehow, I pictured you being bigger."

The voice shocked me out of my almost meditative state of thought. It was light and female and coming from directly behind me.

Please, I thought, let that be Bubbles.

I swiveled around in my chair, and a girl—no, a woman—with dark, glossy hair and even brown eyes stared back at me.

For a single instant, I stopped breathing, and my mind refused to process what I was seeing. Soon, though, it became perfectly clear. I didn't need to find Amelia Juarez. She'd found me.

"What are you doing here?" I kept my voice low, lest Noah burst into my room and attempt to flirt with someone who would in all likelihood kill him for the effort.

"Same thing you are," Amelia replied, leaning against my wall. She had this blatantly casual air about her, as if she routinely showed up in my bedroom and the conversation the two of us were having wasn't strange in the least.

"I live here," I told her, stalling for time as my mind tried desperately to come up with a plan. I scanned her body, trying to identify whether and what she was packing, and then examined the distance between us. If I could take her down before she could draw a knife or a gun or, God forbid, the nanobots, this case would finally be over.

"That's not a good idea," Amelia said, her voice still light and airy, her posture never changing.

"What isn't?"

I mentally prepared myself to attack.

"Attacking me." Without another word, Amelia shifted her position, and just as I was preparing to throw myself at her, she drew a gun. "I don't want to use this."

I snorted. "That makes two of us." If I could just keep her talking, if I could get her off balance . . .

I mean, really, what's a fourth near-death experience when you've already had three?

"I have an offer for you."

Of all the things I expected Amelia to say, which ranged from "Meet your doom" to "It's not my fault; I had a bad childhood," that definitely wasn't one of them.

"An offer?"

"Allow me to explain the concept. I give you something you want, and I get something I want in return."

I knew what I wanted: the nanobots. I couldn't begin to imagine what she thought I could give her.

"I know who has the weapon you're after." Amelia's tone never changed. It would have been more appropriate to a discussion about the weather than one on technobiological warfare. "I know when they're planning to use it, and who they're planning to kill. If you and I can come to an agreement, then nobody has to die."

I stared at her. "So either I help you or you kill someone?" That didn't sound like much of a deal to me. "I don't think so. And for the record, I know who has the weapon, too." I took a step forward, playing the odds that she wouldn't actually shoot me for a single misstep. "You do."

"Are you all this dramatic?" Amelia asked. "Or this stupid?"

I was getting really tired of people calling me a drama queen.

"Allow me to break this down for you. I'm not going to kill anyone. I don't have the weapon. I'm honestly not sure why you think I do." There was no humor in Amelia's voice, nothing that made her words come across as anything but cold, hard fact. "What I *do* have is information that you need, and all I want in return is a promise."

Her words confused me so much that I honestly wasn't sure whether she was speaking English or not. Did she really expect me to believe she didn't have the nanobots? Of the other TCIs, one was in custody, one was dead, and the last one was wandering aimlessly around a park. If Amelia hadn't stolen the weapon, that meant there was another player on the scene, and really, what were the chances of that?

"Give me one good reason I should believe anything that comes out of your mouth," I told her, vaguely aware of the fact that it sounded like something out of a horribly cheesy movie.

"Believe me because it's true," Amelia said, "or believe me because if I had the weapon, your bedroom is the last place I'd be right now. Take your pick."

When she put it in those terms, I realized she was right. If she'd been the one to steal the nanobots, she'd either be sneaking her way into Peyton or halfway to Tahiti by now. Neither of those scenarios involved a detour by my house.

"If you didn't steal the weapon, who did?" I didn't really expect her to answer, but I couldn't help thinking out loud. I'd been so sure that Amelia was the person in black that I hadn't spent any time thinking of alternative hypotheses. Amelia had the motive, she had the intel, and she had the ability to pull the whole thing off. Other than the girls on the Squad, I couldn't think of anyone else for whom that was true.

To my surprise, Amelia had an answer to my question. "If I had to guess who stole the nanobots, I'd go with who-ever blew up Jacob Kann's car."

Originally, the Big Guys had suspected Hassan of the bombing because he'd had the other TCIs under surveillance. Until about forty-five seconds ago, I'd thought Amelia had probably set the bomb herself. Now, I wasn't sure what to think.

"You're saying that you didn't take Kann out?" I had to ask.

Amelia snorted. "He's an idiot, and a womanizer, and he was under the impression that he was going to have sex with me, but I wouldn't have killed him." Amelia never took her eyes off me and the gun never wavered, but some-how, she managed to look exactly like the twins did when they started filing their nails out of boredom in the middle of one of our meetings. "As much fun as chatting is, can we get on with it? I don't know who stole the weapon, but I do know they've disposed of it, and I know who has it now. If you're very, very nice to me, I just might tell you who it is."

"Why would you do that?" I couldn't fathom her reasoning. This whole interaction was so insane that I half-expected my clothes to disappear, revealing that this was just the latest in a long line of twisted naked dreams.

"You act like this is the first time I've dealt your people in," Amelia huffed. "Without me, your bosses wouldn't have Hector Hassan in custody right now, Jacob Kann would have bought the weapon from Ross days ago, and Peyton, Kaufman, and Gray would have intercepted Kann, taken the weapon, and killed Ross just because they could. I've been playing the players and throwing kinks in the firm's plans for days now, and this is the thanks I get? I'm not sure you deserve my offer."

"Kinks?"

Amelia shrugged. "Peyton, Kaufman, and Gray brought me in to act as their little lapdog and fetch the nanobots as soon as Ross sold them. They didn't exactly endear themselves to me, and I figured that if something this big was going down, your people would clue in eventually. I just stalled things for a couple of days. I convinced Peyton to let me bid against Kann for the nanobots instead of stealing them from him after the deal went through. When Ross realized he was dealing with more than one potential buyer, he decided to hold an auction, just like I knew he would."

Amelia was still speaking a language I couldn't quite understand. She'd stalled Peyton and convinced them to wait before moving in? She'd somehow prevented Ross from closing the deal with Kann earlier in the week?

"Why?" I glanced down to make sure my clothes were still in place, because this kept getting stranger and stranger.

Amelia shrugged. "Why not?"

Well, that was less than helpful.

"You want another answer? How about this one: because

I could. Because it was fun. Because my brothers set this job up for me, and they leave the toilet seat up too damn much." I couldn't tell whether she was serious or not on that last one, so I just listened, open-mouthed, as she continued. "An operation as big as Peyton, Kaufman, and Gray—I knew the government had to be all over that, just waiting for these guys to mess up. I figured that if I stretched things out long enough, somebody would catch on, and as far as I'm concerned, the more players, the better the game."

Some game. A bunch of people were fighting over deadly technology, and she was acting like this whole mission ranked right up there with Yahtzee.

"So I'm supposed to think you're a good guy?" I asked, my voice tight. "Because you've been stalling your employers?"

"You're not supposed to think I'm a good guy," Amelia said. "You're just supposed to think I'm good."

"Good?"

"I've been playing you, and I've been playing them. I knew the second one of your girls put a tracker on my car, just like I knew when Peyton brought me here that all they wanted was someone to follow orders and look good doing it." She played with the gun in the tip of her hands, stroking her thumb up and down the side. "They thought they were doing my family a favor by offering me this job." Her lips pulled back into something that looked like a smile, but probably wasn't. "I disagreed."

I forced myself to think through everything Amelia had said. Peyton had brought her in to do a simple job, and somehow Amelia had manipulated them into changing the job description. She'd then orchestrated Ross's decision to host an auction, which had resulted in two more TCIs coming to Bayport. That influx had tipped the Big Guys off to the fact that something was up, and as a result, we'd been brought in on the case. According to Amelia, that had been her intention all along.

"Okay," I said slowly. "So you wanted the government brought in on this case, but once you knew we were on it . . ."

"That's when things got interesting." Amelia's smile looked genuine this time. "I decided to see if I could get you to take out the competition for me."

"The competition you brought here to begin with."

"Except for Jacob, yes."

"And you expect me to believe that you had nothing to do with his car blowing up?"

"Haven't we already been over this? I have no idea who killed Jacob Kann, but whoever they are, they're good. My plan was just to plant a bunch of drugs on him and then lead your people in for the arrest."

She talked about framing someone so glibly. "You framed him," I said. Something about her tone and the words she'd spoken earlier led me to my next conclusion. "Just like you did with Hector Hassan."

Amelia grinned. "I knew somebody would be on this case eventually, and I knew Hassan had some pretty unsavory backing."

If by "unsavory," she meant "terrorists," then yeah.

"I needed to keep track of the others, but figured you guys would be doing the same, so I bugged Connors-Wright and Kann and gave Hassan enough rope to hang himself."

"You bugged yourself to throw us off track." In a word: genius.

"That pointed you guys toward Hassan, since he was the

only one not already bugged, which led to you guys tracking him and bringing him into custody before he could do any real harm." Amelia smiled then, the barest hint of satisfaction playing across her even features. "You're welcome."

"Okay, so you set up Hassan," I said. "That doesn't prove that you weren't the one who took out Kann." I knew I was beating a dead dog here, but I just couldn't help it. Amelia Juarez was apparently some kind of evil mastermind, and she was standing in my bedroom. I wanted her to be the bad guy, because the idea that there was someone out there who'd beaten both of us to the weapon was scarier than the gun still trained on my forehead.

"You don't want to take my word on the fact that I had nothing to do with Jacob's murder? Fine. I'm assuming you guys have some sort of database. You might want to check it, because according to Peyton's reports on the explosion, the bomb was remotely detonated, which means that someone was watching that car and waiting to press the little red button." She smiled, and I could practically hear her thinking "check and mate."

"Coincidentally enough, that was the day your group attempted to plant a tracker on my car. They were tailing me when the bomb went off. Correct me if I'm wrong, but I think the word I'm looking for here is *alibi*."

I would check our files to confirm what she was saying, but I knew without doing so that she was right. We'd had teams tracking and planting surveillance on each of the TCIs, and if the bomb really had been detonated manually, none of them could have done it without one of our teams noticing. I wondered briefly how we could have missed this, how the Big Guys could have missed this, or if they'd actually missed it at all.

If none of the TCIs had planted the bomb, that meant that someone else had, and that meant that there was another player on this case. A player who'd killed Jacob Kann and later stolen the weapon from Ross's lab. A player who, according to Amelia, had already given the nanobots to somebody else.

"Who?" I didn't bother to elaborate. Amelia knew what I was asking.

"No more questions about my motive? No wondering why I'm being such a good little mob princess and sharing what I know?"

"Just. Tell. Me. Who."

"I came here with an offer. If you want to know the information, that means you play by my rules."

"What do you want?" My voice was dull, and the desire to flying tackle her and take my chances with the gun was incredible.

"All I want is a promise that once I tell you who has the bots, you and your little team will be the ones to retrieve them."

"Done." I didn't give even so much as a second's thought to the fact that we'd been taken off the case. Clearly, this diving in headfirst thing was working for me.

"There is one other little thing . . ." Amelia looked me straight in the eye. "I want your word that nobody hears about this conversation until tomorrow, and that whoever your team works for stays in the dark until everything's gone down."

I couldn't tell her no. I could, however, lie through my teeth.

"If you break these rules," she continued, "I reserve the right to blow your cover wide open. I'm sure Peyton,

Kaufman, and Gray would love to know that the government has an entire team here, right under their noses."

For the first time, I realized the full implications of the fact that Amelia was here, in my bedroom. Somehow, she'd figured out who I was. From the sound of it, that wasn't all she knew.

"I saw you yesterday outside of the firm," she explained with no small measure of glee. "You had that same unnaturally natural look about you as the girls who'd been following me, so I took a picture and tracked you down via the Web." She paused. "I never would have guessed cheerleader."

"Shut up."

"Nice website, though."

I knew that class project would come back to bite me in the butt.

"Assuming you play by my rules, your cover is safe with me. And if you win, I'll even let you mind-wipe me, or whatever it is the government does to keep the ten of you its nasty little secret." Amelia somehow made those words sound incredibly reasonable.

"If we win what?" I tried to match her tone, but couldn't quite keep the frustration out of my voice. Being held at gunpoint sucked.

"Since you don't seem to like the word *game*, let's call it a challenge. I'm going to tell you who has the nanobots and what they're planning to do with them, and in the morning, you're going to share the news with your little team. Then, tomorrow afternoon, right before the action goes down, we're going to stop it. Like I said before, I don't particularly want anyone to die, and if we don't do something, someone will."

"You want to work with us?" This kept getting stranger and stranger.

"Not exactly." She looked down the barrel of the gun, straight at me. "Think of it more like a competition. I want the weapon. You guys want the weapon. Neither of us wants it used tomorrow."

Where were the men with the little white coats when you needed them? This was seriously insane. "You're actually challenging us to see who can get to the weapon first?"

She had to realize how little sense that made. If she wanted the weapon for herself, why even clue us in to begin with?

"That's the gist of it," Amelia said. "And stop looking at me like that. I'm not crazy. I'm *bored*, and the person who has the bots isn't exactly a rocket scientist. I could take him with one hand tied behind my back, but what fun would that be? Unfortunately, in addition to being no fun, that would also be stupid on my part. If I did steal the bots back and Peyton, Kaufman, and Gray found out that I'd been holding out on them, I'd be a dead girl. If, however, there's government involvement, then the firm will blame whatever goes down on them. They may not know about your team, but they know they're being watched, and they know there's an operative presence in Bayport. If there's even a hint of government involvement, do you think they'll suspect for even a second that the pretty little piece they hired to run their errands was involved?"

I seriously had to wonder if the fact that she was making sense to me meant that I was a few people short of a pyramid myself.

"How do I know you'll keep up your end of the bargain?" I asked. For all I knew, she'd already blown our cover to the firm. At this rate, I might not have to deal with homecoming after all. If Jack's father found out who I really was, if *Jack* found out who I really was . . .

"Simple. Tomorrow afternoon, we're going after the same thing. Beat me to it and take me down. After that, it's just a matter of lie detectors and memory-altering drugs."

"And if you win?" I had to ask, even though I couldn't imagine Amelia outsmarting the entire Squad. Again.

"If I win," she said, "you're just going to have to trust me. Either way, as long as you play by the rules, my lips are sealed, and your cover is safe. You can believe me or not, but I actually don't have anything against your team. People underestimate you." She smiled, wryly this time. "If there's one thing I understand, it's that. Who knows? If things had been different, maybe I'd be the one running around in one of those stupid skirts."

Was it wrong that I felt a vague feeling of kinship with her when she said the phrase *stupid skirts*?

"Tell me when and where," I said. "We'll be there." I really couldn't see how we had any other choice. If we sat back and did nothing, the weapon would either be deployed, or it would end up in Amelia's possession. Neither one of those was what I'd call a good outcome.

Amelia, keeping her eyes on mine, lowered the gun. "Tomorrow at three in Walford Park, Anthony Connors-Wright is going to kill his father, and he's planning on using the nanobots to do it. There's a political rally, and his father is in charge of security for the good senator. Anthony has some major Daddy Issues and doesn't have the foresight to realize that unless you pick the right target, the nanobots aren't that big a deal."

"Not that big a deal?" I repeated. "How many people at

this rally have to die before it's a big deal? If he releases the weapon—"

Amelia tilted her head to the side. "You really don't know, do you?"

"Know what?"

"There's a reason that so many terrorist groups wanted this thing," Amelia said, "and there's a reason Peyton, Kaufman, and Gray was funding the research. Biological weapons are a dime a dozen. If you want to attack a crowd, there are a half dozen toxic agents a lot less expensive than DNA-wiping nanobots. There aren't, however, many biological weapons that can be programmed to attack a certain individual."

I thought back on what Chloe had told me. The nanobots were revolutionary because of the amount of programming they could carry despite their microscopic size. We had assumed that future development on the programming front would concentrate on identifying the specific base pairs to be attacked within a DNA strand, but what if, instead, the programming identified the DNA to be attacked?

"Are you saying that you can let these things loose in a crowd, and they'll attack only one person?"

"It's called assassination, and yeah, that's what the guys at Peyton seem to think this does."

Suddenly, Chloe's magnet analogy took on a whole new dimension, because Amelia was standing there telling me that like a metal to a magnet, these nanobots would zero in on a single individual, based on their DNA. You let them loose in a crowd, and they set their sights on their preprogrammed target, leaving everyone else unharmed. I wasn't sure exactly how to rate this development. On the one hand, instead of killing thousands of people, this weapon would only kill one. On the other, that one person could be the president.

Suddenly, of the two negative outcomes I'd considered earlier, the one where Connors-Wright deployed the bots and killed his father was looking good, because if Amelia actually got a hold of this technology, there was no telling what she would do with it, or who she would sell it to. The Big Guys were going to freak, or at least, they would have, had I actually been able to tell them about it.

"I said what I came here to say." Amelia raised the gun again and backed toward my window. "You know the rules. Tonight, you tell no one. Tomorrow, Walford Park, three o'clock, winner takes all. You can do all the recon you want, but move in on the target before three, and you can consider your cover blown."

And then, with stealth that would have made Bubbles proud, she disappeared out the window and into the night.

CHAPTER 28

Code Word: Liberty

"I'm in, but I am NOT wearing one of those stupid skirts." I knew even as I said the words that I would, in fact, be wearing many a stupid skirt, and that something about this whole scenario wasn't quite right. I didn't have time to ponder it, though, because the next order of business was filling the last open slot on the Squad.

I listened and talked and made quips about Bitch Quotients, but even as my mouth moved, I knew that I couldn't be here again. I'd already done this. Today wasn't my first day on the Squad, and we'd already chosen April.

Hadn't we?

Kiki McCall. April Manning. Hayley Hoffman.

The names were flung back and forth and the other girls debated in slow motion. It was all "legacy this" and "aptitude for climbing" that. And just as we were getting ready to vote April in, I realized what was wrong with this whole situation—other than the obvious.

I wasn't wearing any clothes.

"Dance with me, Toby."

Jack? What was Jack doing in the Quad? He couldn't be

here. If he knew about us, we'd been exposed—permanently. More importantly, he couldn't be here—I WAS NAKED.

"Come on, Ev. Just one little dance."

DOES NO ONE BUT ME REALIZE HOW BAD THIS IS?

"Dance with him, Toby," the twins ordered, and then they were dancing—with my brother.

"Hey, Tobe," Noah said. "Looks like you're naked, huh?"

I tried to cover myself—I grabbed at papers and books and tried to position my hands to cover the worst of it, but there was no hope.

"Dance with me."

"Dance with him."

"Dance with him."

I DON'T WANT TO FRIGGING DANCE WITH ANYBODY! I WANT TO WEAR CLOTHES!

"Here," Lucy whispered. "Put this on."

Gratefully, I grabbed the clothes she shoved at me, but they disintegrated in my hands until all I was holding was a tiny silver tiara.

And then we weren't in the Quad anymore, and I was wearing clothes and Jack and I were dancing.

"What's that on your head?" he asked.

I reached up and tore the tiara out of my hair. I threw it to the ground, and when it hit, it burst into a million microscopic pieces, and all of a sudden, the pieces were crawling and moving and growing smaller by the second until they were invisible to the naked eye.

I could feel them on my skin, then, burrowing in.

My lungs stopped working. I lost all feeling in my legs. And for some godforsaken reason, Brooke's mother was making out with Mr. J in the corner, and Paris Hilton was standing there, watching.

My body was giving out, my face was contorting, and the last thing I heard before darkness seeped over my mind was a lisping "That's hot."

I bolted straight up and, my mind still all cloudy with unwanted images, I tried to assess the situation. I was lying in bed, fully clothed, it was pitch-black outside, and my necklace had gotten tangled up in my hair as I'd slept. It took me a few seconds to remember why I was sleeping in my clothes. I'd been so busy following the "rules" and NOT calling in my encounter with Amelia Juarez that I hadn't bothered with pajamas, and in the midst of my ceiling staring, I must have fallen asleep.

I blinked several times, trying to get the image of Brooke's mom and Mr. J out of my head. This was one of those times when I was severely glad that my dreams weren't prophetic, because *ew*. And also, the whole naked dreams thing was really starting to get to me. And Jack in the Quad? Hopefully, my subconscious wasn't trying to tell me anything with that one. I was also somewhat disturbed by the fact that in the past two days, Ryan Seacrest and Paris Hilton had both made cameos in my dreams. Before I'd joined the Squad, I hadn't even known who either of them was, and I would have preferred to wipe their existence on this planet from my consciousness altogether.

Groggily, I stumbled out of bed and across the room to my computer. I hit a few keys to wake it up, and then typed in my log-on password, wondering if anyone had discovered my previous night's hacking yet.

I had my answer soon enough. My remote access to the

Squad mainframe had timed out, and all of that information was gone, but the files I'd gotten from the Big Guys' computers were still there, exactly where I'd left them. Slowly and as meticulously as I could, given the fact that it was the middle of the night and I was still half-asleep, I deleted the files from my hard drive one by one, erasing any evidence that they'd ever been here.

I'd hacked into the Big Guys' database to find Amelia Juarez, and instead, she'd found me. I didn't need their files. I didn't need their help. All I needed was the rest of the Squad with me at Walford Park by three o'clock today. Together, the ten of us were a match for anyone. Amelia Juarez wanted competition?

We'd give her competition.

I shut down my computer, careful to disconnect it from the internet first. If the Big Guys hadn't realized I'd hacked them and hadn't hacked into my system to see what I knew, I wasn't going to give them the excuse or opportunity to do so from here on out.

I looked at my watch and then back at my bed and groaned. Five-thirty in the morning was going to come really early. And yet, with the way my throat was burning with secrets I couldn't tell until morning, there was a good chance that it just wouldn't come early enough. I climbed back into bed, and as I closed my eyes and pulled my pillow to the side, I spent a few seconds hoping that my subconscious didn't have anything else in store for me, and then I floated back off into a peaceful, dreamless sleep.

BEEP. BEEP. BEEP.

Unlike most mornings, I didn't bother cursing or slapping at my alarm. I picked it up and threw it against my wall. Hard. I smiled sadistically when it broke into three large pieces and several tinier ones.

Feeling somewhat vindicated, I climbed out of bed and headed directly for the shower. Most of the time, I showered at night, but I could tell already that this morning, coffee wasn't going to be enough to wake me up and prepare me for the day. Somehow, I didn't think Brooke was going to take everything I had to tell her very well.

I stripped off my clothes and stepped into the shower. I turned on the water and basked in the heat and steam and wonderfulness of it for a few minutes before my mind came fully online and I started making a game plan for today.

I needed to tell the others everything Amelia had told me. I needed to tell them about Anthony's plans, and about the fact that none of the TCIs were responsible for killing Jacob Kann. I needed to tell them about Amelia's challenge and the fact that our entire program was riding on our ability to win. More importantly, I needed to convince them to play by Amelia's rules, because they hadn't seen her the night before; I had, and I was one hundred percent positive that she wasn't bluffing. If we told the Big Guys what was going on, if we didn't show up this afternoon or if we brought any kind of backup with us when we did, she would expose us to Peyton, Kaufman, and Gray, and the Squad as we knew it would be over.

I could not imagine this discussion going particularly well. As I tried to figure out the best way of framing my proposition for the others, I finished scrubbing up, and noticed— with no little amount of annoyance—that there was *still* blue glitter on my chest. I attacked it with a nearby bottle of shower gel, and every time I thought I'd gotten it all, I'd shift positions, and light would dance off my skin in a new way.

Darn the twins and their stupid G.A.

After a few minutes, I gave up and turned off the water. I towel-dried off and absentmindedly scratched at my left shoulder, which was itching like crazy. I made a mental note to ask the twins what exactly they put in my Squad-issued shower gel. As a general rule, I tried to avoid using it and usually managed to shower using my own contraband bar soap, which I'd hidden before the twins' last visit so that they couldn't confiscate it, but this morning, I'd been too busy thinking—about my theory and about the glitter—to pay attention to the fact that I was using the gel.

"Okay," I muttered. "Time to wake up."

I wrapped a towel around my body and stumbled back to my room and into some clothing—a pair of low-rise designer jeans with rhinestones on the butt and legs, and a blue silk camisole top. I looked at my shoes and spent a few moments mourning the loss of any and all pairs of comfortable shoes I had once owned, save for the combat boots I'd managed to save from the wrath of Britt and Tiff.

I stared longingly at my old boots, but ultimately decided that today was not the day to start reclaiming my former identity. Today was about credibility. It was about convincing the others to do what I said. It was about breaking the rules for the right reasons, instead of the wrong ones. It was about the ten of us doing what had to be done.

With a wince, I threw on a pair of blue knee-length boots that matched the camisole, and then I grabbed my papers and began to stuff them into my schoolbag. Deciding that leaving sensitive information in with my math and English books probably wasn't a good idea, I rummaged around my room, found the Squad history book that I'd

260

been meaning to give back to Lucy since she'd given it to me, and stuffed the papers inside, before sticking the book in my bag and heading out the door.

I was halfway to practice before I realized I'd forgotten my coffee. This did not bode well for my future. At all.

"You're late." Brooke greeted me with two words the second I walked into the gym. She was a creature of repetition.

"Sorry." This time, I actually offered up a response, but Brooke seemed to sense the fact that I wasn't apologizing for being late so much as I was for the fact that I'd been part of that awful exchange with her mother the day before. Being Brooke, she didn't exactly welcome my sympathy.

"And what are you wearing?" She sounded so aghast that I glanced down, terrified for a split second that somehow, I'd forgotten to get dressed that morning and was not, in fact, wearing anything at all.

I breathed a literal sigh of relief when I saw the top of the camisole. "What's wrong with my clothes?" I asked. The one time I'd actually tried to be relatively fashionable and make a good cheer impression, I'd somehow violated an unwritten mandate of matching?

I really needed my coffee.

"You're not dressed," Brooke informed me, her lips pursed. "For practice."

She said the words like they were two separate sentences, and it took me a while to realize that they weren't, and another second or two after that to process what she was saying.

Everyone else in the gym was dressed in their regular

261

practice clothes—cheer shorts and sports bras and the occasional tank top. How was it that I'd worn cheer clothes the past two days, and we hadn't said so much as a *Go Lions*, but today, I got dressed for school, and all of a sudden it was bona fide practice time?

"Go change," Brooke ordered.

I had to remind myself that she didn't know what I knew, and that there were so many issues behind her captain complex that I couldn't really hold it against her, but her tone still rubbed me the wrong way.

"Listen," I started to say, and then I cut myself off and decided to opt for gestures instead. I tossed my hair over each shoulder and then tucked it behind my ears.

We need to go down to the Quad, I thought. I willed her to understand.

"No." She understood, and she wasn't buying.

"I like found some stuff out last night," I said, pitching my voice into a slight lilt and doing my best to speak in a ditz code she'd understand.

"Practice first," Brooke said. "Stuff later."

And right then, I almost had a meltdown, full-on Toby temper tantrum. I'd spent hours hacking and going through files, trying to come up with a way for her to save face, a way for us, as a Squad, to get the job done and do something right, and then I'd spent a good fifteen minutes with a gun in my face, and she wasn't even going to let me explain.

I felt a hand squeeze my shoulder gently, and I noticed Tara standing next to me. "Practice first," she said softly. "Unless it absolutely can't wait."

I thought about the fact that Amelia had made it quite clear that we weren't allowed to move in until this afternoon, and the fact that taking orders from a known hostile was just crazy enough that Brooke wouldn't need much of an excuse to dismiss it out of hand.

"Fine," I said evenly. "Practice first."

Brooke stalked over to her bag and tossed me a pair of blue shorts and a navy sports bra. "Go change."

I did as I was told. My shoes and socks were still in my locker, and I managed to pull off a pretty quick change, especially considering the fact that the atrocious boots on my feet weren't exactly easy to take off.

When I got back into the gym, the others were in formation for our newest cheer—the one we'd be debuting at the homecoming game on Friday. It was a simple triangle shape, with Brooke on point, the twins behind her, Chloe, Lucy, and Bubbles in the row behind them, and the rest of us in the back row. I was conveniently tucked away in the back row middle, where any mistakes I made would likely go unnoticed.

Under Brooke's sharp commands, we practiced our formation changes, going from our opening formation to spreading out in two lines of five, and finally, to our ending formation. This cheer was the first one they'd ever taught me that included stunting. I was just happy that I'd been relegated to the relatively benign position of "front spot," which basically meant that while the "bases" lifted the "flyer" up into the air, and the "back spot" held everything together and watched out for the flyer's safety—I just kind of stood there and looked pretty, adding in whatever extra balance I could.

The stunt itself was called a liberty. Originally, the plan had been to go for a "scorpion-liberty-heel-stretch, double full down," but ultimately, they'd scaled it back for a variety of reasons, not the least of which was the fact that even as a front spot, I could still send the whole thing crashing down. As much as my cheer skills had improved the past couple of weeks, when it came to life or death maneuvers on the field, no one trusted me farther than they could throw me, which, coincidentally, I'd found out the week before was surprisingly far. Don't ask.

We ran through the cheer again and again and again, sticking the stunts at the end each time, but there was always something about our performance that wasn't quite good enough for Brooke. There was nothing uglier than a cheerleader on the warpath.

An hour later, I was drenched in sweat, my voice was hoarse, and my armpits were killing me. At the end of my rope, I stepped forward, just as Brooke yelled, "Again!"

I met her gaze. I flipped my hair over each shoulder and then tucked it behind my ears, and I stared. This time, there wasn't any pity in my eyes. It was all determination. Our routine was flawless. We'd been working on it for weeks, and until the past couple of days, the spy end of our operation had been limited to training, which we did primarily in the afternoons. We'd practiced enough.

It was time to get down to business.

Brooke narrowed her eyes, and I could practically feel her need to impress her authority upon me, but a second later, Chloe, of all people, came to stand beside me. I could see the question in her eye.

You found something, didn't you? She asked silently.

I nodded, and then Chloe did something that surprised me. She took her hair out of its ponytail, and then flipped it—first over her right shoulder and then over her left, before nodding at Brooke and tucking her hair behind her ears. As a general rule, it was code for using the back stairs to get down to the Quad.

In this case, it was Chloe telling Brooke .that she thought we should go.

I expected the gesture to cause a major catfight. Brooke and Chloe were both really territorial, but whatever they'd talked about on the phone the night before must have temporarily softened the competition between them, because Brooke just sighed and inclined her head slightly.

"Water break," she said. "Back in ten minutes."

I read between the lines. We were going to the Quad, and I had exactly ten minutes to make my case.

CHAPTER 29
Code Word: Itchy

"So you think that based on the recommendation of a hostile TCI, who is, by the way, the lead suspect in yesterday's theft, that we should . . . what?" Brooke just stared at me. "Go to the park? Take down Connors-Wright? It's not like we have jurisdiction here. Not anymore."

"And besides," Tara said beside me, ever the voice of reason, "I'm sure our superiors are still keeping track of the remaining TCIs."

"Like they kept track of Amelia so well that she ended up in my bedroom?"

"You should have incapacitated her." Brooke's tone was stony.

I gave her my best innocent look. "This operation was a Do Not Engage."

"There is no operation!" Brooke was coming close to yelling, and even though the cheer-tone was still present in her voice, the veins in her forehead were starting to pop out, just a little.

"There should be an operation." I was implacable, or at least as implacable as I could be after the stunting torture

I'd just been through. "There *has* to be one. You're acting like Amelia just passed me this information, no strings attached. That's not what happened. You keep talking about her 'recommendation,' but that's not what we're dealing with here. This is blackmail."

"We have no way of knowing if this is a trap." Chloe kept her voice calm, but I could sense the antagonism coming off of her in waves. "For all we know, Peyton put her up to this to confirm some suspicion they had about *you*."

I couldn't miss the emphasis on the last word. Amelia had come to me. She had made me. She'd referred to the others, had alluded to our cheerleading outfits, but she hadn't explicitly identified them.

"This isn't a trap," I said. "And I don't think Amelia Juarez has ever really worked for anyone other than herself. She knows who we are. She could have gone straight to Peyton with it. She didn't." I looked at each person at the table. "And if we play her little game, she won't."

This was it. Either they believed me, or we were screwed.

"If she's telling the truth about Connors-Wright having the nanobots—and I think she is—then we can't afford not to go. Amelia's playing a dangerous game, and I honestly have no idea what she'll do with this technology, or who she'll sell it to, if we don't beat her to it."

Absolute silence greeted my words. If Amelia acquired the nanobots and sold them, then virtually unstoppable assassination technology would be in the hands of terrorists. First they'd study it and attempt to replicate it, but eventually, they'd use it, and somebody important to our national security would die.

I looked around the table, willing the others to snap out

of their horrified states and agree. When they all remained silent, I tried to prod them into talking. "Besides, what do we have to lose?"

Brooke snorted. "Says the girl who hacked into their system last night," she said. The message was clear: *I* didn't have much to lose. "Do you have any idea how pissed they're going to be about that?"

She was totally missing the point. Either we trusted that Amelia would play by the rules of her own sick little game, or we didn't, and if we didn't, we were beyond screwed anyway. "The Big Guys are going to be mad I hacked them? Allow me to pretend that I care." I paused.

"Not very convincing," Tara said mildly.

I shrugged. "That hurts, Tara. Right here." I tapped my heart, and Tara stifled a giggle.

"Tell you what, Toby." Brooke oozed condescension. "We'll look into Connors-Wright's father. I'd be surprised if he's even stationed in Bayport right now."

"And if he is?" I pressed.

"If he is, then we'll see."

At least she was saying "we" instead of "you." That seemed to indicate that she hadn't mentally kicked me off the Squad. Yet.

At the head of the table, Brooke typed in a few short commands and brought up the records for operative individuals currently residing in or visiting Bayport, and as the names flashed across the screen, it occurred to me that the elder Connors-Wright wasn't the only person we should be looking for.

"Whoever stole our target out from underneath us yesterday was good," I said. "Operative-level good, and if it's the same person, they managed to blow up Kann's car without leaving much of a trail. If it wasn't one of the TCIs, what are the chances that it was another operative?"

"A rogue operative?" Brooke was nothing if not skeptical. "You really think there's a rogue operative in Bayport? And that this rogue operative somehow knew about the weapon, piggybacked on our mission to steal it, and then, out of the goodness of his or her heart, gave it to Anthony Connors-Wright so he could waste it on his father?"

"You got a better explanation?"

Brooke stared me down. "Yes. Amelia played you like a fiddle, and for reasons we can't wrap our minds around, she wants us at that park this afternoon."

Her words and tone poked holes in my confidence, but as I replayed the scene with Amelia the day before, I couldn't deny the fact that I still believed Amelia, one hundred percent. She was crazy and she seriously needed to find a hobby that didn't involve becoming a criminal mastermind, but she hadn't lied to me. She hadn't needed to. Rather than making this argument again, I tried the tactic Amelia had taken with me the night before and went with incontrovertible logic. "What about the fact that Amelia couldn't have remotely detonated the bomb, that none of the TCIs could have?"

"We can check that out, too," Tara volunteered. "We'll have to go back over our video and audio surveillance. There's a chance we might not have noticed a remote-detonating mechanism."

"We should also recheck phone records," Chloe volunteered. "Any of the TCIs could have hired someone to detonate the bomb."

Darn them and their logic. Why hadn't I thought of it the night before? Why hadn't I poked holes in Amelia's claims the way the rest of the Squad was poking holes in mine? The only answer I could come up with was that every instinct I had told me that Amelia had been exactly what she'd seemed. Psychotic, but truthful. "Run the data all you want," I said, "but if it checks out, then we do something about it."

As I waited for a response, I brought my hand up to my left shoulder and scratched absentmindedly.

This really wasn't my morning: itchy shoulder, no coffee, antagonism aplenty, and nobody believed a word I was saying. I scratched harder.

"Ummmm . . . are you okay, Toby?" Lucy asked, her voice tentative. "You look . . . uncomfortable," she finished diplomatically.

"I'm fine," I said. "My shoulder itches."

Beside me, Tara leaned closer. "It's awfully red," she said.

"I've been scratching." This had to be the most inane cheerleading operative conversation that had ever taken place. Before it could move forward at all, I suggested we turn our attention to the flat-screen, and all of us began scanning the list for Connors-Wright's name.

Nothing.

I barely registered the I-told-you-so expression that flitted across Brooke's face. "Ummmm . . . Toby?"

"Ummmm . . . Lucy?" I answered.

"Your shoulder is kind of, you know, pink now."

Hadn't we already established this?

"Like neon pink."

I looked down. My shoulder was hot, hot pink. I might have handled that better on a day when I'd had some caffeine, but in retrospect, probably not.

"What the hell did you two put in that shower gel?" I sent the twins dart eyes.

"You actually used the shower gel?" Tiffany asked, impressed. "We thought you'd smuggled in some sucky soap or something, because your scent matrix has been kind of . . ."

Was she trying to say that I smelled? And, on a related note, did she want me to kill her? These were very important questions, but they weren't nearly as important as the one I'd just asked.

"Shoulder," I prompted. "Pink. Why?"

"It's a security thing," Brittany said. "The shower gel has these special chemical thingies in it, and they react and turn different colors for different things." She turned to her twin. "What's pink again?"

"Something electronic, I think," Tiff said, wrinkling her nose. "Like maybe a bug?"

"No," Brittany said. "Bug is blue, remember?"

"Oh yeah."

"It has to be a chip of some kind then, right?"

They seemed to be approaching this whole conversation with the same solemnity with which they considered fall colors. No more, no less.

Brooke, however, snapped to attention. "Somebody get a scalpel. Now."

If you've never heard a cheerleading captain speak these words, then you have never felt true terror. A scalpel? And just what was she planning on scalpeling? Because she had to know that I wasn't letting her come anywhere near me with something of the sharp and pointy variety.

Lucy with the knives had been more than enough.

"Got one!" Somehow, I wasn't surprised that Miss

Knives-Are-Interesting had a scalpel handy. I wasn't going to ask about that. I really didn't want to know.

"Who do you want cutting it out?"

"Cutting what out? There will be no cutting! None. Lucy, step away from the scalpel."

Lucy rolled her eyes and handed the scalpel to Tara.

"You have a chip in your shoulder," Tara said softly, like she was talking a stray puppy out from underneath a car. "Most likely a tracking chip of some kind, just below the skin. The shower gel reacts to certain alloy metals and electrical currents. That's why you're itching, and that's why your shoulder's pink. You've been tagged."

Okay, now this day officially sucked.

"We have to take it out, Toby. For all we know, someone may be tracking you to the Quad as we speak."

I didn't respond. I was too busy thinking. There was a chip in my shoulder. A chip in my freaking shoulder. A freaking chip in my freaking shoulder. Someone was tracking my movements.

"*Amelia* may be tracking you to the Quad as we speak." Brooke amended her original statement.

"She never touched me. She never even came close to me. She was across the room the entire time. She couldn't have done this."

In the privacy of my own mind, I came up with an alternative theory. Not one, but two of the missions I'd gone on in the past two days had gone badly, both times because of the presence of a third party. Someone had blown up Kann's car, and someone had stolen the nanobots. I'd wondered how the intruder could possibly be an unknown player, how they could have known to come to Ross's lab, and now I knew.

Whoever the figure in black was, I'd led them straight to the TCIs. Straight to the weapon. Some independent operative had tagged me to piggyback on our operation, and now that person had some seriously scary technology. And, to add salt to the wound, if I'd used the twins' stupid shower gel before now, we might have discovered this fact before we'd lost the nanobots and before the aforementioned figure had sold them to Anthony Connors-Wright.

"Got it." Tara's words snapped me back to reality, and I realized that she'd already made a small incision in my skin, so small that it barely bled and didn't hurt until I realized that it should have.

"Chloe." Brooke didn't say more than Chloe's name, but our gadget girl snapped into motion, and carefully bagged the chip, leading me to question whether or not she typically carried evidence bags around in her sports bra.

"I'm on it," Chloe said. "I'll have the sample analyzed by lunchtime at the latest." She smiled half of an ironic grin. "Guess our stunting technique is going to have to wait."

"Our stunting technique is already flawless," Brooke said. "Right now, we have other priorities."

Sure, I thought. I got blackmailed by a TCI, and Brooke was all about practicing our cradles, but the moment it turned out that I had a tracker chip in my shoulder, she admitted that we'd already outpracticed ourselves. It figured.

Everyone else was so concentrated on the chip that I was the only one who noticed when the data on the screen in front of us changed. A second, automatic search had just revealed that Anthony Connors-Wright's father was in Bayport, protecting a senator who was scheduled to speak at four that afternoon.

Without a word, Chloe set about examining the chip from

my shoulder, and the others went back over our files, looking for evidence that Amelia had led me astray.

Then one by one, they reported back, confirming everything Amelia had told me.

I took in the information and came to my own conclusion. "Game on."

CHAPTER 30
Code Word: Issues

I'd finally talked the others into stepping up and accepting Amelia's challenge, but nothing I'd said could dissuade Brooke from trying to get authorization to do so. As she pointed out, Amelia had said that we couldn't tell our superiors what she'd told us, or what we were doing. She never said we couldn't make up a reason why we needed to be reinstated on the case.

"Hi . . . Mom? It's me. Listen, there's been a development on the thing." Brooke paused, and walked away from the rest of us a little. "You know, the *thing* thing."

I could hear the voice from the other end of the phone, but couldn't make out the words. Based on whatever Mrs. Camden said, Brooke dropped the cheer-tone in her voice and switched over to operative mode without so much as a bat of her eyelashes. "We've reanalyzed all of the data we collected during the course of this case, and we have reason to believe that somebody should still be keeping an eye on—"

This time, the voice from the other end was louder, and I wondered what exactly it was that finally got a verbal rise out of Brooke's mother, despite her I'm-just-a-sweet-PTA-mom façade.

"We think there may be more to this weapon than previously realized, and that it would behoove us to have as much surveillance on the TCIs as possible until . . ."

Brooke frowned as she listened to the other end. "What do I want you to do? I want you to get us back on this, or short of that, to tell your bosses that we could be looking at something major here."

Hearing Brooke talk to her mother that way cheered me up significantly. She'd just lain down and taken it the day before. At least now she was arguing.

"Yes, I'm aware that the votes for homecoming are cast tomorrow, Moth-er." Brooke broke the last word down into two syllables. "But—"

More talking from the other end of the line.

"What's wrong with my hair?" Brooke asked plaintively. Then she let out a breath. "What about the extra security?" she asked. "Can you at least . . . no, I'm not going to hire a bunch of freshman boys to pretend to be pirates. I don't care how effective you think that would be. Are you even listening to me?"

I think everyone present knew the answer to that question was a resounding no.

"In that case," Brooke said tersely, "I have to go. First period's getting ready to start, and I have to look my best."

And with those words, Brooke hung up the phone. "She wouldn't listen to a word I said, and apparently, all of their resources have been relocated to the airport. They got an anonymous tip this morning."

I was willing to bet a lot of money the tip in question

had come from Amelia herself. This was her game, and she was making damn sure that we played it her way.

"So they wouldn't even sign off on us tailing a TCI they think is harmless?"

Brooke shook her head.

"Can't you go over her head on this?" I asked. "I mean, we could contact the real Big Guys."

I couldn't bring myself to think of Brooke's mom as the end-all-be-all of the Big Guy decision task force. She and Brooke had so many mommy-daughter issues clouding their relationship that it was practically raining passive aggression.

"I could," Brooke said, "but if we go over her head and it turns out to be nothing . . ." She trailed off. "And besides, if I were to officially report in, I'd probably have to clue them in to the fact that your position has been compromised. Twice."

Once by Amelia, once by whoever had tagged me. When she put it that way, I decided that contacting the Really Big Guys probably wasn't a good idea. Brooke had refrained from mentioning the chip literally in my shoulder to her mother, probably as a subtle way of avenging her hair against her mother's criticism. Eventually, she'd tell someone about it, but I knew enough about the way this system worked to know that it would be in my best interest if no one knew that I'd been tagged until after we'd isolated the person who'd seen past my cover, which was now next on my To Do list after taking down Connors-Wright and Amelia, in that order.

Otherwise, I might not have to worry about revisiting all of my homecoming issues by the time prom rolled around, because if my cover was permanently blown, I wouldn't still be on the Squad. If there even was a Squad.

"Even if we take Amelia down, if we don't find the person who stole the weapon in the first place, I'm screwed." There wasn't a person in the room who hadn't already come to this realization, which was saying something, since Bubbles and the twins perpetually had their heads in the clouds. "And the only lead we have on that person is the bomb, the list of operatives in Bayport, and the fact that there aren't many people in this world who can touch me and walk away in one piece."

"We'll deal with that later. Right now, we have to concentrate on Amelia," Chloe said, "because if the unthinkable happens and it turns out that you actually aren't an idiot and Amelia was being straight with you, then we really don't have a choice. The Big Guys aren't going to stop Connors-Wright from using the weapon, and they're not going to stop Amelia from stealing it. Besides, if Amelia steals the weapon, who's to say Connors-Wright won't go ahead with his plan anyway and just shoot somebody?"

The others nodded in agreement—every single one of them. I chose to believe that they were agreeing with Chloe's general assessment, and not the tone with which it was delivered. No one on the Squad wanted to see what would happen if Anthony worked out his Daddy Issues in a very public, very violent way. It went against the unspoken moral code of cheerleading operatives. Rumor mongering? Morally acceptable. Murder and mayhem—not so much.

"We have to do something." Brooke said the words quietly, as if she wished she wasn't saying them. Despite the fact that she'd tried to stand up to her mother, this was taking

Brooke Independence to a completely unprecedented degree. If things went badly, it was her head on the chopping block, and I couldn't think of anything worse than knowing that your own mother would be the executioner.

Brooke breathed out heavily, and then she seemed to realize that she was breaking her own rule and showing way more weakness (if by weakness, you meant actual feeling) than she ever had before. "New plan," she said. "Zee and I are going after Connors-Wright. Amelia said we couldn't take him down until three. She didn't say anything about tailing him. Chloe, you find out whatever you can about the chip, and we'll keep you on constant radio contact. Britt and Tiff, I want you two to get as close as you can to the politician Connors-Wright's father is guarding. A bodyguard will never be far away from his charge, and the good senator doesn't have any public appearances scheduled before the press conference. I'm sure he'll make an exception for his local fan club, especially when the fan club is . . ." Brooke just gestured to the twins.

They weren't the prettiest girls on the Squad. They didn't have Lucy's earnestness or Zee's exotic look, or even Brooke's flawlessly symmetrical face, but they knew how to work what they did have. They were blond, they were built, and they were (I had been told) five times hotter together than either of them was apart. There wasn't a politician alive who could resist the Sheffield twins.

"What about the rest of us?" Tara asked.

"Chloe will keep you guys apprised of the situation," Brooke said. "Unless you hear otherwise, plan to be at the park by no later than three. I'll send you guys exact orders once we manage to do a little recon, but our priorities are getting the weapon and getting Amelia. After that, we'll deal with finding out who planted the tracking chip in Toby's shoulder—assuming it wasn't Amelia herself."

How many times did I have to say "she didn't touch me" before it sank in?

"Lucy, we're going to need every long-range paralyzing weapon you've got. I want Amelia unconscious the second we spot her. It'll have to be something she's not expecting, so get creative. Britt, Tiff, before you guys leave to find the senator, I need you to work your magic on Amelia's picture and give us a rundown of the potential disguises you think would be most effective for her to use. We can't underestimate her, and that means assuming she's as good as you are. Chloe, anyone who comes with you after school needs to be in deep cover. I don't care if you have to dress up like boys—don't let Amelia recognize you."

A buzzer went off then, letting us know that first period was a mere ten minutes away from starting. Without a word, Chloe headed off to her lab, and the twins went to theirs. Zee hung back with Brooke, and the others slowly drifted off toward the locker room, to get changed and get ready for class.

How did they get used to this? Knowing what I knew, how was I supposed to make it through a day at high school, watching three o'clock get closer and closer by the second?

"Toby." Brooke said my name, and I turned around to face her. Was this the part when I said thank you? Or maybe the part when she did?

"You can't go." Apparently, this was the part when she issued more orders.

"Can't go where?" I asked, truly baffled.

"This afternoon. Even if we need every man we've got, even if all the others go, you can't."

I stared at her. I was the one who'd uncovered this whole thing, and now she was telling me I couldn't be a part of it? What a suckfest.

"You've been ID'd," she said. "Whoever this agent is—assuming it's not Amelia—he knows who you are. You'd lead him straight to the rest of us, and there's no way for us to know for sure that you're completely clean. You'll have to go through a complete body scan later, to make sure there aren't any more plants on you, but there's no way I can pull that off without raising some major questions with our superiors. We can't afford to have them questioning us right now."

Damn it. Since when had Brooke become so . . . so . . . reasonable?

"So what am I supposed to do seventh period?" I asked. When I'd first joined the Squad, the biggest perk wasn't the royal treatment I got from the whole school. It was the fact that I was henceforth excused from gym class for seventh-period practice.

"Well," Brooke said, smiling in a way that had me prepping myself for bad, bad news. "We still need to paint the banners for the game on Friday . . ."

Double damn. Damn to the nth degree. Everyone but me was going to go out and save the day, and I was going to be stuck in the practice gym by myself painting banners for a football game.

I forced myself to look at the bright side. If worse came to worse, I could always entertain myself by coming up with some creative banner sayings.

Zee took one look at the expression on my face and shook her head. "Stick with *Go Bayport*," she advised. "Or maybe *Beat Hillside*. No obscenities. No sarcasm. And nothing that even remotely suggests that the football team has the combined IQ of a spider monkey."

She knew me too, too well, but I have to confess—the spider monkey part had never even crossed my mind. Zee may have misjudged Amelia, but there are times when her genius really shines through.

CHAPTER 31

Code Word: Betrayal

By the time I managed to wrangle my way back into the inarguably uncomfortable boots, I didn't have much time to desweatify myself before heading to first period, and for once, the twins weren't there to do it for me, and everyone else was so busy doing their own last-minute primping that no one seemed to notice that for the first time since I'd joined up, I looked somewhat less than Godlike.

Knowing better than to press my luck, I snuck out of the locker room before anyone had a chance to do damage control on my barely made-up face, and for the first time in weeks, I felt like myself. I mean, yeah, I was wearing God Squad clothes, and yes, my hair was still God Squad hair, and practice had done nothing to dampen my Bounce Index, but I wasn't perfect, and I didn't look it.

I didn't look like the old me, either, but it was a start.

Half of me expected to run into Jack on my way to first period, and I purposefully didn't pay much attention to where I was walking, tempting fate to re-create the interaction we'd shared yesterday. And the day before. In just two days, things between us had gotten so much more physical, so much more intense.

Then, just as I was reaching up to open the door to my geometry class, I came to the single most horrible realization of my life. Things had cooled down between Jack and me right after our first kiss. I'd been sending him back-off signals, and he'd respected that, even if he'd done it in a way that let me know that he wouldn't stay away forever. And then, at the pep rally, he'd called off the truce and come up to me.

He'd touched me.

Had he touched my shoulder? Had he squeezed me while we were kissing? Had he planted something in my skin while my mind was too occupied with his lips to notice or care?

I hadn't spent much time thinking about how I'd gotten tagged, or who might have tagged me, but really, there weren't that many options. I went to school, I went to practice, and I went home. Since I was pretty sure I could rule out Noah and my parents, and since the other girls had no reason to tag me, that left either school or some random interaction I'd had in transit.

And if someone at school had tagged me . . .

The thought ate at me, chewed at my skin and my stomach, and crawled up the back of my spine until I thought I was literally going to puke up all of the coffee I hadn't drunk that morning. Except for the Squad, Bayport High wasn't exactly a cesspool of secret identities. There was only one other person at this school who could have possibly had access to the kind of technology that Tara had cut from my skin that morning.

Jack.

I'd thought it myself. Of everyone at our school, he was the one person most likely to figure out our secret, and he was the one whose discovery would devastate our operation the most.

I just hadn't realized how much it would devastate me.

"Thinking about me, Ev?"

For a second, I thought I was imagining his voice, but then his hands were on my neck, and he was leaning in for the kiss.

I don't exactly remember what happened next. It's all a little fuzzy, but the next thing I knew, Jack was on his back halfway down the hall, and my blood was pumping the way it only did after a fight. Most guys probably would have reacted poorly to that kind of violence, but Jack wasn't most guys. He just climbed to his feet and held up his hands. "I come in peace," he said, "and I swear to you, it wasn't my idea."

That was less than comforting. He'd used me. He'd pretended . . . The things he'd said! The way he'd made me . . . And the whole time he was . . .

I couldn't seem to put a whole sentence together, even in the sanctity of my own mind. It didn't occur to me—even for a second—that when we'd first met, our positions had been reversed. I'd been the one using him. The first time we'd kissed had been in his father's office, on the tail end of my part in our first mission of the season.

"It wasn't your idea," I repeated dumbly. "So whose was it? Your father's?"

I was vaguely aware of the fact that we had an ever-growing audience. It's funny how quickly you can get used to that given the right circumstances.

"My father's?" Jack repeated incredulously. "No offense,

Ev, but I don't think dear old dad really cares whether you win homecoming queen or not."

Homecoming queen?

The incredible sense of betrayal in my gut faltered, but I had to remind myself that this guy was a player. He'd made a life out of being on top, and you didn't get there—guy or girl—without knowing the rules of pretense as well as every girl on the Squad did. Jack had explained some of them to me himself.

He was pretending. He had to be.

"If you want to permanently injure someone," Jack said, still keeping a safe distance, "I'd suggest venting your anger on Noah. This whole thing was his doing, not mine. He didn't exactly ask for my permission first."

Noah? Homecoming and Noah? The wheels in my head were turning slowly.

"What did Noah do?" I asked.

"You're going to make me actually say it?" Jack asked. "Come on, Toby. Have a heart. You already kicked my ass."

I had to admire the fact that he could admit it so freely.

Wait, I thought. No. I did not have to admire that! I didn't have to admire ANYTHING about Jack Peyton. Not now. Not when I wasn't at all convinced that he hadn't used me to get to the Squad.

"If I come closer, are you going to go all kung fu on me again?" Jack asked slowly.

My eyes narrowing into teeny-tiny slits, I shrugged. I wasn't about to make any promises.

"Guess I'll have to take my chances then," he said, and then he was by my side again, whispering into my ear. "Anyone ever tell you that you're really cute when you're proving yourself strangely deadly?"

I bristled at the word *cute* and the way he said it. He was taunting me. I'd thrown him clear across the hallway, and now, he was taunting me. He was either very brave or very stupid.

Or maybe, he was perfect.

I tried to keep the sappy thoughts out of my head. I tried not to be affected by how close the two of us were standing. Batting 0-for-2, I tried to remember that nothing he'd said was a guarantee that my original assumption about his guilt was wrong.

About that time, my brother came sauntering down the hall, his arms full of what appeared to be life-sized cutouts.

I looked from Noah to Jack and then back again, just as Noah deposited one of the cutouts in front of the classroom across the hall. It was Jack, in all of his A-list glory, and Noah had pasted a sign into his cutout hand.

JACK PEYTON IS HOT. TOBY KLEIN IS HOTTER. VOTE TOBY AND JACK FOR HOMECOMING COURT.

Noah went merrily on his way down the hall, ignoring me, the look in my eyes, and the fact that Jack had started laughing. The bell rang then, and our audience groaned. Unlike the two of us, the others might actually get into trouble for being late for class. I turned to go to my geometry classroom, but Jack pulled me back toward him.

"For the record," he said, no hint of a smile on his otherwise perfect face, "I still think Mr. Corkin is the hottest."

"For the record," I said, "if I find out you had anything to do with those cutouts, I'm going to kick your ass. Again."

"So noted."

And that was that.

287

CHAPTER 32
Code Word: Girl Talk

By lunchtime, I had concluded that, contrary to my previous belief, that was not that. I felt like Jack was being real with me, but the logical part of my mind kept telling me that I was being an idiotic, emotional, pathetic girly-girl who wanted everything to be flowers and puppy dogs in Crushville. I couldn't ignore the facts. Jack did have access to technology like the tracking chip, and there was no denying the fact that I'd had more physical interaction with him the past few days than I'd had with pretty much anyone my whole life. Amelia couldn't have planted the chip on me. Besides Jack, I just couldn't see who that left as far as suspects went.

I couldn't just waltz into the cafeteria and sit down at our table and play the popularity game with Jack, Chip and the Chiplings, Lucy, Tara, April, and Bubbles. I may have managed to increase my stealth factor significantly the past few weeks, but I still wasn't that smooth, and more to the point, I just wasn't sure I could take it.

So instead, I opted out of lunch and headed for the gym. I doubled back twice to make sure no one was following me, and then I went into the girls' locker room, and after jumping through eight million security hoops, I made my way down to the Quad.

It was quiet, more so than I'd ever seen it. Our flat-screen was turned off, and I couldn't even hear the ghosts of conversations we'd had about training, missions, or who liked who.

"Please tell me you weren't stupid enough to come down here during the day."

I turned and found Chloe giving me one of those patented Chloe Larson looks that made me feel so loved and so special and like everything was right with the world.

I snorted. I couldn't even think that last bit with a straight face.

"Seriously," Chloe said. "Do you have any idea how idiotic it is to just waltz into the Quad in the middle of the day when you know that your cover has been broken? I mean, are you trying to send out engraved invitations to our secret underground lair, or has your brain just stopped working altogether?"

When she put it that way, she actually had a point.

"I think I know who tagged me," I said. "And he's occupied."

Jack was eating lunch with the others, probably wondering where I was and why I'd abandoned him to suffer through the inanity of an A-list lunch on his own.

"Shouldn't you be worrying about Amelia?" I asked, trying to distract Chloe from her dogged criticism by mentioning the reason she was in the Quad during school hours—laying the groundwork for the massive mission she was coordinating that afternoon.

"You know who tagged you, and he's occupied," Chloe

said, repeating my earlier words and not allowing me to sidetrack her. "He as in who?"

I chose not to answer. My suspicions about Jack were my own. I wasn't about to let her know that maybe he didn't like me as much as everyone had thought. I could do without seeing Chloe break into a cheer-dance of victory.

"Because I know you're not talking about him as in Jack," Chloe continued.

Was I really that obvious?

"You really are *special*, aren't you?" Chloe asked. Her tone left absolutely nothing unclear about her meaning. She shook her head, words flying out of her mouth as she did. "I can't even believe I'm doing this," she said. "I can't even believe that I'm . . . never mind," she said.

"What?"

"Just follow me," she snapped.

Completely bewildered, I actually followed her "suggestion."

Two minutes later, Chloe deactivated the security on her lab door and threw it open. "No actual penetration of our perimeter," she said out loud. "Klein just wandered in unannounced." It took me a moment to realize that she was talking to someone other than me. "Your position holding steady?"

"Affirmative," came the reply. I tried to identify where exactly the speakerphone, or communicator or whatever, was, but gave up. Chloe's lab was a mess of accessories, wires, gadgets, gizmos, and clutter. I wouldn't even know where to begin looking.

Satisfied that Brooke and Zee were doing fine in the field, Chloe turned back to me. Rolling her eyes for no apparent reason whatsoever, she picked up a sheet of paper and handed it to me. "It's an analysis of the chip," she said. "It isn't the kind that Peyton uses. Trust me—we've run into their tech before, and this isn't it—it isn't nearly state-of-the-art enough. The good folks at Peyton, Kaufman, and Gray would spit on this chip. It's practically ancient."

I breathed in and out, in and out, letting this information sink in and trying not to let any of my myriad of emotions fly across my face. Chloe didn't need to see how relieved I was that Jack wasn't a part of this. Scratch that—nobody needed to know how relieved I was that Jack wasn't a part of this.

"Do you want to know the truth about Jack Peyton?" Chloe asked, her words coming out in a rush. "The truth is this. You're using him, just like Brooke used him, just like I used him—and just like the two of us, you're starting to fall for him. The difference is that Jack knew that we were using him—he just thought it was all about popularity for us, but in all of his teen boy wisdom, he's decided that you're *different*." Chloe spat out the word.

She was putting into words everything I'd been afraid of, and everything I'd tried not to hope for. Jack wasn't using me. Jack liked me. I was using him.

"Do you know why Brooke and Jack broke up?" Chloe asked suddenly.

"Chlo," Brooke's voice came over the hidden speakers. "Back off."

"Because falling for your mark is the last thing you're supposed to do," Chloe said. "They started off using each other, and then . . . boom . . . there were real feelings involved, and Brooke's mom pulled the plug."

"Chloe!"

"And do you know why Jack and I broke up?" Chloe said softly.

I took a wild guess. "Because you fell for him?"

"No," Chloe said. "Because he wasn't over Brooke."

"Chloe, you need to shut up. Now."

"Don't you have a hostile to be watching?" Chloe huffed. "Don't make me mute you."

It was the first time I'd ever seen Chloe issue a direct threat in Brooke's direction, and for some reason, it made me smile. The two of them weren't acting like part of some crazy hierarchy that I'd never really understood. They weren't captain and cocaptain or commanding officer and second in command. They were friends who had a common ex, and Chloe wasn't about to shut her mouth.

"He's over Brooke now," Chloe said. "And he's sure as hell over me. He's all yours, and you're actually stupid enough to think that he's the one playing you."

"Chloe. Shut. Up." Brooke was clearly on the verge of losing it.

Chloe made good on her threat and turned the communicator off. Given the broader situation, that seemed a little bit shortsighted, but I was the one who'd banged Amelia's rules into their heads over and over again: nothing could happen until three. We could watch, and we could wait, but we couldn't make a move.

"Is there anything else you want to know about Jack Peyton?" Chloe hissed.

"Yes." The simplicity and unexpectedness of my answer took the wind out of Chloe's sails. "What do you know about his uncle?"

"We're not having this conversation," Chloe said.

"We should have had this conversation weeks ago," I countered. "Now, the Squad's cover is in danger, and my cover is pretty much on the critical list. I have no idea what's going to happen next, and I want you to tell me the truth."

Chloe pressed her lips together, hard, but somehow, her expression looked more nervous than angry. "Jack's uncle is one of the Big Guys," she said finally. "So is Brooke's mom."

She stopped speaking then, as if she'd told me something I hadn't already known. "And Brooke doesn't know about Jack's uncle," I said, hoping that would prod her into telling me something new.

"I never told her," Chloe said. "It happened our sophomore year, back when Jack and Brooke were going out. The two of us were in Brooke's room, and I went downstairs to grab some cookies. There was a man there, and he and Brooke's mom were talking. She called him Peyton. I knew it wasn't Jack's dad, and then I recognized his voice—how could I not?—but I didn't really process what he was telling her."

"And what was that?" I asked.

Chloe took a deep breath, like she couldn't possibly have enough oxygen in her lungs to divulge this secret. "He said that history had a way of repeating itself, and that Brooke's mom knew better than anyone how ugly these things could be. I had no idea what he was talking about."

That made two of us.

"That was the night Brooke found out she had to break up with Jack." Chloe shook her head, as if trying to shake off the fact that she'd mentioned any of this to me at all. "If you tell anyone I told you this, *anyone*, I will kill you, and I will make it look like an accident. Are we clear?"

"Crystal," I said, unsure whether to take Chloe's threat literally or with a grain of high school drama salt. Since I didn't plan on mentioning this to anyone ever, it didn't really matter.

Refusing to meet my eyes, Chloe leaned forward and flipped the communicator back on. "Sorry," she said. "Technical malfunction."

"Connors-Wright still hasn't made a move," Zee said from the other side of the feed, "and there's no sign of Amelia. I'm uploading my footage of the park so we can divide it up and decide the most likely angle of entries for our hostiles."

Chloe glanced at me, and I nodded. If they were talking entry angles, this afternoon really was going to happen, and since Chloe couldn't exactly leave the audio feeds behind long enough to do a cameo upstairs, it was up to me to pass the message along.

"I'm going back up now," I said.

Chloe huffed.

I thought about thanking her for reading me the riot act about Jack and telling me a secret she'd kept from Brooke for years, but decided against it. This was Chloe, and she didn't want to hear it from me.

CHAPTER 33
Code Word: Answers

By the time I made my way back up to the cafeteria, my presence had definitely been missed. The other girls' eyes registered my entrance the moment I walked into the room, and the decibel level of conversation in general went up a couple of notches when the rest of the school saw me.

I was going to go out on a limb and guess that my . . . errrr . . . tumultuous relationship with Jack and my . . . creative display of "affection" that morning was the reason why. Luckily, people didn't get a chance to stare at me for long. One guess as to why.

"Four score and seven years ago, our forefathers brought forth on this nation the sacred tradition of homecoming."

First the homecoming pirates, and now this? Where was Noah coming up with this stuff?

"That one girl might be named queen." Noah paused for just a moment, and it occurred to me that he hadn't prepared a speech and that perhaps he was having more difficulty with his Abraham Lincoln persona than he had foreseen. Unsure exactly what to say, he continued babbling on, his voice getting louder by the moment. "You!

You there!" he yelled, pointing to a random guy who'd just gotten up to throw his trash away. The guy in question couldn't decide whether or not everyone thought Noah's outbursts were secretly funny, or whether they were just weird, but when Noah called on him again, he answered.

"Uhhh . . . yeah?"

"Do you swear to tell the truth, the whole truth, and nothing but the truth, so help you God?"

"Uhhhh . . . God?" the kid asked.

"Answer the question!" Noah boomed, sounding for all the world like a courtroom lawyer.

"I guess so," the kid said finally.

"Who are you voting for?" Noah asked.

"Uhhhhhh . . ." The kid clearly wasn't sure how to answer the question, but none of Noah's freshman friends suffered from any such doubt.

"To-by! To-by! To-by!"

For the love of all things good and coffeelike, I thought. The chant was catching on.

"For truth! For justice! For the American way! Vote Toby Klein!"

"Actually," I said, speaking up for the first time during one of Noah's little performances. "Please don't." I tried to phrase this in terms that wouldn't compromise whatever cover I still had left after the last couple of days, which meant I couldn't tell the entire student body that I would prefer to eat my own tongue than wear a tiara at that stupid dance.

"I'm just a sophomore," I said. "And there are four seniors nominated, even though none of them are here today, because they're . . . posing for *Seventeen* magazine. . . ."

The lie seemed like the kind of thing everyone would buy, and by the time the magazine actually came out, another rumor would have jumped to the forefront of the gossip mill. "Even though the seniors aren't here right now," I said, "I know that it would mean a lot to them if you voted for someone who'd been at and loved this school for four years. So don't vote for me. Vote for one of them."

Done with my speech, I walked to our table and sat down, mentally daring any of the others to comment on anything I'd just said. The girls knew me well enough to keep quiet. Chip didn't know anything or anyone well enough to do the same.

"That was kind of cool," he said. "You're a really strange girl."

All things considered, it was probably the nicest thing Chip had ever said to me. For the first time since I'd met him, I didn't feel even slightly compelled to castrate him with a butter knife.

"Where'd you go?" Bubbles asked me.

"I had to check on the banner paint," I said. "I thought we left it in Brooke's car, but we didn't."

"Banner paint?" Jack asked. "Really."

"Yes," I deadpanned. Then I turned to the other girls. "About the thing. The thingy-thing after school?" The other girls nodded.

"Yeah huh?" Lucy asked.

"It's like thinging," I said. I probably could have thought of a better word to tell them that our plan this afternoon was still on, but a better word might have actually made sense to someone other than the five of us, so I didn't bother.

"And FYI, Chip," I added. "If you don't stop trying to look down my shirt, I'm going to castrate you with a butter knife."

This time, Jack's grin was sincere. The others just laughed off my threat, though Chip's laughter definitely fell under the heading of *nervous*.

Sometimes, in the midst of all of this, it felt good to be me.

The rest of the period flew by in a blur, and I managed to make it through the rest of the day without causing a single scene, which was impressive given my track record. The closer seventh period got, the quieter and more withdrawn I got, and the less I thought about Jack and the more my mind played over every piece of data I'd encountered during my hacking spree the night before.

If things had gone differently, I'd have been getting ready to go out into the world and fight the good fight. I'd have been the one taking Amelia Juarez down, the one making sure that Anthony Connors-Wright didn't unleash the bots. If we hadn't been taken off this case to begin with, I might have been tracking down the person who'd stolen the bots in the first place, the person who had tagged me.

If I'd been part of our last line of defense against biotechnological warfare and the dangerous precedent that Ross's invention could set, my adrenaline would already be pumping. I would have barely been able to sit still in my seat. As it was, I felt drained. Empty.

Uneasy.

What if I'd been wrong about Amelia? What if I was missing something? What if the other girls went and something happened to one of them? What if Amelia won?

Under the influence of the what-if game, I didn't even

register the occasional barb that Mr. Corkin threw my way during history, and during computer science, I just stared at my screen. By the time seventh period came around, all I could think about was the fact that despite all of the what-ifs and everything that had happened in the last few days, the one feeling that I couldn't shake was that I hated being left out.

It was a strange thing for me to realize. I'd never been part of a group before, let alone a team. I'd always been a loner. I'd never liked sitting on the sidelines, but that wasn't what was getting to me about this. It was the fact that all of the others were part of something, and I wasn't.

For the first time, I considered what it would really mean if we couldn't figure out who had tagged me. If there was a person out there who knew my identity, and we didn't catch them, I wouldn't be able to go on any more missions. I wondered briefly if they'd replace me and thought about what it would be like to go back to being the old me. I wouldn't have to worry about wearing the right clothes or saying the right things. I could see if Jack really liked me for me, or if part of the draw was who and what I appeared to be, even though he knew better than to believe a word of it. I wouldn't have to feel guilty about using the only guy who'd ever kissed me.

I would never have to go to a pep rally again.

The twins would stop fussing over my makeup, and I could go back to using regular soap, and I wouldn't have to take any more crap from Chloe or deal with the fact that Lucy was way, way too perky before noon. Zee would stop psychoanalyzing me, and Brooke's totalitarian tendencies would be none of my concern. I'd never fully figure out what the deal was with Jack's family.

Tara wouldn't be my partner.

I wouldn't have a partner.

I wouldn't have a team.

Life would suck.

In my head, the whole thing wasn't laid out sequentially. The thoughts hit me all at once, and I couldn't sort them apart enough to really analyze the fact that my entire stomach dropped at the idea of not being a part of something bigger than just me. The Squad had ruined me for being a loner. As much as I wanted to insist that I hadn't, I had changed, and if all of a sudden I wasn't a cheerleader anymore, there was a distinct chance that I would miss it. Not just the missions and the training and the overall purpose in life, but the other girls and the games and maybe even the actual cheering.

On the tail end of this realization, it occurred to me that if they did replace me, I seriously hoped that they transferred somebody in. If they brought one of the JV cheerleaders up to varsity, I was not going to be a happy camper.

I thought of Hayley's words to me the day before. "If you're still a part of the God Squad," she'd sniffed. "I wouldn't want to be."

It was official. If Hayley Hoffman got my spot on the Squad, I was going rogue. I had some secret-agent skills now, and I'd use them to do something drastic.

That cheerful thought in my mind, I resigned myself to the fact that while the others were out determining whether or not I even had a future, I was stuck here painting banners. I thought about painting them down in the Quad, where I could at least keep tabs on how the mission was going, but thought of the way Chloe had reamed me that afternoon and decided against it.

I might have been going down, but strangely enough, the last thing I wanted was to bring the rest of the girls with me.

The practice gym was eerily quiet as I unrolled the banner paper and filled two tins with paint. Blue and gold, the colors of Bayport. Unsure what to do next, I stared at the blank paper. Zee had been pretty explicit about what not to write, but no one had actually versed me on the finer points of making banners. I vaguely remembered holding one up for the boys to run through at our last game, but the task of actually making it had fallen to one of the girls whose bubble letters were far superior to my own.

Needless to say, girly script was not my forte.

"Oh, well," I muttered. "Here goes nothing."

I dipped my foam brush into the blue paint, and set about writing GO LIONS! on one banner and GO BIG GOLD! on the other. The whole process was strangely soothing, though I wouldn't have admitted my lack of enmity for it under threat of death.

"Toby?"

I jumped at Mr. J's voice. Something about thinking the phrase *threat of death* and then having someone call out my name when I'd thought I was alone put me a little on edge.

"Oh, hey, Mr. J," I said.

"Why aren't you at the Spirit Lunch?" he asked.

"The whatsit?"

"The Spirit Lunch, honoring the state's most esteemed cheerleaders," Mr. J said. "I believe that's where Brooke said she and the seniors were going this afternoon, and the rest of the girls appear to have gone as well."

Personally, I thought my *Seventeen* magazine excuse had

more oomph, but I wasn't going to quibble with the vice-principal.

"Someone had to stay and paint the banners," I said simply.

"Oh," he replied. "Good girl." Then he paused and turned back over his shoulder. "She's in here, Joanne," he called. "I'll let you tell her the exciting news yourself."

Joanne. My mind took in the name and recognized the reference. Joanne McCall. The PTA president. The nauseatingly reminiscent mom.

"Exciting news?" I asked.

Mrs. McCall came into the room, her smile proving that as Botox-ed as her face was, she still had control over at least a few of her facial muscles. "The homecoming game is going to be televised," she said. "Including your halftime routine and the coronation ceremony. Isn't that wonderful news?"

Wonderful wasn't the word I would have chosen myself, even with my newfound insight into my feelings about my cheer identity. Cheerdentity. Whatever.

"If you girls will excuse me," Mr. J said, "I have a student in my office. Something about Abraham Lincoln and streaking."

Mr. J left, and I looked down at the banner, hoping the NRM would get the hint and leave, but she didn't. Instead, she came further into the gym, blathering on about the "excitement" as she did.

"It's the Game of the Week, you know," she said. "For the entire state. There's a chance that the feed may even be picked up nationwide. It's such an exciting opportunity for you girls!"

Blah, blah, blah . . .

"It's so unfortunate that you won't be there to enjoy it."

The tone of her voice never changed, but my body reacted as if it had. Even before my mind processed her words, a chill ran up my spine, and I made my way to my feet.

"What did you just say?" I asked her.

She pursed her lips. "I said it's unfortunate that you won't be there," she repeated. "These are such precious and wonderful times. It really is a shame that I have to do this. I didn't want to, you know, but you girls make these things so difficult."

I stared at her, and comprehension dawned on me. "You?" asked. "Seriously?"

Mrs. McCall came closer. "I know, I know," she said. "Nobody ever suspects the soccer mom."

It was when she said the word *mom* that my brain connected the dots and I thought about Kiki McCall and the fact that more than anything, she wanted to make varsity. There was something else, too. Something from my dream the night before, or maybe something from my first day on the Squad. Or maybe both.

"When you went to see Karen, I thought you'd figure it out," Mrs. McCall continued.

"Karen?"

"Karen Madden. Oh, I suppose her last name is Camden now. It's so hard to keep these things straight."

The PTA president was planning to take me out, and here she was talking about Brooke's mom? And then I remembered the last piece of information about Kiki. She wasn't a very good cheerleader, and she clearly wasn't cut out for espionage, but the reason she'd been strongly considered for the Squad was that she, like Brooke, was a legacy.

And that meant that once upon a time, her mother had been on a Squad.

That morning, I'd tried to convince the others that a rogue agent had tagged me, that the very same rogue agent had planted the bomb in Kann's car and stolen the biotechnological weapon right out from underneath us at Ross's office.

"You're the rogue operative," I said. "You're the one who planted the chip on me." I'd always thought that this woman had no respect for personal space, but really, she'd had ulterior motives. "You stole the nanobots and blew up the car."

"I was trying to make things easy," she replied. "At first, I thought I could scare you off, but the bomb didn't seem to bother you much once you regained consciousness. I thought that when I crashed your retrieval mission, the other girls would realize they'd made a mistake and that you were never cut out for any of this." She sighed. "And I thought for sure that when they discovered that you'd been tagged, they'd report it and you'd be gone, but no. They didn't, did they? If they had, you wouldn't be in school today." She blew a wisp of hair out of her face. "It's the darnedest thing."

Half of me thought I should just take her out then and there. She might have been trained as an operative back in the day, but she was old and I was young, and I was willing to bet a lot of money that she couldn't move like I could. There weren't very many people who could.

"Nuh-uh-uh," Joanne McCall said, making a tsking sound with her tongue. She pulled something out of her pocket, and I recognized the silver box in her hands. "You take so much as a single step toward me, and I'll let these little darlings do their thing. I had a piece of your hair on file, you know. All that lovely DNA. So very convenient. I was so glad I'd gotten a hold of a sample that first day, when I saw you in the mall."

"How can you . . . I thought . . . Anthony . . ."

"The TCI?" The fact that she used the acronym freaked me out. "I needed a diversion, and he was more than willing to buy a decoy. That boy is a bit slow. I knew he was bugged, and I figured you girls were listening, and that orders or no orders, you wouldn't be able to resist saving the day." She sighed nostalgically. "We never were."

This was just freaking unbelievable. The president of the PTA was a former agent who'd been stalking me for weeks. She'd duped Anthony into believing he had the actual weapon, assuming that we'd be listening, but instead, she'd tricked Amelia, who must have replaced our bug with one of her own. If Amelia hadn't come to me, hadn't issued her little challenge, Mrs. McCall's decoy wouldn't have worked, and I wouldn't be here now, by myself, with a madwoman.

Her words echoed in my mind, and I wished I wasn't processing them as fast as I was. She had my DNA, she had the nanobots, and she was saying that I wasn't going to be around to enjoy the game on Friday.

It didn't take someone with my mathematical prowess to finish the equation.

She was actually going to kill me. Psycho Mom was actually going to kill me. Again, I say: This was freaking unbelievable.

I had to keep her talking long enough to come up with another plan. There had to be a way out. She couldn't just use a prototype biotechnological weapon to kill me in

Bayport High's practice gym. Well, she could, but I certainly wasn't going to let her.

If I had a choice.

So I did the only thing I could do to keep her talking. I asked a question I already knew the answer to, even though I really didn't want to hear her talking about it.

"Why?"

She giggled then, a high-pitched sound that made me realize just how crazy she really was. "If you have to ask that, Toby, you really don't belong on the Squad. I knew that, of course, but still, I thought you'd be brighter than this. I guess I give those other girls too much credit."

Just keep talking, I urged her silently, as I examined the exits in the room and the distance between us, trying to gauge whether or not I could make a run for it or knock the container from her hands before she could flip the lid.

"And that's why this has to get so ugly," Mrs. McCall sighed. "Because those girls chose you, and the government signed off on it, even though they knew that I'd been prepping my Kiki for this her whole life. She didn't know why, of course. She's a sensitive girl, and she wasn't ready to learn, but she would have been ready if they'd picked her. I worked too hard and too long to make her ready to just sit back and let them pick somebody like you."

My mom's spiel about the mother who'd hired the assassin didn't seem quite as outlandish anymore. In fact, compared to the situation at hand, it seemed almost reasonable. I mean, that mom hired an assassin. This mom was playing assassin herself—with stolen technology to boot.

If I got out of this alive, I was never going to dismiss one of my mom's random stories ever, ever again.

"Once you're gone, the others will see. They'll have to

give the tenth spot to Kiki. She'll be wonderful, you know. She has to be."

I thought of poor, clumsy Kiki, whose only distinguishing characteristic was the fact that she was Hayley's lapdog. She'd never make the Squad. I thought about telling Mrs. McCall that, but one look at her crazy eyes told me that such a comment might send her right off the deep end.

Think, I told myself. There has to be a way out of this.

"Enough talk," Mrs. McCall said. "I know you'd love for me to carry on until someone comes to save the day, but I'm afraid that isn't going to happen, Toby. It's sad," she said. "It really is, and I am sorry. These are supposed to be such precious years, but I'm afraid I have no choice—"

"Freeze!"

I'd never been so glad to hear a bossy, clear, more-popular-than-thou voice in my life. I looked past Mrs. McCall and saw Brooke standing in the doorway.

She was holding a gun.

CHAPTER 34

Code Word: Teamwork

I never thought I'd be so glad to see my school's Queen Beeyotch holding a gun, but my joy was short-lived. Psycho Mom was way too psycho to go down without a fight.

"Move at all, and I'll shoot," Brooke said, her voice pleasantly deadly.

"You must be Karen's girl," Psycho Mom said, her voice equally pleasant and twice as unhinged. "You look just like her, you know."

"Thank you. Drop the box. Now."

"We weren't in the same program," Mrs. McCall continued. "But I heard about her. I went to Quantico when I graduated, you know, and all anybody could talk about was your mother. And then I met my Larry, and we got married, and well . . . sometimes, family just has to come first. I dropped off the radar, but when Kiki was born, I put in my notice, let them know that I'd be training her, and that if the program was still operational, she'd be ready."

Mrs. McCall frowned. "I never heard back, but I did some digging and when I realized your mother was living in

Bayport, well, I knew this must be the place. I talked Larry into moving here. This school has one of the best cheer-leading programs in the country, I told him. And it does. And Kiki's done so well in it!"

Brooke cocked the gun. "Box. Floor. Now." Her voice was absolute steel. Gone was the teenager, gone was even the artifice of pleasantries. This was the warrior. I wondered how she was doing it—holding the gun, preparing to fire, doing it all without showing any external signs of weakness.

Then again, this was Brooke Camden. Team Captain. Showing weakness wasn't exactly part of her MO.

Mrs. McCall held her hands out in front of her, like she was going to drop the box, but I knew beyond all knowing that she was going to open it instead. I flew toward her then, driven by the pull of survival.

I should have known that Brooke had another trick up her sleeve, and I should have known that the trick in question had a PhD. Brooke never went anywhere without a partner. Girls traveled in flocks, and the Squad wasn't an exception to this. There was safety in numbers.

In the instant before Psycho Mom opened the box and I took her out (no idea which one of those possibilities was going to come first), I heard someone entering a number into a cell phone and turned to look at Zee. I didn't have to glance down at the Bayport High emblem beneath my feet to know what Zee was doing, and I short-circuited my attack plan, putting every ounce of momentum I had into jumping straight up into the air.

Mrs. McCall moved to open the box.

And the floor beneath her feet gave way to nothing as

Zee's code activated the trapdoor mechanism on the emblem. Mrs. McCall disappeared, and then the emblem came back up into place, just as I crashed to the ground.

Remember when I said that some of the entrances to the Quad were less convenient than others?

This was one of them.

If you were standing within a six-foot radius of the center of the gym when the mechanism was engaged, you fell down and landed on the world's largest trampoline in the middle of the Quad. Lucky for me, the floor mechanism was blindingly quick—otherwise, I would have fallen, too, and if I'd fallen with Psycho Mom and the bots, I'd be dead.

"They can't get through the floor, can they?" I asked.

Brooke gave me a look. "Puh-lease," she said. "You think we're not equipped for nanoattacks? What do you think we are, amateurs?"

Her hands shaking, Brooke lowered the gun to her side even as she smirked in my general direction.

"Shouldn't someone go after her?" I asked. "I would, but I've got this funny fondness of living."

"Yeah," Zee said, managing to keep a straight face. "You have a real love of life. It's a major contributing factor to that sunny disposition of yours."

Considering she'd just saved my life, I refrained from retorting.

"And we don't need to go down there," Brooke said. "The others are already there. Chloe's working on something to catch the bots, and the others are all ambush-ready."

"All of them?" I asked. Brooke nodded.

"How?" I opted to stick with simple, one-syllable questions. As the reality of the situation sank in, I couldn't handle much more.

"Amelia took Connors-Wright down. We took her down. It was all very food chain–like."

Zee picked up where Brooke left off. "Then we confiscated the weapon."

"Did you realize it was a decoy?" I asked. After all, Brooke had never seen the real deal. Mrs. McCall had stolen it before she'd had the chance.

"Not at first," Brooke said, "but then Connors-Wright came to and started babbling about how much he'd paid for the right to kill his father, and we realized pretty quickly that it wasn't nearly as much as a professional would have charged for the real deal."

"Of course, the fact that the payment was funneled through the Bayport PTA was a pretty big tip-off, too," Zee added. "So we started thinking about what you said, about it being a rogue operative, and then it finally occurred to us to look at things from a different angle. Connors-Wright's motivation for getting the nanobots was personal. What if the enemy operative's was, too?"

"What if," Brooke said, "that person just really didn't like you?"

Oddly enough, this was apparently a really easy idea for Brooke to wrap her mind around.

"What if Kann was never the target?" Brooke continued. "What if you were? What if the whole purpose of stealing the weapon from Ross's office was to discredit you?" She paused. "And then there was that minivan that tried to run you off the road . . ."

"If you were the target all along, and the enemy realized we'd left you alone . . ." She shrugged. "We hurried back."

"What about Amelia?" I asked.

Brooke smiled. "Let's just say that this time, my mom

came through. Amelia won't be playing any games any time soon."

I couldn't help but wonder how long it would be before Amelia would find her way back out into the world. Somehow, I didn't think she was the type to roll over and die, just because she'd been apprehended. In fact, she'd probably just see this as the next stage of the game.

Beside me, Brooke looked down at the gun in her hand, as if realizing suddenly that it was there, and her skin went very pale. I tried to figure out a way to say thanks, but couldn't quite form the words.

"You okay?" Zee asked Brooke. Apparently, our profiler had already come to the conclusion that I was going to be just fine. Forget the fact that I'd almost died . . .

"I'm not," Brooke said, the gun still in her hand. "But I will be. My mom was right. I had to get over the gun thing eventually."

Whoa, whoa, whoa. Hold up there, I thought. There were lots of take-home lessons from what had just happened—for instance, "Never underestimate the PTA" and "Don't put Toby on banner duty"—but none of those lessons involved even the hint of the suggestion that Brooke's mom had been right about anything.

I opened my mouth to say this, but Zee shook her head. I bit back the words and almost choked on them, but figured that Zee had her reasons. She always did.

"Look on the bright side," Zee said, changing the subject.

"What bright side?" Brooke asked.

Hello! Saving me! Bright side! Our covers were safe! Bright side!

"When the floor gave way, Toby's banners bit the dust," Zee said.

That was supposed to be the bright side?

"No offense," Brooke said, and I prepared myself to be offended. "You're a great hacker, but your bubble letters really suck."

CHAPTER 35
Code Word: Catfight

When I walked into the Quad the next morning, I wasn't sure what I expected to find. I knew that the Big Guys had taken Mrs. McCall into custody, and that with their help, Chloe had been able to locate and deprogram the nanobots. Or so I'd been told. If I suddenly keeled over in the middle of the debriefing, I was going to know who to blame. I also knew that the Big Guys (and Brooke's mom) had decided to forgive me my breach of protocol with Amelia, and Brooke her rogue operation. After all, in a roundabout way, we'd been right, and in a not-so-round-about way, we'd saved the day. Again.

Besides, as far as the Big Guys were concerned, the threat was contained, and all was right with the world. And the fact that they were the ones who'd dropped the ball and actually left Joanne McCall off of their watch lists didn't exactly give them much room to cast stones. I mean, come on—she was clearly unhinged, and they'd known she was in Bayport all along.

Walking into the Quad, half of me expected some kind

of celebration. Ribbons. Confetti. Ice cream would have been nice. Cookies would have been better.

What I found was a half dozen girls gathered round a single screen.

"New mission?" I asked. "Already?"

"Homecoming vote projections," Lucy answered. "Our old hacker wrote the program a couple of years ago, and we just entered in the last piece of data. It's some algorithm thingy."

I winced at the phrase *algorithm thingy*, but figured that, depending on what the aforementioned thingy had to say about homecoming, I'd save any more dramatic reaction for later.

"You're in the lead," Chloe told me, her voice tight. "By a lot."

Brooke flipped her hair over her shoulder. "I can't believe we actually saved you," she huffed. "This is our senior year."

I looked at the other nonsenior cheerleaders. Hadn't any of them bothered to fill the seniors in on my little speech yesterday? "I practically begged the student body not to vote for me," I said. "It's not my fault my little brother is a spaz."

"The problem is that you did ask people not to vote for you," Zee said. "Now half of them are supporting you because they think you're nice, and the other half are voting for you because they honestly believe you don't want to win, and they're just being petty."

"Though, to be fair," Tara added, "Noah's pirate speech did have some effect as well. His Abraham Lincoln speech, not so much so."

I didn't ask how this program somehow had the capability to analyze my brother's wacky campaign ideas. I really didn't want to know.

"Just tell me what I can do to lose," I said. "Please."

Brooke said something along the lines of, "I don't think there's a point," but what I heard was, "I am going to make your life a living hell for this."

"Turn that thing off," Chloe said darkly. "Let's go upstairs and practice."

Brooke smiled then. It was a chilling sight. "Let's," she said. "I was thinking we'd teach Toby how to fly."

Fly? As in give up my lovely, benign front spot position in order to let a bunch of girls with hardcore grudges against me throw me up into the air and hold me there? That so wasn't going to happen.

Except I looked at Brooke's face again and knew that it would.

The thing about being a flyer is this. If you think you're going to fall, you will. If you think the bases are going to drop you, they do. And if you think this whole thing is some sort of twisted punishment for past sins, you're absolutely one hundred percent correct.

An hour later, I still hadn't managed to stick a liberty, but I had managed to acquire several new bruises that would look just lovely with the homecoming dress the twins had picked out for me.

"By the way," Tiffany said, proving herself remarkably in tune with my thoughts. "We got you a new dress. It's pink."

The torture, it appeared, was just beginning. The worst part of it was that as hellish as this was and as catty as they were all being, I knew that if things had gone differently

316

and I'd woken up this morning as a noncheerleader, my life would have been a whole lot worse.

"Let's go again," Brooke said. "One, two, down, up, down . . . up." She counted off the movement, and this time, as they hoisted me none-too-gently into the air, I actually managed to stay there. My form wasn't pretty, and it wasn't so much a liberty as a "get me the hell down from here," but I stuck it.

And from down below, Lucy took that exact moment to announce in her own perky, innocent, not-at-all-vindictive way that she'd asked my brother to homecoming.

"Aggggggkkkkkk!" The noise I made as I fell off the stunt was only vaguely identifiable. The others didn't let me hit the ground, but they did catch me in a way specifically designed to give me a wedgie, and I was about ninety-nine percent sure that they were doing it on purpose.

CHAPTER 36
Code Word: Homecoming

"That was the award-winning Bayport High Varsity Spirit Squad!"

Usually, making it through a halftime routine was a cathartic experience for me. I wouldn't say that I enjoyed it (perish the thought), but there's something about that last "Bayport!" that gave me the same kind of rush that I had a tendency to crave. That said, the past few days had more or less cured me of my adrenaline addiction. For the time being, at least.

I also typically enjoyed the end of our halftime routine because it meant that I could slink back to the sidelines. Not so today. Not so at all.

"And now, we proudly present the members of this year's homecoming court."

Each of us was matched up with an escort. Mine was supposed to be a sophomore named David, but at the last second, Jack redirected David toward one of the twins and took my arm.

"You ready to find out the voting results?" he asked, as he escorted me to the center of the field.

"Do I look ready to you?"

Jack smiled. "Ev, you were born ready."

"Bite me."

He leaned a little closer and whispered so that only I could hear him. "Don't tempt me."

I tried very hard not to smile, and succeeded only because I knew what was coming. I'd run into enough programs built by the Squad's previous hacker to know that she was good. The projections were accurate, and I was going to win. I had to wonder—where were the homicidal psychopaths when you really needed one? Right now, I could use the distraction.

For a brief instant, I considered bolting off the field, but Jack tightened his hold on my arm as we came to stand on the fifty-yard line, facing the stands.

"What would you say if I told you I already knew the outcome?" Jack asked quietly.

"I'd say something along the lines of 'join the club,'" I mumbled miserably.

"What would you give me if I told you that you were wrong?" Jack murmured, as Chip and Brooke came to stand on one side of us, and Chloe and her escort came to stand on the other.

"Anything," I told him. "You name it, and it's yours."

"What if I want a dance?" Jack asked.

What the hell? I thought. This was a bet that I very unfortunately wasn't going to lose. "Whatever you want," I reiterated. Jack smiled.

"That's exactly what I wanted to hear."

"The Bayport High homecoming court is a long-standing tradition here at Bayport. Each year, four seniors, three juniors, and two sophomores are nominated for the coveted roles of king and queen respectively. The nominated seniors are . . ." The announcer was dead set on extending my misery as far as was humanly possible, and he read through each of our names, pausing for applause with each one. Finally, he got to the point, and I winced in anticipation of his words.

"And this year, the homecoming king and queen are Chip Warner and Brooke Camden."

I turned to stare at Jack, but his face was absolutely blank.

"Each year the sophomore attendant with the most votes is named the homecoming princess," the announcer continued, and I prepared myself—gladly—for the indignity. At least next year, I wouldn't be eligible for princess and would only have the queen thing to worry about. The junior girls didn't know how lucky they had it.

"This year's homecoming princess is April Manning."

As April and her escort walked forward to get her tiara, I jerked Jack downward. "Explain," I said.

"I can neither confirm nor deny that any such explanation is necessary," he whispered, "but let's just say that I'm not a stranger to rigging elections and leave it at that."

I should have been disturbed at the reference to the fact that he'd been brought up to be corruption incarnate, but I wasn't. I was too busy thinking that my not-a-boyfriend was the sweetest, most wonderful, ingenious boy in the world.

"Remember," he murmured, as the entire court was presented once more. "You owe me a dance."

I didn't even scowl in response to those words. I wasn't a queen, I wasn't a princess, and with any luck, I'd never have to suffer through a stunting wedgie again. Life was good.

After the game, we went to put on our dresses, and the change in the others was palpable. Brittany and Tiffany produced a new dress that was black and only borderline girly, and neither of them made so much as a single lewd suggestion about Lucy and Noah. Meanwhile, Lucy was blowing off nervous energy by bouncing repeatedly up and down as Bubbles added the finishing touches to the weapons expert's hair.

Getting ready for a dance, it turned out, was a communal experience. For once, I wasn't the only one being primped and fluffed by somebody else. Spirits were higher than the ponytails we'd worn on our heads for the game. Even Chloe spared me a smile.

"Done," Britt announced, giving my hair one last spray of a newly developed supersonic holding serum.

"Done," Bubbles echoed. Lucy spun around, giddy, and the movement caught on, until all of us were spinning. Even me. It was weird. If you'd asked me, I would have put money on me being the stick in the proverbial mud, especially considering the torture they'd put me through the day before, but here, getting ready, none of that seemed to matter.

Of course, the fact that they'd saved my life before they'd starting making it miserable did buy them a little bit of leeway.

Brooke clapped her hands, and a few seconds later, the spinning stopped. "Let's do this," she said, and with one last glance in the mirror to confirm that her tiara was still in place, she led us out of the room and off to meet our dates.

"*Enchanté, mademoiselle*," Noah said the moment he saw Lucy. His accent was French and over the top and ridiculous, and for some reason, Lucy seemed to think it was funny. He took her hand and kissed it, and a happy blush rose on her cheeks.

Maybe I'd been hanging around Zee too long, but I couldn't help but analyze their body language and come to the only possible conclusion. There was a distinct chance that peppy Lucy, designer of the bulletproof push-up bra and the bobby-sock grenade, actually had a thing for my freak-of-nature brother.

Go figure.

"*Enchanté, mademoiselle.*" Jack's French accent was predictably flawless. Rolling my eyes, I punched him in the stomach.

"Anyone ever tell you you're one of a kind, Ev?"

His arm settled around my shoulder as I answered. "Every day."

To Jack's credit, he didn't make me dance at first. For the first hour of the dance, I twitched at every slow song that came on, but he didn't mention our bet so much as once. For the most part, we just watched Noah and Lucy. She was a fabulous dancer. He seemed to think that every song required disco moves.

"If dancing ability is hereditary," Jack told me, "I think I know why you avoid it."

This time, he dodged before I had the chance to punch him.

"Chickening out?" I asked him finally. "Afraid to be seen with me on the dance floor?"

"Me? Afraid of you?" He took my arm and pulled me up. "Never."

Because my timing was either very, very good or very,

very bad, the music transitioned to a slow song then, and Jack met my eyes. "Afraid?" he asked me.

I thought of the dreams I'd had for the past few nights and looked down at my body. I was still wearing clothes, and as far as I could tell, Ryan Seacrest and Paris Hilton were nowhere in sight. Plus, the PTA chaperones didn't appear to be armed—always a good thing.

"Me? Afraid?" I mimicked. "Never."

We walked onto the floor, and as we started dancing, I realized that even though he was the hottest guy in school, and I'd been forced to become one of the hottest girls, and everyone's eyes were on the two of us, I felt like myself. And Jack? Well, I had to admit it, at least to myself—as he pulled me in for a kiss at the end of the song, he felt distinctly like my boyfriend.

Some time later, I floated off to the bathroom, still in a happy daze that probably should have disturbed me, but didn't.

Zee and Tara came with me. Squad Rule Number One: never go to the bathroom by yourself.

"You look . . . happy," Zee told me.

"Shut up," I replied, but I ruined the effect with a girly sigh.

"Shutting up," Zee returned, and then she mimicked my sigh.

"Don't pay any attention to her," Tara said. "I think it's nice."

I could count on one hand how many times the word *nice* had been applied to me.

"And besides, once competition season starts up, you won't have that much time for romance. You should savor it while you still can."

My kiss-punch-drunk brain was a little slow in processing, and it wasn't until a good thirty seconds later that my mouth responded to Tara's words. "Competition season? What do you mean by competition season?"

"Nobody told you?" Zee asked, hooking her arm through mine and smiling. "When you're on the Squad, football season is only the beginning."

ACKNOWLEDGMENTS

With any series, half the battle is knowing that there are people who care about the characters as much as you do, and for that, I'm grateful to the people who helped shape the Squad—my editor, Krista Marino; my agent, Elizabeth Harding; my first reader (and mom!), Marsha Barnes; and my second reader (and roommate!), Neha Mahajan. Jack, Noah, Toby, and the girls wouldn't be who they are without you, and neither would I. I'd also like to thank Noreen Marchisi, who's seen me through five books now and done an incredible job with each and every one, and Sarah Fogleman, who's always on hand for moral support. You guys are the best!

Jennifer Lynn Barnes is a recent graduate of both Yale University and Cambridge University—and a former competitive cheerleader. In 1997, she was named an All-American Cheerleader by the National Cheerleading Association. She can neither confirm nor deny any experience she may or may not have had as a secret agent, but she can tell you that she's the author of four other teen novels: *Golden*, *Platinum*, *Tattoo*, and *The Squad: Perfect Cover*. Jennifer wrote her first book when she was still a teenager, and she is currently hard at work on her next. Visit her online at www.jenniferlynnbarnes.com.